MERRY AND BRIGHT

A COLLECTION OF HAPPY ENDINGS

NICOLE FRENCH

raglan

To every reader,

including those who love these characters.

and those just discovering them.

DEAR READER

The pieces you are about to read are just that: pieces. With the exception of "After Party," none of the chapters in this book are complete stories, instead building on or perhaps taken from the writing process itself.

This book is a collection of separate collections, one per series I have published so far. A sort of gallery or walk into the mind of a writer (well, me) comprised of three primary entries: epilogues, alternate points of view, and snippets.

You see, when I write, it's rarely in a linear fashion. While I do outline my series (generally three books at a time), the beginning is much more organic. As I get to know my characters, think through the things that motivate them, the moments that drive them, or the bits and pieces that give them (and therefore us as readers) pleasure, those separate little "kernels" (as Diana Gabaldon calls them) often to come to me randomly. Sometimes it's right when I wake up. Sometimes it's right when I'm outlining. As I write, I often keep a separate document where I can jot down these little snippets. Some of them make it into the final manuscript. Many don't.

I've chosen to keep these bits and pieces as organic as possible. As a result, you may find the occasional error or incomplete sentence. You may find a word choice that doesn't quite sound right, or perhaps a plot point that doesn't actually work with the story you know. That's okay. There is a reason they didn't make it into the final manuscript.

All of them, however, gave me distinct pleasure because they were part of the process of getting to know the characters. They also give me that thrill when I watch or feel a character do something I may have wanted to feel before. Often it's one of those cathartic moments—another way of saying "I love you," or maybe another moment of discovering how much they "hate" each other. Maybe it's backstory for a plot point that is talked over in the story; maybe it yet one more kiss in a dark corner. It's all valuable. It's all pleasure. And isn't that what romance is really about?

Alternate points of view are also immensely helpful when I'm first getting to know a character—so much so that I recently started rewriting the entire Spitfire series from the perspective of Brandon Sterling, the male protagonist, for my newsletter. I've included a chapter from that rewrite here—a scene where he chases Skylar into the snow and they meet for the first time. Knowing what Skylar is thinking is helping me a lot to describe her actions here. But even years later, I'm learning so much more about Brandon than I realized. Oddly, it gives a story I've already written so much more depth.

Usually, I write these at the beginning of the manuscript. I originally intended, for instance, for the *The Hate Vow* to be a dual perspective novel. However, as it ended up primarily Jane's story, most of the scenes I wrote from Eric's perspective, including the first chapter, had to be translated into Jane's or discarded altogether. Still, knowing Eric's mind allowed me to write his actions more intuitively. This is where the chapter from his thoughts, "Marry Me," comes from.

Lastly are the extended epilogues. These, of course, are generally written after the primary story has finished, a way of gaining adequate closure when a story has taken the emotional toll of three full books. I'm sure you know what I'm talking about. None of these series particularly shies away from raw emotions or trauma. Our characters go through things. Lots of things. And so do we make that journey with them. It follows that we as readers (and yes, as the writer, I too) need to see a little bit more of their happy ending than a single chapter at the end.

All of them, however, are for you. Unfinished and raw. It's my way of saying "Take me as I am." Or as these are.

My love letter to you.

xo,
Nic

SPITFIRE

Even after seven years of marriage and two children, it's easy to wonder if your flaming hot billionaire husband still wants you. On Christmas Eve, Skylar Crosby comes face-to-face with her greatest fears. And her greatest fantasies.

The Spitfire Collection includes:

- "Merry Always"
- Sterling (from Brandon's POV)
- An extra scene

MERRY ALWAYS

"Oh, look, it's snowing."

I turned from where I was wrapping packages on the kitchen island to where my best friend, Jane, was standing under windows of the adjacent solarium, gazing at the small orchard of apple trees quickly accumulating a bright white trim.

She sighed. "It never looks the same in New York, you know? There's something about snow and Boston that's just fucking magical."

I snorted. "Snow is snow. We get it for about eight months, and then it's blazing hot until it comes back again."

"Since when did you become such a cynic?" Jane returned to the breakfast bar, where she took a seat next to me as I wrestled with a long strip of ribbon.

I shrugged. "Sometime between two kids and a job that never ends."

I didn't mean to sound so cynical. The truth was, my life was pretty great. Most days.

And it had all started one snowy night in law school, when I had landed in the living room of a reclusive billionaire during a blizzard. Seemingly overnight, Brandon Sterling became the love of my life. Transformed everything I thought I knew about love. Swept me off my feet and then some for most of the past seven years. I was married to a brilliant Adonis who adored me, had two perfect children and a beautiful home in Brookline, and I had a successful legal practice where I helped women escape marriages that were actually terrible. Most days, my job made me all the more grateful for my blessed life.

Snow had made this life happen. But the thrill of magic I usually felt whenever it started was tinged with something else these days.

"It means you'll probably need to get back to Boston tonight, then, won't you?" I said, not even bothering to hide my disappointment. "Eric won't chance you being stranded here over the holidays."

It was December twenty-third. Jane had come up to Boston from New York for the week to Christmas shop with me and the kids and basically do best friend stuff together for the holidays, since we couldn't spend them together.

"Probably," she agreed. "Although it's more that he won't chance being stuck alone with my mother when she arrives tomorrow morning."

I yanked at a ribbon with the blade of my scissors, then scowled at it when it failed to curl correctly around the knot.

"Let me do that." Jane took the scissors. "You're going against the grain, Skylar." She shook her head. "Crafty shit never has been your forte, has it?"

Instead of swearing the way I wanted, I allowed her to take over and collapsed at one of the stools at the counter. "Don't act like you aren't dying to go home anyway," I said. "Your husband worships the ground you walk on. You know it, and I know it."

"Well. Perhaps," Jane said, looking very much like a cat preening in the sun. "But that's something we have in common, isn't it? I'm sure the second I leave, Brandon's going to run through those doors and sweep you off for some magical night, since the kids are with your grandma."

I didn't reply.

"Sky?"

I looked up. "Hmm?"

Everything I was thinking must have been showing on my face because Jane immediately dropped the scissors atop the box.

"What's wrong?" she demanded.

I sighed. No use hiding anything now. "I think...I don't know..." I toyed with a ribbon, wrapping and unwrapping it around my fingers. Just spit it out. "I think Brandon might be having an affair."

The words sounded ridiculous the moment they came out of my mouth.

Jane, to her credit, didn't tell me I was crazy. She sighed and rubbed my shoulder. "Well, shit. You mentioned this the last time you came to see me. About things being off."

I nodded, suddenly blinking back tears. It was one thing to think this. Another to say it out loud.

"I thought at first it was just tunnel vision. You know how he gets with his work projects. The kids." I shook my head. "Once upon a time, that attention was on me too. But for the last few months, I don't know. He's been so distracted. He comes home late, sometimes not until ten or eleven o'clock at night."

Jane tipped her head. "Is that all, though? He could be distracted for a lot of reasons."

I shook my head. "I—ugh, I can't believe I'm going to say this. But he left some receipts on the nightstand a few weeks ago. Two receipts—one for this ridiculous lingerie shop, another for The Martin."

Jane whistled. "That fancy restaurant downtown?"

I nodded sadly. "The one where he used to take me. When he didn't want anyone to see us."

Jane frowned, clearly trying to sort this out. "Look, you also said he used to take business meetings there. And the lingerie—Christmas is in three days, Sky. That could just be a gift for you."

"There was also a card for a real estate agent," I whispered. "Jane, don't you remember the first thing he ever asked me? It wasn't for a date."

Jane cringed, clearly remembering with me Brandon's first horrible attempts at courtship.

"'No strings. No sleepovers,'" I quoted. "'Nothing to get in the way of both of our very busy lives…An apartment near campus, your office, a car, whatever you need. The idea is to make this as convenient as possible.'"

Jane's black brow arched over her glasses. "That was an admirable impression. You even got the South Boston accent right."

But I wasn't in the mood for jokes. "Jane! He's obviously doing something behind my back! What if it's another woman?"

"Then you'll take his ass to court and take him for half his billions, like the kick-ass divorce attorney you are!" Jane grabbed me by the shoulder and shook me a little. "Don't forget! You're a force to be reckoned with, too, my dear friend. This weepy act doesn't suit you, and you know it. If you think Brandon's messing around, hold his ass to the fire. Don't wait to get burned yourself. You never have in the past. I know you won't start now."

"That was different," I whispered.

She let me go. "Different how?"

"Because," I said. "Back then, I didn't have as much to lose."

Before she could answer, the sound of her cell phone rang—the Clash's "Rock the Casbah"—burst through the air. Which meant it could only be one person.

"Go ahead," I said ruefully. "You know he won't stop until you answer."

Looking sorry, Jane grabbed her phone off the table and dashed out of the room to talk to Eric. I finished mangling ribbon on the last few packages, trying not to cry as the snow started coming down even harder.

Jane returned a few minutes later, overnight bag in hand, jacket on, but looking regretful.

"He called. A car will be here in a few minutes to take me to Logan," she confirmed. "That control freak already has a charter on standby. Can you believe that?"

"That's not controlling. It's thoughtful." I glanced at my phone, which had sat silent since Brandon's text, sent around two, informed me he would be home late tonight. Again.

"I hate to leave you like this, though. And a few days before Christmas..."

I waved away her concerns. "I'll be fine. I won't say anything until after the holidays anyway. The kids will be back tomorrow, I've got a mountain of Santa stuff to do, and I'll be too busy to think about whether my husband is sleeping around."

Maybe that would be true for the next day, but it wasn't true for tonight. After Jane left, I waited a bit for Brandon to return from his day's "errands" before I finally gave up around eight, heated up some Chinese leftovers, and buried myself in our king-sized bed, trying not to feel desperate while I watched old movies and hugged his Brandon-scented pillow to my face.

I fell asleep sometime around when Cary Grant was asking Deborah Kerr to meet him at the top of the Empire State Building. Dreams of another proposition haunted my restless mind.

You'll come over Friday nights. Every other Saturday, as long as my schedule permits.

You'll have an allowance for whatever clothes and salon services you need. You'll benefit too.

You want me to be your mistress.

Should we establish a rate, Mr. Sterling? A Harvard brain like mine doesn't come cheap, you know.

Well, it's not really your brain I'm after right now, Red.

"Fuck you!" I shouted into the darkness, waking up only to realize that it was nearly midnight. And the other side of the bed was still empty.

My stomach immediately tied itself into a very uncomfortable knot.

Suddenly, my phone buzzed loudly on the nightstand. Sweaty and disheveled, I grabbed at it.

"Brandon?" I answered. "What's going on? Where are you?"

"Hey, Red. I, um, I'm sort of stuck," he said. "My, um, car broke down in the snow. And I need you to come get me."

I frowned. "What? Where is David?" I asked about Brandon's longtime driver with a frown.

"David went with the, uh, tow truck. Come on, you know I don't trust just anyone around the Mercedes."

He was lying. That much was clear. He used to tease me for

being the one with the glass face, but over the years, I'd come to read this man's tics like a book. I'd bet anything that right now he was running his hand through his hair and staring out a window too.

"Can't you just call a car?" I asked. "You wake Margie up for a lot less."

"Please, Red," he said. "Just come get me. I—I need your help."

The low hum surrounding the familiar moniker had me rising out of bed. There was an urgency in his voice I hadn't heard in years.

Bad news, probably.

He was nervous.

Oh God, this was it. I knew how Brandon worked. When something was on his conscience, he usually couldn't wait until morning. This was the man who once stood outside in the rain for hours to confront me.

I shoved on a pair of sneakers and was down the stairs within minutes.

"Send me the address," I said, my voice low as the knot in my stomach tangled even more. "I'm on my way."

The address was for a brick building off Acorn Street, one of those buildings on Beacon Hill that looked like it sprang right out of a Longfellow poem. I parked on Beacon and walked in my plaid pajamas and Sorel boots, not wanting to hazard driving over the crooked cobblestones. Snow was piling inches thick now—by morning, I guessed the city would have close to a foot.

When I reached the address Brandon had given me on the mostly darkened street, I called him again, looking up at the darkened windows of the building.

"Brandon?"

What was he doing here? Was he confronting me with his infidelity? Showing me where he was going to live from now on?

You're spiraling, Sky. Jane's dry voice grounded me.

Until, that is, my errant husband picked up the phone.

"Hey. You here?"

"I, um, yeah. I'm standing outside."

"I'll let you in. Apartment 3A."

The call ended. A buzzer sounded at the door.

I walked to the top floor with dread sinking every step. When I reached the door bearing the number 3A in brass lettering, I was almost too drowned in it to knock.

But in the end, my curiosity got the better of me. If I was greeting the end of my life, I might as well do it with a stiff upper lip.

Brandon, however, couldn't wait. Just as I raised my hand, the door swung open, and I was greeted by the sight of my very tired-looking, but still incredibly gorgeous husband.

Seven years after we first met, the sight of him still made me breathless. Six feet, four inches of muscled, charismatic billionaire filled the doorway completely with a pair of shoulders that spanned the doorframe, denim-clad legs that went on for miles, and a jawline that, even at forty-five, could still cut class. Sure, there were a few differences. His piercing blue eyes had a few more tiny crinkles at the edges. His thick, dirty blond waves that were always just slightly overgrown were now threaded with a bit of hidden silver here and there.

When I had first met him, I grew used to seeing him in the immaculately tailored suits he wore to the office as the CEO and name partner of two different firms. Now, retired to a self-funded lab where he tinkered with inventions most of the day, he wore a daily uniform of jeans, T-shirts, and his favorite old Red Sox cap.

Either way, he was still the tower of charisma I'd fallen in love with from the first moment I'd seen him.

But that face, as piercing as ever, wasn't exactly smiling. In fact, it was downright unreadable.

"Took you long enough," he said. "I was worried you got stuck in the snow."

I shook my head apprehensively. "Um, no. Just drove slowly because of it. There is about four inches on the ground right now."

This was awkward. So awkward. We had been together for nearly seven years, but here we were, discussing the weather.

"So, um, are you ready to go?" I wondered.

Brandon's brow rose as he glanced behind him, then back at me. He was clearly wondering why I wasn't giving him the third degree. After all, I'd given him hell for a lot less than calling me to a strange apartment in the middle of the night.

What would he say, though, if he knew I was too scared to know the truth?

He sighed. "Um, yeah. But first...come in for a second, Red."

I blinked. And suddenly, I realized that was the very last thing I intended to do. "Um, no, that's all right. If you're ready, let's just go."

Brandon frowned. "Um, I'm not. Actually, there is something I need to talk to you about."

I shook my head woodenly, causing my bright red hair to escape from its loose braid. Oh God, this was it. I wanted to vomit. "No, let's wait on it, please."

"Skylar, this will really only just take a second. Why won't you come in?"

"Because I don't want to see the stupid love shack you've set up for yourself now that you're leaving me!" I blurted out.

The smile was replaced by shock. "What?"

I backed away. "I'm going to go..."

"Skylar—"

"Don't."

"Skylar, seriously, just come inside so we can talk about this."

"No!" Like I was still a temperamental twenty-seven-year-old student and not a venerated lawyer and mother of two, I turned and fled down the stairs.

"Goddammit, Skylar!"

I almost made it outside. Brandon had longer legs, but I was small and quick. Unfortunately, just when I reached for the door handle, I was grabbed from behind and swiftly whirled around against the plaster.

"Is that what you really think?" Brandon asked as he caged me there on the landing. "That I've been having an affair? That I'd just leave you and the kids like that?"

I sniffed miserably. His scent surrounded me—almonds and soap, the same delicious combination that infused his pillow. "People have done it before."

"We aren't just fuckin' people, Red!"

"You're going to wake up your neighbors," I mumbled weakly.

Brandon stared at me for a moment, then slammed his palm against the wall over my head. "I don't give a fuck if I wake up all of Boston, baby. I'll be as loud as I have to if that's what it takes to convince my wife I still love her."

"God," I muttered. "You always do this. Just railroad over everything I. Don't. Want. To. Talk. About. It!"

"Fine," Brandon said. "Well, fine. You don't have to talk about it. But you're damn well going to see it."

And before I could reply, he bent down and tipped me over his shoulder, keeping one strong arm wrapped around my legs as he turned and started hoofing me up the stairs.

"Hey!" I cried out, batting at his shoulder. "Let me down!"

"Not until you see what I have to show you."

He jogged up the stairs, ignoring my smacks and attempted kicks. It made no difference—the man was made of steel. Finally, we reached the third floor, and he kicked open the door, which fell closed with a bang once we were finally inside.

I pressed my hands over my face. I was acting childish, I knew. But it was two—well, only one, now—days before Christmas. I wasn't sure I could bear it if Santa left me a divorce under the tree.

"Come on, Red," Brandon cajoled. "Open your eyes."

Apparently, I had no choice.

I took a deep breath, then removed my hands. And found myself standing in the middle of one of the most beautiful apartments I'd ever seen.

"This is it, huh?" I whimpered.

Brandon tipped his head. "No, Red. This is for you." He gestured toward the space around him. "Merry Christmas, baby."

It was modest. Nothing huge or ostentatious. Just a one-bedroom apartment with a bedroom and bath down a hallway, plus the living area we were standing in, which included a kitchenette and small island. Modest, yes, but pristine. The floors shone, the crown molding gleamed a bright white, all the furniture—a couch, a TV set, and a small desk against the bay window—was polished bright. The walls were blue—the same color as my room in the apartment I'd lived in briefly before we got married. The furniture was similar, albeit a more expensive version of the secondhand mid-century modern stuff I'd used to outfit that place. And in one corner, he had set up a small Christmas tree, lit with white lights that danced across the ceiling like stars.

I turned around. "What...what is all this?"

"It's for you. And for me, when you want me here. But mainly for you."

Brandon toed the floor nervously with his sneaker. His South

Boston accent was creeping out—it didn't usually do that unless he was emotional.

"I know I'm early, but I wanted to give it to you when the kids weren't around," he continued. "It didn't seem fair, you know. You gave me one of the guesthouses for the lab, plus I have my office upstairs. You go to your offices every day, but that's not the same as having your own space. Where you can get away from me and the kids when you need to recharge. Just be yourself."

I turned. "And you thought I needed an entire apartment for that?"

Brandon shrugged. "You hate hotels. And especially since Luis came, you haven't wanted to go all out to the Cape for some time away. And don't think I haven't noticed how much you resent the lab." He peered at me curiously. "Did I...did I do okay?"

The nervousness on his handsome face was disarming. Even after seven years, he still worried he couldn't make me happy.

Well, you didn't help here, did you?

"I wasn't sure," he echoed my inner thoughts. "Sometimes you don't like it when I go overboard—"

"Brandon," I interrupted gently.

He looked up. "What, Red?"

"It's been seven years. I know you're not trying to buy my love anymore."

"Baby, ten minutes ago, you thought I was having an affair. I have to cover my bases here."

I opened my mouth to protest, but he had me there. Instead, I took a slow walk around the modest living area. "So this is why you've been gone constantly? This is where your mind has been?"

He nodded. "I bought the building and had it renovated. The other three apartments will be rented out, but this one's for you. Do you...do you want it?"

I opened my mouth to say no, but found I couldn't. "I...I do." I shook my head. "But honestly, I feel bad about that."

Brandon frowned. "Why?"

I shook my head. "I don't mean for you to think I don't support you. I do, Brandon. I'm so proud of what you're doing in your lab—"

"Yeah, but—"

"And I know you gave up so much time so that I could get my practice going. I was gone a lot, and that couldn't have been easy," I rattled on. Now that I was going, it was hard to stop. Maybe that's really what that pit in my stomach was about. Guilt, not suspicion.

"But?" Brandon prodded.

I crossed the room to look at the desk, ran a finger over its shining surface, then toyed with the modest diamond on my hand. This was the hard part.

"Sometimes I feel like...that's all I got. A hard beginning, then a few years where our life prioritized my career instead of yours. But now we're back to you. And I'm left to deal with my job, running our house, and often the kids on my own too."

Brandon opened and closed his mouth a few times. But then, he simply nodded.

"Yeah, baby. I know. It's why..." He gestured at the space around us. "Well, it's why I did this. I felt like I've been failing you lately. And I wanted to make up for it."

"So you feel guilty too?" I whispered.

"Baby, I feel guilty about every waking minute I can't spend worshipping you. There just aren't enough hours in the day. But, Red?"

I looked up. "Yeah?"

Brandon slipped a finger under my chin and tipped my face toward his. "Guilt aside...please tell me what in the hell I did that made you think I could even see other women besides you?"

"I-I don't know."

I pulled my chin away, too shy to look at him. Here he was, looking like he walked out of GQ despite wearing nothing but torn jeans and stained cotton. I, on the other hand, had jumped right out of bed. My hair was undoubtedly a mess, and I probably still had pillow creases on my cheeks.

"I don't exactly look twenty-six anymore, do I?" I admitted. "I look like a thirty-four-year-old mother of two who spends most of her days at the office, has more gray hairs than she'd like to count, and never gets enough sleep. Why wouldn't you look at other women?"

Brandon tugged me closer, then took my face between his big hands and stroked my cheekbones gently with his thumbs. "I've told you once before. I'll tell you again. This face was and still is the most beautiful thing I have ever seen in my sad, sorry life. This face is my heart, Red. Even if I could, I wouldn't want to see anyone else."

Gently, he leaned down and pressed a kiss to my lips. A tear trickled down my cheek. I hadn't realized how deeply these insecurities ran until I voiced them out loud.

We stayed like that for a few minutes, kissing slowly, gently, allowing our tongues and lips to say the words we couldn't find otherwise. When finally I broke away to lay my head on my husband's warm, broad chest, he rocked me back and forth for a few moments before his hands traveled back up to clasp my head.

I tried to pull back. "What are you doing up there?"

"Hold on," Brandon said as his fingers moved over my scalp. "I'm counting."

"Counting what?"

"The gray hairs you insist you have." He pulled my hair apart, like he was really looking. "One, two...oh, wait, that last one was just really light blond." He stood back. "You must be talking about somewhere else."

And before I could stop him, he was pushing the elastic of my pajama pants and underwear down to the floor while he sank swiftly to his knees.

"Brandon!" I squealed. "What are you doing?"

He had already pressed his nose between my legs, inhaling deeply in that way that was utterly animalistic

"I told you," he said. "I'm checking for gray hairs."

"Brandon!"

His nose pressed against my clit, rubbing lightly before he sat back again. "You're a liar, baby. None here. I do see something very interesting, though."

"Oh?" I asked. "And what is tha—oh!"

His tongue swept up as he slipped one finger, then two, inside me.

"Brandon." My head hung back, fingers threading into his thick, golden curls. "Brandon—oh! Someone...might..."

I looked over his shoulder to the windows across the living room. The lights across the street were off, but that didn't mean no one was there.

To my regret, he stopped. "See us? Yeah, but baby, after all this time, I sort of wonder if you like it."

With a chuckle, he returned to his work, and soon I was too overcome to argue. After all, maybe he was right. I wasn't totally opposed to the idea that someone out there might see how this man completely undid all my pretenses.

"Oh..." I moaned as his fingers quickened along with his tongue. "Oh...God."

It was all I could manage. Braced against the desk, Brandon between my legs, I was limp and at his mercy as his tongue urged me higher and higher on an invisible plane of pleasure.

And then the familiar but no less exciting cliff approached.

"Brandon!" I shouted as I dropped off.

My entire body seized.

I began to shake.

The stars beyond the windows of the apartment blurred.

I was consumed with pleasure.

It took minutes, maybe more, for me to return to earth again. Brandon rubbed his cheek, roughened by the effects of a day's growth, against my inner thigh, then lightly kissed the skin before standing.

"The truth, Red?" he said as I slowly came down from my high while sagging against his chest. "I'll think you're the most beautiful thing on the planet, even when we're old and wrinkled. You don't ever have to doubt that."

"That seems a bit unreasonable," I said lightly into his shirt. "Even for you."

"Who ever said love had anything to do with reason?" Brandon asked as he reached down, grabbed between my legs, and gently lifted me to sit on the desktop. He pressed himself between my legs, so I could feel the strong, highly unreasonable desire through his jeans.

And before I could answer, his lips closed over mine, taking my mouth with a kiss I hadn't tasted in months. It was full of heat. Fury. Desire. Longing. The kiss that was always too much and at the same time shouted "not enough!" The same kiss that, seven years ago, made my toes curl and my gut clench with need in exactly the same way.

"Brandon, I—" I croaked.

"Hush, Red," he said with a smirk before kissing me again. "And before you tell me not to silence you, I just want to say—why don't we say things in other ways for a minute or two?"

Oh, he knew me. He knew me better than anyone. Knew that

even as an argument was bubbling to my lips, it would disappear the moment he stripped off his shirt and allowed me to feel the smooth muscles of his chest and abdominals. Knew that I'd lose my ability to think right when I felt him enter me, solid and warm. Knew I'd lose all conscious thought as his fingers slipped between us, one hand to my breast, the other to my clit.

"B-Brandon!" His name escaped my lips like a siren.

"That's it, baby," he growled, now starting to pick up the pace. "You don't need to be quiet in here. No sleeping kids. No family or housekeeper to overhear. Shout my name, Red. Let me hear it!"

And I did. Again and again as he pummeled into me, finding my darkest spaces the way only this man had ever done.

Seven years together.

It could have been seven days.

Slowly, I was learning the truth.

A lifetime isn't long enough when it comes to your soul mate.

"Holy fuck, Red!" Brandon growled as he thrust forward a few more times. His entire big body tensed, and mine, sensing his pending release, tightened around him. "Jesus, baby, that feels so fucking good!"

"I'm close," I managed before biting his shoulder.

He hissed. "Oh God, I'm about to come!"

"Do it!"

And then we fell apart together, shaking atop the desk he had purchased for my desire, making the entire apartment glow with the remnants of our love

---

Sometime later, I leaned into his chest, allowing me to fold against his big body. This was my happiest place, wrapped up in his warmth.

"You didn't have to do this, you know," I murmured.

"What, give you three orgasms on your new desk?"

"Buy me an entire building. Do you think you'll ever learn not to be so over-the-top?"

Brandon chuckled. "Probably not. But you deserve a space for yourself, Red. More than I do, considering how much you do for all of us."

"I don't know about that," I said, hugging him close. "You are an incredible father and husband."

"Except for the last few months?"

I snorted and didn't answer that.

Instead, I just said, "I think we both deserve the space to grow. Maybe we can do it together."

He tipped my head up so I was looking at him, and then blessed me with his smile—a thousand-watt expression that lit up any room, certainly more than the Christmas lights that twinkled all around us.

"Sounds like a plan," he murmured. "I do love to see you soar."

I smiled back. "Right back at you, Mr. Sterling."

The smile broadened into a grin. "Merry Christmas, Red."

I returned his kiss. "Merry Always."

Thanks for reading!

Did you know that the first full book of Brandon and Skylar's story is totally FREE on all platforms?

Start reading here: www.nicolefrenchromance.com/LegallyYours

STERLING

AN EXCERPT FROM BRANDON'S POV

She wasn't hard to track. The snow that had already coated the city with a solid inch or two that evening was coming down in wads and already starting to cover her footsteps, but they ran right across Beacon Street and into the Common. I tracked her around the Carousel and past Frog Pond, which would have been full of ice skaters a few hours earlier, but was now dead quiet.

"Jesus," I muttered as I slipped for the second time. My leather-soled Grensons looked good in the courtroom, but they were hell on ice.

I was about to hook a right toward the visitor's center when I caught her up head, red hair glinting under one of the lone street-lights. Her body was bent forward as she tromped doggedly through the storm, legs practically shaking with every step. My guess was that she was aiming for the Park Street T-stop. Interesting. Red line. Was she heading to Cambridge, or did she live south? Would a girl like that even step foot in my old neighborhood?

I almost got lost myself, imagining it. But then I almost lost her too.

"Wait!" I shouted, picking up my pace. Fuck, it was cold. "Miss—fuck—I don't know your name, but will you just *stop!*"

To my honest-to-God surprise, she did. I wouldn't have. Small girl, middle of the park, stopping for a man twice her size yelling at her in the dark?

I mean, I wanted her to. For me. But the fact that she did kind of made me want to yell at her a little too.

After nearly falling twice, I finally caught up to where she was waiting, finding myself breathing like I'd just run a marathon despite being maybe a quarter-mile from the house. Pathetic. Especially for someone who runs about eight miles a day every morning.

"Do you always go wandering around the Common after midnight?" I demanded, a little more harshly than I really intended. "It's not exactly safe. Especially for someone like you."

When I stood back up to my full height of six feet, four inches, and change, her eyes rounded with green curiosity that glowed through the snow. Christ, they were more expressive than I had originally thought. Light enough that they reminded me of the jade medicine balls I'd picked up in China last time I was there, with the same kind of depth, a green you wanted to dive head first. A green you could drown in.

Those eyes slowly drew up my body, sparking even more as they rested briefly on the products of my morning training sessions and runs along the river: my flat stomach, big shoulders, and yeah, that face everyone seemed to like.

What do you know? She liked what she saw too.

"You left without saying goodbye," I said, shifting to a friendlier tone and flashing the smile that usually got me whatever I wanted. "I'm sorry, I didn't catch your name. Or what you were doing in my house."

"God."

One word, husky, almost a whisper. It might have been an exclamation, except she could barely get it out. She didn't look dim —not with the clear intelligence in her expression. But her mouth opened and closed for a moment, looking a bit starstruck, like a deer caught in headlights, and her skin pinked from more than just the cold.

Shit. I knew what that meant.

I saw it a lot. That starstruck expression a lot of women and some men got when they met me. I was a decent-looking guy. Apparently, the tall, blue-eyed, blond thing worked for some. A pretty face, yeah. Although I wasn't sure I wanted that to be *all* this one liked.

The question was: why?

I blinked and realized she was talking again. Babbling, actually. Something about being a friend of my housekeeper, and that she'd taken refuge in the storm, and a lost cell phone signal, and, and, and...

God, she was adorable. Earnest and nervous in that way that made it clear she had no idea I wasn't angry, and so was doing her best to prevent an inevitable explosion. Her hands, graceful even encased in gloves, were moving a mile a minute, and I thought I detected a slight trace of a New York accent. Out of towner, then. Maybe a student?

Christ, she really was too young for me, wasn't she?

Did I even fucking care?

"She had no idea, really, so please don't blame her," the girl was saying as she pushed a loose lock of her bright hair out of her face. "I didn't mean to intrude in your, space, truly, and, um..."

Suddenly, I couldn't take it anymore. There were places where I was just fine with people being intimidated by me. The courthouse. Conference rooms. Hell, even a street corner.

But not here. Not now. Not her.

Without even considering her personal space, I set my hands on her shoulders and bent down about a foot so our faces were even. Her mouth stopped moving, and her eyes met mine full-on with an intensity that almost forced me a step back.

God, she really was beautiful. Unusual. Almost otherworldly. And that voice, with its slightly husky timbre, was the stuff of dreams. Really, really dirty ones.

"It's okay," I said as much to myself as to her, overemphasizing each word like I was speaking to someone with hearing loss.

It was supposed to be funny. And it almost worked. She didn't smile, but her daze broke when she rolled her eyes.

"Sorry," she said shortly, but offered nothing more as she glanced at my hands still resting atop her shoulders.

"Your name?" I asked as I forced myself to release her. I didn't want to. What I *wanted* to do was pull her closer. Find out if the rest of her felt as good as the tiny bit I'd touched.

Her gaze drew slowly up my body as I straightened, flickering over me as she took in details all over again. Something told me she wasn't missing a beat. The fancy shoes and the Zegna suit. The Rolex and the slicked-back hair. All parts of a costume that hid the fact that I wasn't anything more than a scrappy kid from Dorchester.

Once again, her eyes lingered on the body, the pretty face. She definitely liked those.

Well, fine. I could work with that.

"Yum," she whispered.

I swallowed a laugh. What do you know? Red here was as hypnotized as I was.

"Your name is Yum?" I teased. I couldn't help myself.

"Oh—no," she sputtered, her skin flushing even more. Fuck me, I wanted to tear apart her jacket apart and rip open her shirt.

See if that gorgeous shade extended over her body. See if I could make her do it again.

"Christ. Sorry," she continued. "It's Skylar."

I frowned. Something about that name sounded familiar. Something—

"Skylar Crosby?" I asked.

The files Kieran had held up earlier. The interns at Sterling Grove. Don't say yes. *Please* don't say yes.

"Yes..." she said with an adorable frown that created a divot between her brows. She took a few steps back. "How did you know that?"

Great, she thought I was a stalker.

I offered her my very best "don't worry, I'm not going to rape you" smile, but I had a feeling I just looked like a shark. "I make it a point to know all of my employees' names. Even the interns. Skylar's a memorable one."

I could practically see the dots connecting right along with the dread knotting in my gut. It was bad enough that I'd just chased a very off-limits intern into the dark and snowy night like a madman. But she was realizing something even worse.

That I was her boss.

Fuck.

"Oh, Jesus," she breathed. "Jesus *Christ.*"

You could say that again, beautiful.

"No, just me, I'm afraid. Although it's a nice comparison." I was grinning like a friggin' clown, but what else was I supposed to do? Chastise her? Be the dickhead boss and tell her to be more professional?

Her eyes grew with sudden panic, and she started babbling all over again.

"I'm so sorry, sir. Oh my God, oh God, I was intruding on your home, and I really shouldn't have. A friend of a friend invited me to wait for a car inside because of the weather, but it was completely inappropriate. I only went upstairs to find cell reception, I swear, and then you walked in..."

Goddammit. I didn't know this girl at all, but in two minutes, I could see that she did not like messing things up. She was smart and motivated, and if she was an intern at *my* firm, that means she was going places. Or wanted to, anyway.

Suddenly the only thing I wanted was to put her at ease. For her to know I was a decent guy.

For her to trust me.

"Ms. Crosby," I interrupted as gently as I could. "Really. Don't worry about it."

She stopped babbling and looked up, green eyes full of fear. "I'm just...very sorry for intruding. And for babbling. It's something I do when I'm..."

"When you're what?"

"Um, nervous," she admitted in a half-whisper.

"You'll have to fix that if you want to be a litigator," I teased again.

Again, her skin turned that delicious bright red. Out of embarrassment? Irritation? Maybe both? I couldn't tell. Not yet. But I knew right then I needed to know all her secrets. That was just the first of them.

"It's all right," I said yet again, reaching out to pat her on the arm. I was a robot, unable to stop myself. I needed to touch her. I needed a lot more than that. patting me gently on the arm.

Good fuckin' God, what was I doing?

Her eyes dropped to my hand, then followed it as I drew it back. But she hadn't asked me to stop. Maybe she wouldn't. I was technically her boss. She wouldn't want to be on my bad side. Nobody did.

The idea put a very sour taste in my mouth.

A gust of wind whistled through the trees, causing a shower of snow to fall around us. Skylar shivered. Suddenly I was extremely aware that I had run out of the house in nothing but a suit that was probably ruined, and it was a cool twenty-two degrees outside and snowing harder than ever. Just beyond the hill, the lights of the Park Street station shone like a beacon. For a moment, I imagined her making her waiting in the station. Sitting on the cold concrete steps, avoiding the last remnants of the city who had no other place to take shelter but a T stop in the dead of night.

And just like I knew I had to follow her out into the storm, I knew there was no way in hell I was letting her stay out in it.

"I'm going to head back inside," I said, nodding toward the house and the fire that had to be crackling by now. "Care to join me?"

She blinked, looking particularly feline. "Oh no, sir, I'm really fine. The T is just down this path, and it goes right back to Cambridge."

Cambridge. Intern. That meant she was probably at Harvard Law. Smart cookie. But of course she was smart. Sterling Grove didn't hire idiots.

I just looked at my watch. "It's almost one," I lied. Whatever. It was twelve-thirty. So I rounded up. "You probably already missed the last train, if you don't get robbed in the park on your way there. Come on. My driver's out of town, but I can call you a car while you wait."

Another lie, yes. But I was already halfway to hell at this point. Might as well go all the way there.

She hesitated, one of her hands fidgeting nervously as she appeared to weigh her options. She clearly didn't *want* to take the notoriously unreliable train home in the middle of the night. Who would? But at the same time, she was clearly thinking with a lot more rationality than I was.

I caught the hand and squeezed it, startling her out of her slight daze. Her fingers unconsciously curled around mine, palm fitting palm eerily well despite the differences in our sizes.

I swallowed thickly, then did what I did best. I took charge.

"What kind of boss would I be if I made my interns stay until after midnight and didn't give them a ride home?"

"Um..."

She only looked confused. I didn't blame her. I had no idea if she ended up at my house after work or what had happened. I honestly wasn't sure I cared.

So I tried another tack, one that generally got whatever I wanted.

"Let's go," I said, in the exact tone I used when I wanted my associates to get shit done.

And then, without waiting, I turned and started back toward the house. It took everything I had, but I didn't look back to see if she followed. Instead, I did something I hadn't been in the habit of for a very long time.

Please, I prayed, thinking as hard as I could toward the big man upstairs, while just as intently *not* thinking about why I would ask him this in the first place.

A few seconds later, though, I heard the distinct swish of footsteps behind me.

EXTRA SCENE

Brandon puts Jenny to bed

"Do you think someone will visit the moon, Daddy?"

"Someone already did, kid. A bunch of people, in fact."

"Really?"

"Yeah. They haven't been for a while, you know. But they'll probably go again. To Mars too. Maybe even some of the

Jenny and I stare up at the ceiling, where a bunch of glow-in-the-dark stars glimmers from the ceiling. Space has been a topic of discussion a lot in our house, ever since Ray and I developed a technology to improve atmospheric interference on the space station. She might look and talk and, okay, act just like her mother, but Jenny's still my daughter. My baby girl's got a head for math and science, just like me.

"But Dad, don't you think that's impossible? I mean, it's really cold up there, and then what would we do if the space ships failed? Freeze to death?"

"Maybe. But we'll have to talk about it more tomorrow, bean. It's time for sleep."

I get up from her bed, but she keeps talking.

"And then if they freeze, you said there's no water, so wouldn't they just float away like dust?"

"Jenny." That was my "time to button it up" voice. Like usual, however, she didn't listen.

"And if it *were* like that, Daddy, why would we want to go there in the first place? Earth is so nice, and—"

"*Jenny.*"

She stops talking with a squeak, and immediately, I want to walk it back. It's my papa bear voice, the deep one that tells her she needs to stop whatever she's doing and listen. Sometimes it works, sometimes it doesn't—usually when she has her dander up since my baby girl has her mother's temper. Set it off, and...yeah. No amount of *Jenny*s is going to get her to do a damn thing.

But right now she's content to be quiet and look up at the stars, counting their neon shapes until finally, her breathing starts to lengthen in the dark.

"Daddy?" she asks right when I start thinking about leaving the room..

"Yeah, cub?"

There's a long sigh. "Would *you* go to Mars if you had the chance?"

I run a hand through my hair, thinking about the question. Ten years ago, the answer would have been easy. Ten years ago, I was mired in two companies that sucked the life out of me, a long-term marriage that had barely been arranged. My life was work and nothing more. I would have taken a ticket to Mars in a heartbeat to get away from it all.

Until, of course, I met her mother.

"No, cub," I tell her. "I'd miss you too much."

"Sometimes it takes a while to miss people," she said. "You might not right away."

"I would."

"You're quiet. You're not saying something."

I smirk. Smart kid. "I'm quiet now because I was thinking about everything I have. Everything I'd never want to leave. It takes a while when you're as lucky as me."

She's quiet herself for a while—long enough that I think she's finally asleep. But again, right when I'm about to lift myself out of the armchair, her little voice, full of sleep, floats through the air.

"I'm lucky too." She yawns and turns over.

"Yeah, cub," I whisper. "You are."

Three, two, one, and...she's out. Slowly, carefully, wincing when my weight causes one of the old floorboards to squeak, I tiptoe out of Jenny's bedroom and escape into the hall. To my right is another escapee—Skylar, closing the door to Luis's bedroom.

"How was he?" I ask, tucking her under my arm as she comes to me.

She sighs. "Okay. Still scared to go to sleep."

My boy. My little guy. He's haunted by demons he still doesn't have the words to tell us about, things that happened before he came to us. The only thing I can do is hold him tight and tell him again and again that the bad guys won't return. I know what it's like for him, wrestling with those kinds of memories. I had my own set of horrors as a kid, that kind that made me afraid to close my eyes at night too.

I shudder and push a hand over my face. "Maybe I should do bed with him from now on. Jenny's okay with you."

Skylar purses her lips, like she's considering it. Jenny's the easy one right now, though I never thought that would be the case. My daughter is as stubborn and prickly as her mother, outspoken, with a mind that never stops moving. She's never been a good sleeper, but at least she never had nigh terrors.

BAD IDEA

Four years after fighting for their chance at happiness, Layla is about to get her master's degree. But on the way to the celebration, she and Nico will learn something else: the sex of their second baby.

The Bad Idea Collection includes:

- Two extended epilogues
- Several extra scenes and cut snippets

EXTENDED EPILOGUE I

Nico

"What do you think, *papi*? Red or pink?"

Mattie shakes his head, making his black curls flop over his forehead.

"*Violeta*," he pronounces. "Mommy likes the purple best."

My son's Spanish is probably better than mine, thanks to the fancy-ass preschool he's attending. Thank you, Grandma, although if Cheryl ever hears me say that Layla says I'll get a drink in my face. Of course, that only makes me want to say it more.

I look back at the rows of flowers, searching for the dusky shade of eggplant he means. It's the color I usually buy my wife— the one I've been bringing her for the last five years, since we first met. I would see it at sidewalk stands just like this one, and the purple, the same color as the flags hung from the downtown buildings owned by her school, would remind me of that sweet, beautiful girl I met in the middle of my delivery route. The one I should have stayed away from. The one I could never forget. The nickname is a joke now, since she graduated almost four years ago, but Layla will always be my NYU.

I turn back to Mattie, who's giving the flower selection the same critical eye. Mateo Christopher Barros Soltero, otherwise known as Mattie, because that name is *way* too grown up for a person who still can't tie his own shoes, is picky. Too picky for someone who barely comes past my knee.

"*Papi*, they don't have purple," I say, holding out the two bunches again. "Come on, man. We need to meet up with *Abuela* so I have time to pick up Mommy. We got an appointment, and we can't be late."

Mattie scowls at the flowers and shakes his head again. "*No.*"

I sigh. That was a Spanish *no* right there, the kind he learned from Ma and Maggie and Allie and Selena—all the women of my family who manage to shove "what the fuck are you thinking?" and "are you kidding?" and "try again, you idiot" into two tiny letters. This kid has two main personality traits: he's stubborn like his aunties, and he fuckin' adores his mother, maybe even more than me. Only the best for her, and he doesn't settle. Even at three.

I put the flowers back. "Okay, okay, fine. You choose. But for real, Mattie, you got two minutes."

Mattie strides up the sidewalk and back to reexamine the selection, his chest sticking out. He's short for his age, but a little soldier, no matter if his shoelaces are always untied or he always has a little bit of chocolate smudged on his cheek.

When he comes back, he's carrying a spray of bright blue flowers that pretty much match his eyes, the ones he inherited from his mother. Everything else on the outside is all me, from the thick black hair to the shoulders that promise to be a little too wide for his frame one day. But his eyes? His heart? That's all Layla.

"These," he says. "Because they match her school now." He

frowns. "Wait, is it still her school since she finished yesterday? The funny hat means she was done, right?"

I smile. It's stuff like this that amazes me about this kid. Three years old, and he remembers that the school colors for Columbia are blue and white. I doubt I could have remembered my own name at that age.

"Close enough, man. It's still her school." I take the flowers and hold them up to the vendor. "Yo, man. How much are these?"

"For the hydrangeas? Ten dollars."

I fish a crumpled bill from my wallet and hand it to the guy before turning to Mattie. "All right, kid. Let's go. We got a train to catch."

We spend the forty-five-minute subway and then PATH ride across the Hudson into Hoboken, chatting about pretty much whatever goes through Mattie's head. Superheroes and why does that guy have a funny ear and how his friend Henry has a super-hero cape and he'd like one too and, and, and...

"Daddy?"

"*Que pa'o, papi?*"

I look down at my little man. That's really what Mattie is. Living in the city makes kids grow up faster than they should—I would know. And as much as Layla and I try to keep his innocence intact as best we can, the truth is, you see shit in this city, whether you grow up on Park Avenue or in the projects. I wish Mattie didn't know what it sounds like to have his mom catcalled or see someone with so little they have to sleep on the street. But that's New York. Highs and the lows. Skyscrapers and tent cities. You can't tell a three-year-old to keep his eyes closed; just teach him how to understand it all as best you can.

But I'll give him this: you can't tell a three-year-old to be quiet either. And when Mattie sees someone doing wrong, *especially* if it's to his mom, he calls that shit out. I almost fainted when he yelled, "GIVE THAT LADY BACK HER WALLET!" across a subway car two months ago, but you know what? The asshole did, and then he was tossed out of the car on the next stop. And then the entire jam-packed subway car started clapping. For my kid.

Yeah, you could call me a proud dad.

Mattie looks up at me, twisting his lips around in thought. "Why don't you call Mommy Columbia instead of NYU, since that's her school?"

I mimic his expression. We both do that when we're thinking—make weird shapes with our mouths. Layla laughs at it all the time, which, to be honest, only makes me do it more. I love that sound.

At first, I'm not sure how to answer. I mean, I can't really tell Mattie that I call his mom NYU because it makes her turn the color of a peach, the exact color of her skin after I smack her on the ass. I can't tell him that it reminds us both of when we first met, when I'd shove her up against the brick wall of her dorm and kiss her until she'd run out of breath. Or that just a name will sometimes make her do the same thing to me, even after four years of marriage.

"It bugs her," is all I tell him. "And she likes it."

Mattie frowns. He's a very literal little dude, and usually if something doesn't make sense, he'll push me until it does.

Luckily, he doesn't press it this time. A group of panhandlers starts singing at the other end of the train, their rendition of "A Hard Day's Night" a distraction from slightly naughty nicknames and even naughtier memories. They're pretty good, actually. You can't be busking for money in this city and not have some talent.

When they're done, Mattie turns to me, and I already know he's going to ask for some money. He's so much like his mother—

he can't stand to see people hurting, people in need, without doing something to help. Unfortunately, there are a lot of people in New York who need help. My wallet doesn't have enough singles.

"Here," I say, pressing another few bills into his chubby hand.

He grins, and when one of the singers comes around with his hat, Mattie gleefully delivers the bills.

"Good song!" he tells the guy, and the guy grins, showing a big gold tooth in the back of his mouth along with a few others that look like they need some dental work. Mattie, to his credit, just keeps smiling. It's just another way he's more like his mom than me—he sees the inside of people, not the outside.

About twenty minutes later, we get off in Hoboken. At one point, I hoist Mattie up with one arm to help him avoid the rush. Some people are just dicks, through and through—they won't even slow down for a little kid.

"I'm *fine*, Dad," he says, kicking his little legs to be put down when we emerge from the station.

"I know, I know," I tell him as I set him on the sidewalk. "I just gotta look out, you know?"

He brushes out his sweatshirt, then goes about taking off his backpack and digging out his baseball hat—a little black Yankees cap, just like mine. He claps it on, looks back up at me, and grins.

"Now we're twins," he says. "See?"

I nod. I can't help but smile back when my kid looks at me that way. "Yeah, *papi*, we're twins. Come on, everybody's waiting."

We walk the few blocks to K.C.'s townhouse near the river. The girls are all almost ready for the party—there's a bunch of big blue balloons tied to the iron rail of the brownstone. When we enter the apartment upstairs, I'm hit in the face by a giant cluster of blue, white, and gold streamers and a shit ton of tinsel hanging from the doorframe.

"Ah!" I cry out, spitting them out while Mattie runs into the decor.

"Be careful!" snaps Maggie as she walks out of the kitchen carrying an arm full of blue and white plates.

I toss the streamers over my shoulder and stride in. My sad blue flowers look ridiculous compared to the fuckin' flower shop my sisters—and I'm guessing Cheryl, because some of these bouquets look expensive—have set up in here.

"Maggie, what the fuck—I mean, freak?" I hastily correct myself when Mattie beelines back across the room. Shit. I mean, shoot. It's a habit I still haven't been able to break since having a kid. It doesn't help that everyone in my family swears like sailors, and the guys at the firehouse are twice as bad.

"That was a cuss, Daddy," he calls out with his tiny palm turned over. "A dollar for the swear jar at home. I'll put it in my pocket for later."

Maggie snorts. "Please. *Papito*, you gotta bill him more than a dollar if you want your daddy to quit using the f-word. I've been trying to get him to clean his mouth out since Allie was born."

"Please. Like you got any right to call me out. You need to take some Palmolive to your mouth, *gata*, that's what's up." I roll my eyes, then fish out my last dollar and hand it to Mattie. "Don't tell Mommy," I tell him, and clap him on the head while he runs off to find his cousin.

"Ma's here?" I ask. "Where is she? Or Selena and Alba?"

Maggie tosses her head back to the kitchen. "Alba and Selena are in there making the rest of the pasteles. Ma went with Scott to the store to get some more fruit for the punch." She clicks her tongue. "I'm glad. They are freaking nauseating."

I snort. After Ma got her Green Card, the first thing she did was start taking English classes. And wouldn't you know it—she fell for her teacher, Scott. Scott is a nice dude—a retired community college instructor who teaches free ESL classes for immigrants at the library. Apparently, Ma was his star student, and since then, they've been pretty much inseparable. Ma moved into his apartment in Queens last summer, and two weeks ago, the dude actually asked my permission for her hand in marriage.

"Head of household," he said, like that was supposed to make a difference.

But the thing is, it does. It matters that, for once, my mother found a man who cares enough about her to care what her family thinks of him. It matters that he treats her like gold, like a whole person, not someone to clean his shit and do whatever he says. And it matters, *really* fuckin' matters, that she's happier than I've ever seen her in my life.

So, of course, I said yes and bought the guy a couple of beers. Now we're just waiting for the announcement.

"Seriously, though," I say as I take the plates from Maggie and bring them over to the table. She takes my flowers and examines them critically. "You don't think this is a bit much? It looks like a *quinceañera*. It's just her master's degree. Layla doesn't like this kind of craziness."

"Boy, please. You are not the only person in this family proud of my sister. First person in our family to go to graduate school. And now she's going to do good with it? Your fucking sad little flowers don't cut it. Everyone wanted to do this for her, and she deserves it, so let us throw her a real party."

I look around, waiting for Mattie to charge back in, but he doesn't. Of course not. I'm the only one who ever gets caught cussing.

I can't argue with my sister's words, though—both that she considers my wife her sister too or that her accomplishments are something to be fuckin' proud of. I can't lie. I was practically busting at the seams when I watched my girl accept her diploma yesterday. I was maybe even prouder than when she graduated from NYU, because this degree was hers in a way that the first one wasn't. After Layla was accepted to Columbia, she worked her ass off and won four different scholarships to pay for school and living expenses so she could get her master's in social work instead of going to law school like her dad wanted.

Sergio never stopped bugging about it. In fact, once he knew his daughter was pregnant, would you believe the asshole actually took a sabbatical and moved to New York for the birth? Three fuckin' months I had to put up with that dickhead poking his controlling face around my apartment, checking on my kid, giving me dirty looks every time I had to pull a two or three-day shift. If it wasn't for how pissed he got every time I called him *Mister* Barros instead of Doctor, I don't know how I would have survived.

But I can't say I wasn't ever grateful, either. Like that time Mattie got croup—he was the only one who knew how to loosen that shit in his throat to keep him from choking to death. Scared the fuck out of me, let me tell you. Or when Mattie got hand, foot, and mouth disease from his first daycare, Dr. Barros was the one to calm us down and assure us that Mattie wasn't dying of measles.

So, yeah. Maybe the guy's not all bad.

In another year, though, Sergio Barros won't be the only doctor in the family. Gabe has two more years at NYU medical school, and then he'll be officially Dr. Soltero, ready to start an internship in family medicine. And even though I know we'll be throwing a *hell* of a party when he does graduate, Maggie's right. Layla is the first to get some fancy initials after her name. After Soltero.

"Hey." Maggie snaps me out of my thoughts with her fingers two inches in front of my face.

"Yo!" I cry out, batting her hand away. "Why do you *always* have to do that?"

Maggie smirks. "Because you *always* ignore me when I'm talking."

I frown. "What is it?"

"I said, don't you have an appointment you need to get to?"

I blink, then check my watch. Shit, yeah. If I'm going to have time with the graduate herself at home, I have to jam.

I grab the keys to K.C.'s Yukon off the table and start for the door. Mattie won't miss me—he's probably knee-deep in Allie's Barbie collection by now, poor kid.

"K.C. know you're taking his car?" Maggie asks as she heads back to the kitchen.

I jingle the keys. "It's all part of the plan. See you at seven."

"Don't be late!" Maggie shouts, but I'm already halfway out the door.

Layla

I glance at the wall clock above the chair, but it still says the same time. Still five after two. Still twenty minutes past the time my freaking husband was supposed to be here to pick me up.

I stand up from the couch and smooth out my skirt. After our appointment, Nico and I are meeting with my parents, who both came to town for my graduation last night, for a small celebration. I should probably go change my shirt, a thin cotton tank top that's more comfortable than dressy, but Nico's unreasonable enjoyment of irritating my dad seems to have rubbed off on me. He'll take one look at my outfit, a simple red skirt and cotton tank top, and give me a lecture for lacking appropriateness.

Well, whatever. Going for drinks at the Plaza isn't really my idea of celebrating, but it's fine. It's their comfort zone. Really, though, a master's degree isn't *that* big of a deal. Not compared to the fact that Gabe is going to be a freaking doctor in a few more years. It's a two-year degree that I finished with the help of a lot of people. If anyone should be celebrated, it's them.

I glance around our small living room, checking for things out of place. This is the first time in a long time I actually had some time to myself without the threat of papers to write or housework to catch up on. Since we moved here, I've been in school, balancing the hectic life of having a husband whose job takes him away for days at a time, living with a toddler who would just as soon knock things over as look at them, and trying to get through the intense two-year program that would allow me to do the kind of work I've dreamed of since that day I watched Carmen find her freedom.

My job starts next week, but first things came first. As soon as my final paper was submitted, Mom, Carmen, and I went through every piece of junk that Nico and I had accumulated over the past few years and tossed it, getting ready for the changes up ahead, and today I spent the morning cleaning my house.

It's weird to call it that—*my* house. I mean, I'm still not quite twenty-six. Most people my age spend their extra money on drinks or vacations. No one is spending them on a new furnace or toddler clothes.

But honestly, I couldn't be happier. We're so lucky. Our little townhouse is nothing massive—maybe a quarter of the size of the house where I grew up outside of Seattle. But it's a lot bigger than most apartments in New York, with three full bedrooms, an actual living room, even a washer and dryer. Is it weird that a washer and dryer excites me now? There is a *lot* more laundry to do with two boys in my house.

I wouldn't have thought I'd like living this far from Manhattan, but things change when you have a kid. We kept the apartment in

Chinatown until Mateo was about a year old, but you get tired of walking up and down five flights of stairs *really* quickly when you're carrying a baby, a stroller, and all the other crap that somehow magically materializes when you have a kid.

Mateo brought other changes too. When he was born, something clicked in both of my parents. They might have finally gotten their act together and finalized their own divorce, but they realized that this life I had been building in New York wasn't going anywhere. So instead of alienating my new family and distancing themselves from what I had embraced, they gifted Nico and I with a down payment on this place in Riverdale, in time for our first anniversary. Nico was speechless. He literally couldn't speak for almost an hour.

I wander out the back door, to the tiny patio that takes up our "backyard," if you could even call it that. Having a yard at all in New York City is a luxury. This space was my birthday present last year from Nico and Gabe. Together they landscaped the two hundred square feet of nothing into a mini-paradise, laying down a brick patio, exchanging the chain-link fence for a taller wood one, and building a fire pit in the middle. They planted a few trees that now block out most of the surrounding buildings, and a bunch of different flowers that make it smell sweet in the spring. It's my happy place.

I sit down on one of the lounge chairs and look up through the foliage, past strings of lights to the blue sky that's dappled with clouds. Even from here, you can hear the chatter of the city, although it's quieter in this part of the Bronx. Not far is the Metro line both of us take into Manhattan almost daily, and the sounds of kids playing at the park a half a block away filter through the fence. But the sounds blend together with the wind coming off the Hudson and laughing through the trees. It's peaceful, not frenetic. Just what I need.

I close my eyes and listen, turning my face to the sun.

Please, I find myself praying to a God that, over the years, I've come to believe in more and more. *Please protect it. Please don't take it away.*

I listen, but there's no answer. There never is, but I know He's there. He must be.

"I thought you might be out here."

Nico's deep voice seeps into me, and immediately, even though I'm annoyed he's late, I'm calmer. That's just what his presence does. It's why, though he'll never know, I'm that much more anxious when he goes to work. Nico's job isn't the safest in the world. As interesting as his stories about climbing into burning buildings or broken sewers are, there's a part of me that doesn't want to hear them. Is it terrible that I kind of wish my husband were the kind of firefighter who rescued cats in trees?

But I'd never stop him from talking about his job, one of the loves of his life, because I love every damn bit of himself that Nico Soltero has ever been willing to share with me. Even the scary parts.

I turn and smile. "It's so nice, and the weather is beautiful. We have to enjoy it while we can, right?"

Nico leans against the doorframe, making no move to come get me, though I kind of wish he would. He looks as freaking delectable as ever in his uniform—the navy pants that hug his slim hips and round backside *just* right, the short-sleeved button-down shirt that really doesn't leave enough room for his biceps, the curved-billed Yankees hat that he'll never, ever toss out. He smiles and crosses his arms, making the tattoo sleeve that now reaches over his forearm ripple. He let Milo try out a few more patterns over his forearm, including several dates into the curving lines. The day he was released from Tryon. The day he graduated high school. Our first date. The day he was accepted into the FDNY academy. The day his mother was granted permanent residency. Two days later, when we got married. Mateo's birthday.

There are others too, etched so small in black you can only see them when you're close enough to kiss them, as I often do. His arm has become a map of his life, and I'm honored to be a part of it.

By the time my gaze drifts back up to meet his, Nico's no longer smiling. Suddenly the air, despite the balmy spring weather, crackles.

Even more than six years after we first met, it's still like that between us. There's an energy, something between us that connects on a cellular level. Something in Nico's body, in his blood, his veins, calls directly to mine. Sure, sometimes it gets swallowed up by everyday life. It's hard to want to jump each other's bones when a baby is crying, and you've got a term paper due in two days, or when you've been working for seventy-two hours straight, and the water heater is broken. But even so, there are still times when he will just look at me—across the dinner table, over a mountain of laundry, when I walk in the front door—and I swear, it's like the wind was knocked out of me. Every single, solitary part of me reorients toward him. And for just a moment, it feels like there's nothing else.

"You're late," I whisper, although I'm done caring about that. It's occurring to me, just as I'm sure it's occurring to him, that we have the house to ourselves, which almost *never* happens.

Nico smiles again, this time slow and deliberate, gradually baring his bright white teeth in that sly way that hints of something much more wicked. "No, I'm not. I borrowed K.C.'s car. No train today, so we have plenty of time."

His deep brown eyes, almost black, slide over my body, tracing over the shirt that clings to my breasts and waist and the skirt that stops mid-thigh. It's not a particularly revealing outfit—comfortable and light, appropriate for the warm May weather. As if on command, though, goose bumps rise all over my skin, down my bare legs. Nico's eyes gleam, and finally, he pushes off the doorway and joins me on the lounge.

"How you doin,' Mrs. Soltero?" he asks as he squats down for a kiss. "You're looking pretty fine over here in the sunshine."

"You are so corny. Nice rhyme."

He doesn't answer, just reveals one of his dimples before he slips a big hand around the nape of my neck and plants a long, slow kiss on my lips. His tongue teases them open, and I oblige, eager to taste him thoroughly. We don't often get moments like these when we can take our time.

"Mmm." His voice rumbles low in his throat as he pushes me back into the chair. His other hand drifts down my shoulder to palm one breast. "What the..." He breaks away and looks down. "Baby, you're not wearing a bra."

I raise a brow and bite my lip. "I was home alone. Didn't really see the point."

"Yeah, but..." He licks his lower lip. "Baby, look at you. What if you had to answer the door like that?"

I follow his gaze. Okay, to look at me, you'd probably think I was freezing.

I look back up and grin. "Afraid I'm going to attract the attention of another deliveryman?"

That only elicits a growl and a kiss that's much more possessive that the first. Both hands find my breasts now, take full handfuls, knead, and caress, while mine slide up his neck and into his thick black hair, knocking the baseball cap to the ground. Nico drops his lips down my neck, and then, as he breaks away, plays with the straps of my shirt, pulling one strap over my shoulder, then the other until the entire neckline is below my breasts.

Keeping the strap wound around his fingers, he teases my nipples with the tightened fabric. Up and down over the sensitive nubs until my breath grows shallow, keeping his eyes on mine the entire time. When I moan a little, he drops the straps, and his thumbs feather down over the soft skin of my breasts, then over my nipples, making them rise even more. My back arches slightly into his touch. Then he pinches, and any and all thinking ceases entirely.

"You got jokes, huh?" Nico asks as he tugs slightly on the tips of my aching breasts. They're more sensitive than ever, and I know that feeling is only going to get worse in the months to come. If it's anything like Mattie, I'll be tempted to run to the firehouse in the middle of the night just so he can take care of it.

He pulls again, this time harder. My eyes close against that intoxicating combination of pain and pleasure as he pulls even harder, forcing me to follow the movement and sit completely up until my lips meets his full, eager mouth. He kisses me deeply, pairing a bit of sweetness with the pain he inflicts.

Then, just as suddenly, his hands and mouth pull away, and I'm released back into the chair cushion with a light thump.

My eyes fly open. "Are you kidding?"

Nico sits up, black eyes dancing. "What?"

I shake my head. "There is no way you're going to get me all turned on like that and stop midway. That's just cruel for a woman in my condition."

That wicked smile makes it return, just like I knew it would.

"And what condition would that be?"

I tip my head. "Pregnant, as you well know. And everyone knows, you're supposed to do what your wife tells you. You're not supposed to stress her out, so you have to give her what she wants, whether it's weird foods at three a.m. or sex with her hot firefighter husband."

Nico tips his head back and laughs, and then, before I can say anything else, he slips one big arm under my back and another under my knees and sweeps me off the lounge against his very broad shoulders. There won't be any more carrying me over his shoulder for the next several months, but that doesn't stop him from picking me up in other ways. He'll do it when I weigh another thirty pounds more, too, as he proved the last time around. I was honestly scared he was going to break his back, carrying me up six flights of stairs.

"We could just keep doing it out here, you know," I suggest as I bury my nose in his neck, inhaling his salty-sweet scent. Soap. Sweat. Smoke. The combination is intoxicating.

"We could," he agrees, though he's already moving toward the house. "But the last time we tried that, Mrs. Ortiz gave me dirty looks for a week." He kicks the door shut behind him and gives me a long kiss, full of tongue and promise. "Face it, NYU. You're too damn loud."

I smack him on the shoulder, but I don't argue as he continues carrying me up the stairs and into our bedroom, maintaining our kiss the entire time. The man is seriously talented with that tongue of his. I should have known better than to let him use it when we were outside, where the neighbors could hear.

He lays me on the bed, but when he tries to stand up, I snake a hand around his neck, keeping his face close for a moment more.

"Please," I whisper. "You know. You know how I need it right now."

Nico stands up, clearly checking me over. It's not often I make this request, and when I do, it's usually because I'm scared of something. Sometimes he doesn't know what. The demons that used to visit me from time to time rarely stop by these days, but our life has replaced them with some others. I have more to lose now, just like him.

I stare as he removes his shirt, reveals every delectable muscle, every beautiful line of his chest and stomach, one button at a time.

The funny thing is, I don't even think he notices the way I'm drooling over him. He's too busy thinking about what I'm asking, making sure I'm really okay.

"I don't—I don't want to hurt you. Either of you," he says, though I can see with the way his hands are clenching at his sides that he wants to do exactly what I'm asking for. Today, we're both scared. We're both searching for a bit of control, in the other way we know best.

"If it's going to happen again, it's going to happen again," I say, struggling to keep my voice from warbling. It's one thing to think it to myself, but it's another completely to say it out loud. "But you remember what the doctor said. Sex has nothing to do with it. Neither does any of the other things we normally do together. The best thing we can do is just be ourselves. Together."

Nico swallows, causing a muscle in the side of his jaw to tic. His hands flex again—he's dying to do it. Flip me over. Ram inside. Release his frustrations into my body the same way I'm dying to let him.

But still, he pauses.

He thinks too much. At least, that's what I always tell him. Even though we've been together for as long as we have, Nico still doesn't always believe I completely understand what I'm asking for. Or maybe he still can't believe I like it as much as he does. Nico understands that deep inside, there is always going to be a part of me that burns a little, an anger that needs to be let out, a need to hurt, just a little. He gets it because he feels it too. But that doesn't stop him from feeling bad about it.

Even though he spends most of his downtime at the firehouse working out, he still has to take off for Frank's a few times a week just to rid himself of the tension that builds up. Sometimes it's just too much for my man to bear, and hitting something, whether it's one of the heavy bags or Nate's mitts, is one of the only ways to get rid of it.

This is the other. I wish he didn't feel guilty about it, but the reality is, we both get what we need when he takes control, gets a little aggressive. I need to feel just a little pinch of pain. And sometimes he needs to give it.

I get up on my knees and shuffle to the edge of the bed, where I slip off my shirt and skirt so that I'm kneeling in front of him, almost naked. He watches me unbuckle his pants and pull them down so that, after he removes his shoes, he can shimmy out of them the rest of the way. I toy with the elastic of his boxer briefs, but only tug them only a little lower than his hip bones. There is something so crazy sexy about the combination of muscle, bone, and tendon that converges right above the band. I lean in and lick the spot, then sit back up to kiss him properly.

"Please," I whisper against his lips. "I'm not going to break. *We're* not going to break."

Then I clap his hand to my ass, which is *still* his favorite part of my body. Seriously, I could probably get this man to do anything I wanted if I kept his hand right here. It's not a privilege I take advantage of a lot, but it's nice to know it's there.

Nico moans a little into my mouth, and his hand automatically kneads the full flesh.

"Fuck," he breathes before sucking on my lip again with a slight bite. His other hand grabs the other cheek, and he massages them together, pulling me up against his hard length. "Jesus. *Christ.*"

I reach behind and cover his hands with mine. Then I clamp down, grabbing with them, and make him do it hard. Hard enough to leave a bruise.

"Ah!" he bites out.

Suddenly, I'm flipped over so I'm on my knees, my face presses into the bedding while my hands are held together behind my back. My underwear is dragged down my legs, and before I know it, he's pressed against my entrance, sliding in slowly at first, and then thrusting deeply into that warm, slick place where he still fits so perfectly.

There's no wait. No gently touch or kisses to get me ready. He doesn't take the time to lick or play with his hand—but he doesn't need to, not today. His little game on the patio had me ready and willing well before he picked me up, and he knows it too.

And he knows I'm looking for something else anyway.

The crack of his hand meeting my flesh echoes through the air, and I shudder, in the best possible way.

"Again," I call, low because my voice is muffled in the sheets. But he hears me.

His hand smacks my ass again and again, alternating between a light, brushing swat, and a full-on smack as he pounds harder, filling me completely with every push, every grunt. I press my elbows down, pressing back against each blow, groaning into the sheets every time his palm lands on my skin. I'll be bright red by the time he's done, and I'm absolutely loving it.

With the last, particularly rough slap, I scream into the sheets, and Nico pauses.

"Layla," he barks. "Up. Now."

I push up awkwardly, and he helps me the rest of the way so that my back is resting against his front, both of us on our knees together while he remains buried inside. He twists us toward the shelves mounted over the bed, the ones that are doubly reinforced for moments like these and sets my hands on the edge of the lowest one so that I'm bent at a slight angle, It's one of our favorite positions, one that allows me to take him deeply, yet gives him full access to the front of my body.

He lifts one knee and sets his foot down on the bed, almost in a parody of a proposal, except he's buried seven inches deep and giving me one of the hardest fucks of my life instead of an engagement ring.

"Is that how you want it, baby?" he asks as his hand slams down again. "You want it hard like this?"

"Ummm, yesssssss!" I shout, holding on to the shelf for dear life. When he takes me this way, I can barely think, much less speak in full sentences.

Nico's hands float up my sides, resting briefly over my ribs, where my half of our matching tattoos, stretches over my ribs. In his handwriting, *saudade para tí*. His fingers trace the lines as he continues to thrust, harder and harder, while his fingers curl and his nails scrape my skin just a bit as he drops that hand down between my legs.

The effect is instantaneous. He pinches my clit, and it's that tricky combination of pleasure and pain, the one that Nico always manages to find *exactly* right, that sets me off.

I begin to shake. He pulls the hand away.

"Nico!" I cry out hoarsely as my muscles tense. "Oh...*fuck!* Baby, I'm so close, *sooooooo* close."

He slams in again, and again, but his words are no longer intelligible. I can feel him expand within me, growing bigger, longer, harder. It only brings me even closer to that critical edge, the place where I can't hold myself back anymore.

"Hold on, baby." He grunts. *Thrust. Smack.* He winds a hand into my hair and yanks me back up against him. The hand at my clit works a little harder, then pinches a bit and pulls.

"Now, Layla," Nico croaks. "Come with me, baby. *Now!*"

His teeth find my neck, and he bites. Hard.

"Fuck!" I shout as my orgasm launches through me.

My entire body shakes, seizing up against his strong, solid warmth, kept from toppling over by the arm wound around my hips and the other hand clasping my hair. I don't know how he doesn't come apart too, but it's Nico's strength that keeps us from falling over together. But he's shattered too—I can tell by the way every muscle wound around me is flexed, muscle, vein, and tendon all in high relief. His teeth still clamp down hard enough that I swear he's going to draw blood, and he emits a long, almost pained groan against my skin as his release floods me.

Our life together has never been easy. We've had our battles to fight to be together, both coming from inside and outside of ourselves. Money. Family. This city and all the memories it holds.

We both have our outlets, our ways of coping, so that when we come together, we can give each other the best we have to offer. Most days they work, but sometimes they aren't enough.

But this. This connection. This outlet. This heat. This love. This is *always* enough.

EXTENDED EPILOGUE II

Nico

"I'm going to hell," I state clearly about ten minutes later, though I couldn't be happier about it.

"You always say that after we do that."

Layla pushes her hair out of her face. A few strands are stuck to her forehead, which glows a little from what we just did. I don't know if I've ever told her, but she really is most beautiful after sex. She didn't come—she's still scared to, and I know she won't *really* let go until after the baby's born. But her face is still high and flushed, with a glow of happiness that emits around her like a halo. But the fuck if I don't still want to corrupt all that angelic goodness.

"A good man wouldn't think about his pregnant wife this way. And he sure as shit wouldn't do some of the things I do to you." I turn over onto my side and give her a gentle kiss, the kiss she deserves.

"Hush," Layla says. "A good man does *exactly* what his pregnant wife asks for. And you did it. So good job."

I look her over, observing the fullness of her body. She looked like this before too—nipples slightly darker, hips a little fuller. Everything just a little more, I don't know, ripe somehow. She shines, like a peach that's just been picked. She was sick for a few weeks in the beginning, but it's now, when she's just beginning to show a little, that she looks fucking breathtaking.

Her fingers drift over my chest, playing over the compass under her cheek. Tracing the letters of her name at the top. My true north. That's her, always.

I kiss her again, full of gratitude. Seriously, how the fuck did an asshole like me get this lucky? "So I guess that means I'm perfect, huh?"

Layla smiles. "Perfect for me."

"For us," I confirm.

Then, with a groan, I gently roll her onto the pillow and get out of bed. I could stay in here all day, especially now, after a forty-eight-hour shift, when my bones are so tired I could fall asleep standing up. Sometimes, when I have a day off that lands on a Saturday, we do camp out here for the day. Mattie goes to my mom's, and we get the quality time we desperately need and never seem to find enough of.

But today is not one of those days.

"Come on, *mami*," I tell her, reaching out to help her out of bed. "If we don't get going, we really are going to be late."

Layla takes my hand and stands up, the sheet falling off her naked body, and the fuck if I'm not hard all over again. Damn. We *really* need to get a few more of those lazy Saturdays in before the baby comes.

Layla's mind is already on other things, though, as she moves around the bedroom getting dressed again. I watch her for a few seconds. Looks like sex didn't completely work to distract her from her worries. Not that I can blame her. Today is a big day.

"It's going to be all right," I tell her, though I'm already moving to the closet for a change of clothes. As much as I like the way my girl looks at me when I'm wearing my uniform, after wearing it for three days straight, I'm more than ready for jeans and a T-shirt when I finish my shift, though. Not this time, though. Layla thinks we're going out to dinner after our appointment, and we usually do a little something to look nice for our "date nights."

I pull on a pair of black pants and a sky-blue shirt that Layla bought me last year for my birthday. "Baby," I say again as I tuck it in. "It's going to be fine."

Layla sighs, but says nothing—just keeps her gaze focused in the mirror as she brushes out her hair. She has on one of her endless black dresses, a relatively modest one with thread-thin straps that clings to the rest of her body down to her knees. It's totally appropriate for a family party or a casual dinner, but it still makes me want her. Then again, I'd probably want her if she wore a garbage bag.

I finish putting on my shoes, then walk up behind her so I can wrap my arms around her chest and set my chin on her shoulder. I meet her eyes in the mirror and have to brace myself not to look away when I see the fear pouring out of them.

"*Mami*," I say quietly. "It's going to be okay. I promise."

Her eyes gloss over. "But what if it's not? Nico, what if it's—"

"Shh," I cut her off and press a kiss to her cheek. To tell you the truth, I don't even want to think it. I don't want to say it out loud or hear it either. "Let's just go, okay? Let the tech show you herself."

It doesn't work. We're both silent for most of the ride back into the city, to the midtown offices of the fancy fuckin' specialist that Layla's parents insisted on this time around.

The past still haunts us both. I can tell what she's thinking about, because I'm remembering the same things. The look on her face when she first discovered blood between her legs just before the end of her first trimester. The tears that streamed down her cheeks when the doctor told her what was happening. The way she fell onto my shoulder and wept while I held her all the way to the hospital. And the way we sat together, forehead to forehead, clutching each other while the doctors gave her drugs that would help her deliver the baby we'd never know. The little girl who was no longer living.

You don't realize how much you want someone until they're gone. Even if they were never there to begin with.

Saudade, that longing for something that's never happened, never felt more acute.

A few days later, when Ma, Maggie, and Selena came over, and even Cheryl flew out to help Layla in ways that I'm pretty sure only women can, Gabe took Mattie for the afternoon while I went down to Milo's tattoo parlor on Second Avenue and had my friend start the next part of my sleeve. That was when we got the idea to ink the dates in between the swirling designs he was printing all over my skin. Grace's birthday was the first—the day my baby girl came into the world and left it at the same time. Next came the others, all the good and the bad, the most important days of my life. Everything that made me who I was.

That was the day I realized I never wanted to forget a thing. That you have to take the bad along with the good, or you'll never make sense of either.

"Hey," I say once I've parked the car, and Layla and I are walking down the sidewalk, hand in hand. "It's going to be all right. The doctor said you were in the clear after twelve. You're at twenty weeks now."

But today is different, and we both know it. This is the full scan. The day we find out the sex of the baby. Look at all its parts. Watch it move. This is the day that things get very real.

Or not.

Layla stays quiet all the way up the elevator, while we wait to be called into the ultrasound, while she changes out of her dress, and while we wait for the technician to arrive.

Even after she does, my girl is tight-lipped, blinking furiously against a tide of emotion that's always threatening and made worse by the crazy hormones circulating through her body. She holds my hand with a death grip while the gel is applied to her belly and the probe is placed on top. We both watch the screen, searching the static for the one thing we are desperate to know. That she-it-he-whoever...is still alive.

Ba-dum.

The sound breaks through the technician's chatter and my cloudy thoughts loud and clear. It's a whisper, a rushing rhythm against the static, quick and lively. Layla's mouth is open, and I'm pretty sure mine is too—but I honestly can't tell, since neither of us seems to be breathing.

"God," I whisper as I stare at the screen. Something moves— a hand, a little foot. Some kind of limb that waves back and forth, swiping through the static noise to announce itself to the world.

"Oh, yes," says the tech as she looks at the screen. "I'd say you have a very healthy little girl here."

And at that word—that one little word—I swear to God, my heart drops all fourteen stories back to the asphalt.

"W-what?" I ask. "Did you say we're having a g-girl?"

Layla grins. Usually, she's the one who stutters when she's

nervous, not me. I kiss her knuckles absently, but I'm focused on the technician. I need to hear this news again to be sure.

"Well, there's always a chance we're not seeing something, but usually it's pretty clear at this point." The tech moves the sensor a little more. "See there? She's doing a great job of showing us what she's got. If it's a boy, you can usually see the penis from a few different angles, but when it's a girl, you really need her to spread her legs nicely, just like she's doing right now."

Layla giggles. I literally have to stifle a growl.

"Miss?"

The tech looks up.

"You're very nice and all," I say. "But I'm going to need you to stop talking about my daughter spreading her anything, okay?"

"Nico!"

Layla swats at my shoulder, but I'm dead serious. Jesus. If this is how I'm feeling about a blip on the screen, I don't even want to think about how I'm going to be when this tiny creature becomes a full-fledged person. As the tech continues moving the stick around and taking pictures of different parts of anatomy and answering Layla's questions, I'm imagining all sorts of things. Not death, but life. Because the baby on that screen is kicking up a fuckin' storm. There ain't nothing on that screen but bold, take-no-prisoners *life*, one cell at a time.

Me. Nico Soltero. With a daughter. A black-haired, blue-eyed girl who's probably going to be even more beautiful than her mother and have more attitude than her aunties. A daughter who will attract every motherfuckin' asshole New York City has to offer.

And just like that, my heart stops all over again and doesn't start beating until the ultrasound is over, Layla's cleaned up, and we're back on the street, walking to the car.

"Hey." Layla tugs my hand, pulling me to a stop somewhere

around Lexington and Seventy-Fourth. I think. I really can't tell. "Say something. Are you all right?"

"How are we going to protect her?" I whisper. "How are we going to make sure that she doesn't go through what you did? My mom did? Maggie did?"

Visions of the women I love most in the world, with their faces black and blue, flash through my head, and right there on the street, I have to stop. I have to lean against the sturdy brick wall of the building to calm my racing heart.

I thought it would kill me when I saw Layla torn up that way. I felt like committing murder, and I came closer to it than I'd like to admit. And to be honest, she's never fully recovered either. When something happens to you like that, you never totally do.

I don't think I'd survive if someone did that to my daughter. I really do think I'd keel over dead. Right after I buried the fuckin' bastard first.

Layla frames my face with her slim hands and presses her forehead to mine, ignoring the curious looks of New Yorkers walking past us on Lexington Avenue. The touch soothes me, but only just.

"That's not going to happen to her," Layla says. "I know it."

"But how do you know?" I ask. "How?"

She inhales as she pulls back but doesn't avert her gaze and doesn't move her hands. Those blue eyes could always see straight through me, and right now, they're holding me up.

"I know," she says, "because she's going to grow up with something different. Baby..." She trails off with that common name, the one I always used to call her, but now she's come to call me too. I like it. No, I love it.

She leans in and touches her nose to mine, then brushes her lips to mine.

"Don't you see?" she whispers in a voice that would be swept up by the city if we weren't so close.

My hands find her waist to pull her closer. This woman is my lifeline. My everything.

"You and I never knew the kind of love we have now. That's why it took us so long to figure out what we really had." She sighs, then kisses me again. "Our love doesn't just save us, Nico. It saves our kids. Our families. And their families too. That's how we'll protect our daughter. By loving her. But most of all, by loving each other."

It takes a few seconds, but she doesn't look away. Layla holds me with her wide blue gaze, straight and true, until her words nestle deep inside me and bloom with their truth. I pull her even closer, enjoy for a moment the feel of her in my arms. I remind myself that the past is in the past, and this woman has been my present for years now, and God willing, many more to come.

"You," I tell her. "I love you. You know that?"

She smiles against my lips. "I know that. And I love you too. Always."

"You hear that?" I look down at the bump that's barely visible under Layla's dress, then spread my palms over it. "I love your mom, baby girl. And don't you forget it, okay?"

Layla laughs, and the clear sound breaks through the fear and worry clouding my sad, sorry mind. Leave it to her to remind me of how much we have rather than how much we stand to lose. We won't get everything right. We'll make mistakes. But my girl's right about this, one hundred percent. What we are together saves us. Every single time.

"Do we really have to take the car back tonight?" I wonder as Nico steers K.C.'s big Yukon down one of the narrow streets in Hoboken. "I thought K.C. is touring through Europe this summer."

"He is." Nico pulls into a parking space about a block from K.C.'s brownstone and turns off the engine. "He left last week. But, uh, I think Alba needs it for something."

I arch a brow. He's lying—Nico's almost as bad of a liar as I am —but I don't know what about. Over the years, I've learned to read this man like a book, and never in the last five years have I *ever* known Alba to drive K.C.'s car. I'm not even sure she has a license.

"Come on," Nico says, jangling the keys. "She's inside cleaning for him. We'll just drop these off and go to dinner, okay?"

I get out of the car, and Nico takes my hand, humming a little as we walk, sometimes bouncing on his toes. Something shifted between the ultrasound office and here. Nico is lighter than he was twenty minutes ago. We're both buoyed by the news that the baby is good. That *she* is healthy and happy.

"This will be quick," Nico assures me as he unlocks the door to the apartment, though his eyes sparkle like black diamonds.

What is going on...

"SURPRISE!"

I'm practically tossed back into Nico's chest by the energy of all the people in the room who spring shouting and laughing as we walk in. K.C.'s big living room has been transformed from a sophisticated bachelor's pad into a sparkly blue pom-pom, covered pretty much floor to ceiling.

We're quickly engulfed by at least fifty different party guests, and it becomes evident just what this is: a graduation party.

In between kisses on the cheeks, I look around to find familiar faces of people I've come to know and love over the years, and some new ones too. Maggie and Allie sweep me up into a hug and are quickly joined by Selena and Carmen. I return their embraces and kisses whole-heartedly. None of my life would be possible without these incredible, strong women there to support me. They have been the ones who have watched Mateo when Nico was at the firehouse and I needed to study. They have been the ones who taught me how to cook well enough that I didn't completely gross out my family or burn down the house. They have been the ones who have provided untold emotional support over the years. My life is full and whole because I have them in it.

"You're late."

"Here we go," Maggie mutters to Selena.

I turn around to find Dad weaving through the small crowd. He leans in to give me a kiss on both cheeks, then, as if thinking better of it, gives me a hug too. Nico rolls his eyes, but I take it. My dad may never be the warmest man in the world, but he's definitely better than he used to be.

When he releases me, I smile. "We're not late. It's my party, right? I'm right on time."

"Where were you?" Dad asks as I give Mom a hug too. She rolls her eyes at me when we finish, as if to say, "I tried to stop him."

I turn to my dad. "We had an appointment with the ultrasound tech, if you must know. It was my twenty-week scan today, on top of all of this."

At the words, my dad's dark eyes bug out. "Layla, I told you I wanted to be there at the scan. You don't know if this technician is any good, *linda*. I'm a doctor. I know things she may not."

"Dad, you're a plastic surgeon, not a neonatal specialist. Plus, the technician works for the specialist *you* sent me too," I argue gently. "We wanted it to be just us this time, okay? But if you want to look at the ultrasounds, they are in my purse."

"That's not the point, Layla! The point is that we had an agreement, and as your father and a doctor, I have a right to be there—"

"Dr. Soltero," Nico breaks in, his voice tightening a little. "Let's let it go, all right? It's done, and ultimately, it was Layla's and my decision to make."

"Serge," Mom adds. "Come on, it's a party..."

Dad turns back to me, frustration and stubbornness warring across his features as he looks down at my stomach and back up to me. He opens his mouth to unleash another tirade, but it's quickly interrupted by another little voice shouting across the room.

"*Vovô! Pare!*"

Mateo comes tearing out of the kitchen, his little legs zipping him around Carmen's legs. Dad swivels around and immediately drops the attitude.

"*Vovô*, you said you would be nice today," Mateo chastises my dad openly in front of at least ten people watching us. He shakes his little finger, and behind Dad, my mom has to cover her mouth to keep from laughing.

"You promised," he says again, then tips his face up to his grandfather and waits.

Dad opens and closes his mouth a few times before sighing and squatting down so he's face-to-face with Mateo. Even though Mateo still looks mostly like Nico at this point, I can see little things of me in him too. Other than his blue eyes, which he obviously gets from me and Mom, Mateo gets that same divot between his eyebrows when he frowns that my dad does—right now they are mirroring each other.

"Nice?" Dad repeats.

Mateo nods. "You *promised*, Vovô."

Dad sighs. "Okay, okay. You win." He claps a hand on Mateo's head and stands up. "It's done. And yes, it's a party. We are here to celebrate." He turns to Mom, who is now watching with a raised brow. She's impressed with Mateo's technique. So am I, for that matter.

"Cher, where are the drinks?" Dad asks. "I could use a scotch."

"Come on, Serge," Mom says, pointing toward the refreshments table. "Let's get you sorted."

I turn back to Mateo, who immediately launches himself at my legs.

I reach down to pick him up, but before I can, Nico sweeps him off the floor and brings him eye level with me.

"Whoa there, dude. You got to be careful around *Mami*, all right? She's carrying some precious cargo."

"Stop. Let me hug my love, will you?" I accept Mateo's tight embrace when he tips toward me with outstretched arms. It's then I notice he's carrying a bouquet of ratty hydrangeas that have lost most of their blooms.

"Did we surprise you?" Mateo asks after he's done squeezing my neck.

I kiss him on the cheek and watch his eyelashes flutter on top. "Yeah, sweets, you did. Did you do this?"

Mateo, now content to sit in his dad's strong arms, nods, his blue eyes the same color as the decorations all around us. "Daddy and I got you these. *I* picked them out though, because Daddy couldn't remember which school you go to."

I take the hydrangeas from Mateo's chubby hands and make a big ordeal of sniffing them while he watches. They don't smell like anything—the flowers on the street rarely do—but the look on my kiddo's face turns me into the best actress on the planet.

"They are amazing," I assure him. "Thank goodness Daddy had you there to help."

Mateo puffs out his chest proudly and gives Nico a look that clearly says *I told you so.* "I helped *Abuela* make the cake too, see?"

He points to a big table at the far end of the room, which is already crowded with people.

I turn to Nico. "Did you do this too?"

My husband grins, that signature smiles of his lighting up the entire room. "I might have had something to do with it."

I look around again. Most of the people here are friends of Alba and Carmen—people Nico considers family just because they are part of the tight community he grew up in. Cousins galore, most of whom are related to K.C. directly. Flaco and his parents. Dozens of aunts and uncles, people who have blessed me and my child over and over again. There are other faces I know too —Shama, home from LA, where she took a job with an advertising agency. Gabe, taking a night off studying with his girlfriend, Sarah, another medical student in his cohort. Vinnie is back there somewhere, though he won't stay long, usually preferring to spend his weekends bar hopping with other investment bankers.

I turn back to Nico. "This is crazy. It's way too much."

He shrugs. "Try telling my mom that. You know you can't stop her and Alba when they want to throw a party. Add in Cheryl, and things go a bit crazy."

"What are they going to do when you graduate?"

It's hard to tell, but I think my man flushes a little. Just a few weeks ago, we received a letter from John Jay College of Criminal Justice admitting him for the fall semester as a part-time student, along with all of his previous community college credits and the prereqs he finished last year. He's nervous, but Nico decided in the end he wanted to do more than just follow orders at his station. Eventually, he wants to be the one giving them, and at some point, that requires a degree.

He doesn't even have to answer my question. I already know

that I'm going to plan the biggest party this city has ever seen when my man graduates from college. Between me, Carmen, his sisters, Alba, and K.C., it's basically going to be like New Year's Eve times ten.

So Nico just smiles again. "I might be a little proud of you, NYU. Not a lot of people could get their master's while they have a kid running around at home, especially this guy."

"Columbia!" Mateo shouts. "Her school is Columbia, Daddy. See, Mommy, he *still* doesn't know!"

Nico just grins even wider, and, though he speaks to Mateo, his twinkling black eyes are still trained on me, with a little more focus, carrying intent for later. When we are alone again. "What'd I say, huh? Mommy is always going to be my NYU."

I blush. I can't help it. Nico sucks on his bottom lip for a second, and my face turns even redder.

"*Ven,*" he says, tugging me close so that I'm wrapped up in the two men in my life, big and little arms together, while my husband kisses me. It's not the kind of kiss that anyone would accuse of being inappropriate, but it carries heat, nonetheless.

"I love you," he whispers into my ear, his deep voice thrilling down my spine. "And I am proud of you, so you better get used to it, baby."

I don't have to say I love you too—he knows it, every day, all day. But I still want to. That's the thing about love, something that Nico and I always seemed to understand. You want to tell them, every day, because when you love, really love someone, you want to see them lifted up. You thrive when you make them happy.

So I kiss him again while Mateo watches happily. "I love you too. Thank you."

Nico grins, then sets Mateo down on the floor. "All right, Mattie. Let's get this party started, shall we? First up, let's get your ma some punch."

Two hours later, my feet hurt from dancing so much, but I'm still swaying on the floor, held in a cocoon of my husband's strong arms. Without the benefit of K.C.'s musical stylings, our parents chose the playlist, which basically meant starting the evening with a few hours' worth of old-school salsa, followed by the string of bossa nova that's calming everyone down. Mateo is asleep under the table with a bunch of his other cousins, and the adults who haven't left or collapsed around the couch in food comas are grooving lightly to the saxophone and piano soothing the room to sleep.

I lay my head on Nico's shoulder, letting him slowly turn us around the middle of the living room. I haven't had a drop of alcohol, but I feel drunk—with happiness.

Across the room, my parents are dancing, close and in a way they haven't for years. As if sensing the change, Nico follows my gaze.

"Look at that," he murmurs. "Something happening there?"

I turn my face into his neck. "I doubt it. That looks more like goodbye to me."

After five years of separation, my mom finally put her foot down and demanded a divorce. She hasn't mentioned anything yet, but I suspect she's met someone new. Grandpa died just after Mateo's birth, so it's been just her and Grandma in that big house in Pasadena. I wouldn't blame her at all for wanting something more than country club dinners.

But still. What kid doesn't like seeing their parents together? I never miss the dreamy look on Mateo's face when he sees Nico and I kiss after a few days apart—sometimes he's more excited for our reunion than for his own after Nico finishes a long shift.

As if he knows what I'm thinking, Nico rubs a broad hand up

and down my back. The simple touch warms me. This is what he does—always takes care of me.

"Not everyone can be as lucky as us," he says.

I close my eyes, content to feel his touch lingering over my neck, shoulders, and spine. It's true. We are lucky—incredibly so. And the crazy thing is, I know there's more to come.

Maybe that's why I still feel that melancholy from time to time —that longing, that desire, for something a little more. Brazilians call it *saudade*, the word that's printed on my ribs and Nico's, twin statements of that yearning neither of us can ever quite shake. A desire for something that maybe hasn't even happened. The future that lies before us.

There are so many things coming. My new job, starting as a children's social worker. My entire career will be to make sure that kids who find themselves here alone don't get lost the way she was. That they always have someone to help them find their way. Nico's school, which I know he'll attack with the same gusto with which he approaches every new thing he sets out to accomplish. Our daughter, on her way, and who will no doubt be as much of a delight and challenge as her big brother.

I long for these events because I know they'll bring us more happiness, more joy, more heartache, more fulfillment.

"I love you," I whisper, lower than the music, low enough that he probably doesn't even hear me.

But he does. Nico hears more than my words. He hears my soul.

The hand at my back moves up to cradle my head to his shoulder, while his other arm remains tight around my waist. He strokes my hair and murmurs something unintelligible in what sounds like Spanish. My own Spanish is good enough now that I'd be able to understand it if I could hear it at all. But it's okay. Right now, I'm content just to feel.

We stand like that for a few more moments, catching the eyes of a few onlookers. All our parents glance over with clear fondness —it swims out of Carmen, and even my father's normally stern features soften. It's because they know what this is. They know what we are.

Nico hums a little as he plays with my hair, and I feel the truth sink in before he even says the words.

"I love you too," he whispers back, his soft lips dusting lightly over my ear. "Always."

***

Catch up with the rest of the series here: www.nicole frenchromance.com/badidea

EXTRA SCENES & SNIPPETS

In another world, Layla finagles a date...

But things start to slow down after five. Karen actually leaves by 5:30 with a few curt reminders to lock up before I go. I find myself unable to focus on the dry chapters of Aphra Behn, instead watching the seconds tick by on the clock, always conscious as the time draws closer to six

At 6:03, the elevator doors chime open. I look up from my book and am sorely disappointed when a middle-aged man wearing a bland brown suit shuffles in.

"Hello, I'm Jared Blake, here to see Steven Fox, please," he says as he approaches my desk.

I smile politely. "Of course, sir." I dial Mr. Fox's assistant. "Hi, Mae. Jared Blake for Mr. Fox."

Mae assures me she'll be up soon; in the meantime, I am to offer Mr. Blake a drink.

"Just water is fine," he says, taking a seat in one of the plush green chairs in the lobby. I hurry off to grab a cup of water from the cooler in the back, hoping the phones won't ring while I'm gone.

The elevator door opens just as I'm handing Mr. Blake his drink, and I turn around to find Nico wheeling out another large stack of packages. *Damn.* I can't flirt in front of clients.

"Hey, NYU!" he greets me, flashing that light-bulb smile that makes my knees buckle all over again.

I can't help but note the way his FedEx jacket pulls against the muscles in his broad shoulders. And now I'm wondering just how many times I'll fantasize about being carried away on those shoulders before I can actually get him to do it. The thought again occurs to me that this guy can probably get any girl he wants with that grin. I am way out of my league here.

What the hell was I thinking?

"H-hi Nico," I greet him.

Come on, Layla. Get it together. I have practiced this conversation in my head at least fifty times today. My plan isn't going to work if I'm too lust-struck to speak.

Mae walks out with a huge smile for Nico.

"Hi, there," she greets him brightly.

Another smile. This guy has a smile for everyone. Nico tips his hat at her as he unloads the packages.

Mae looks like she's about to combust, then reluctantly ushers Mr. Blake down the hall to her boss's office, leaving Nico and me standing alone in the lobby together. The only thing between us is the foot-wide barrier of the desktop.

"Need some help?" I venture.

Somehow, I manage to walk around the back of the desk so I can actually stand next to him. It's not just for my benefit; I'm angling to give him a view of how I look in my carefully chosen outfit. Unfortunately, I didn't account for the fact that being this close to him reveals that he smells almost as good as he looks, with some indistinguishable men's scent and a faint musk that has got to be all him. I have to grip the edge of the desk to stand up straight—that's how good he smells. Seriously, what is going on here?

In my three-inch stilettos, I'm maybe a half-inch below him, nearly eye-to-eye. He notices my proximity and offers another heart-stopping grin. *Jesus*, I think as I reregister the deep thumps in my chest, *this guy must get more tail than a stray dog.*

"Nah, that's okay, sweetie," he's saying kindly. "But you can give me your autograph right there."

He points a large finger at the space on his digital scanner for a signature. I resist the urge to write my phone number as well. That would be too obvious, I think.

"There you go," I say, handing the small device back to him. He uses it to scan the packages on the floor, and then wheels the dolly back to the elevator without so much as a second look my way. Crap. This is where I have to make a move if I'm going to get things going. Valentine's Day is next Friday.

"Ah, Nico?"

I clear my throat awkwardly, but he stops and turns mid-reach for the elevator button.

"Whatcha need, NYU?"

I smooth my sweater as I try and probably fail to lean nonchalantly against the edge of the desk. But I'm not a total amateur, so I intentionally brush the fabric with a long, slow stroke. I smile to myself as I note his eyes flicker over my body for a half-second before returning to my face as if he hadn't just been checking me out.

"Well," I say slowly, as if pondering some great question.

He's fixated on my face, his mouth slightly open before he starts chewing on his lip. When his gaze flickers down to my own mouth for a nanosecond, I'm extremely thankful I took a bathroom break to retouch my lipstick just before he arrived.

"I was wondering. Some friends of mine want to meet me for drinks up here tonight, but I don't really know this neighborhood very well. Do you know anywhere that's good?"

Nico purses his lips, his extremely kissable lips. God, this man is gorgeous. Seriously, there is a very strong likelihood that with all this daydreaming, I am probably turning myself on more than him. Go figure.

"Well, my favorite bar in this neighborhood is The Traveler," he says. "Me and the boys go there after work a lot. But other than that, I don't really go out much around here since I live uptown."

Bingo. There's my in. I lean over the desktop and grab a Post-It notepad and a pen. It gives me a reason to arch my back and perk up my ass; when I stand up, I'm happy to see that his line of sight it glued to that part of my anatomy. Doing my best, to stifle my triumph, I smile politely.

"Traveler's," I say phonetically as I scrawl the name of the pub on my pad. "So, where *do* you go, then?"

Nico jerks his gaze back up to my face, looking slightly dazed. "Oh, ah, well, that depends on what I'm into. I don't have much time to go out, actually."

"FedEx working you too hard?" I give him a sly half-smile as I stand up straight, tracing a finger over the wood grain on the desk next to my hip. He follows the path of my finger for a moment before looking back up to me.

He snorts at my statement, tossing that idea aside with the flick of a big hand. "Nah, I have another job on the weekends. I work the door at AJ's on Saturday nights."

Jackpot.

"AJ's?" I asked, trying to look like I hadn't just heard him mention the club last night. I know exactly where AJ's is. I even tried to go there once with the girls, but we were turned away when there were too many people.

"It's a little club over Chelsea," Nico's saying. "Kind of over by the Piers. They do some live music and dancing. You and your friends should come by sometime. This Saturday is dancehall night."

Double jackpot. There's my invitation.

"Maybe we will," I say sweetly.

I take my time walking back around the desk, aware that he is watching my progress. It's not until I actually take my seat that he reaches back to push the elevator button. He has to tap the wall a few times to find it, since his eyes don't move from me. I hide a smile behind my computer screen. Another point, Layla.

"How old are you, NYU?" Nico asks out of nowhere, tipping up the curved bill of his FedEx hat to see me more clearly. His eyes are somehow darker in the light, and my heart speeds up just a touch under his gaze.

"Twenty-one," I reply automatically. I don't want to lie, but it hasn't escaped me that he's a doorman to a place I might go this weekend.

Unfortunately, I can't lie to save my life.

Nico tips his nose down at me and arches one eyebrow. "How old are you really?"

I sigh. "Nineteen. How old are *you*?"

He clicks his tongue and let out a whistle. "Too old," he says reluctantly. The elevator doors open and he wheels the dolly back inside.

"No, really, how old are you?" I call as he pushes the button. He grins as they close, but I hear the number "twenty-six" float from between the doors along with that bright smile just before they close.

I sat down with a thump, and my heart did the same thing inside my chest. Damn, I'd really been hoping for twenty-three, twenty-four at most. The better part of a decade spans between us.

Well, at least he's not quite old enough to make me keep my promise to Quinn. It's not much of a consolation, but it's something. Besides, I'll be twenty in just a few months, so it is really more like six years. Not *that* bad, really.

By the end of my shift, I have almost completely convinced myself that decade age difference means nothing, despite the fact that the oldest guy I have dated up until that point hasn't quite graduated college. But this is New York, and I practically live like I'm an adult on my own anyway. Half my friends have dated guys in their mid to late twenties already—it's too easy, when we all have fake IDs and spend most of our weekends going to bars along with the rest of New York's single population. It won't matter a bit. And anyone that gorgeous is worth a little difference in age.

By the time I lock the elevator door and walk out to the street at seven, I have already formulated my next move. It'll require a short skirt and a posse, but a trip up to Chelsea this weekend is definitely in order.

After the hospital

After I'm released from the hospital, Quinn, Nico, and I all shove into a cab back downtown to the dorms. It's warm, but I feel loads better after getting the IV treatment. I sit in the middle, tucked securely into Nico's side while Quinn jabbers on about finals coming up and her plans for the summer (she's spending it in Corpus Christi with her grandparents). His thumb runs over my shoulder, toying with the thin strap of my dress. The movement consistently reminds me of what we missed out on this afternoon. I don't feel like I've been in the hospital. I feel like I was on a date that was very rudely interrupted.

We all file into the dorm lobby, where I sign Nico in with the front desk. Quinn talks the whole time, almost as if she's nervous about something. Maybe she can feel the tension between Nico and me—every time he touches me, electricity practically pops off my skin. There is nothing I want more than an empty apartment right now.

"Aren't you coming?" I ask when she stays in the lobby instead of following us to the elevator bank.

"Ah, no," she says, glancing between the two of us. "Jamie and Shams and I are going to grab some Chinese." She looks to Nico. "You staying the night, FedEx?"

Nico grimaces slightly. I know how much he's ready to be done with that identifier. "Only if Layla wants me to," he says.

"I want," I assure him with a squeeze to his hand.

He flashes me a bright smile—there go my knees. "I want," he says.

"Then it's settled. But don't—ah—wear her out too much, all right, Chachi? You've got a couple of hours, but this one doesn't need to land back in the hospital."

I roll my eyes. "Thanks, *Mom*."

Quinn just smirks. "You got it, babe. Later, kids."

The apartment is empty when we make it up. Nico and I move silently about it. "I like you like this," he says as he drifts both hands up and down the sides of my body. "I like you anyway."

Some spicy time

I suck in a harsh breath as his mouth starts to follow his hands, drifting lightly up and down my rib cage, floating over the sensitive skin just under my arms, around my navel, up the edges of my ribs, and finally feathering over my breasts. He places a soft, gentle kiss between them and inhales deeply.

"You smell so good right here," he murmurs as he rubs his nose lightly over the soft, untouched flesh there. My hands find a place in his thick curls while his mouth kisses me lightly. It's an erogenous zone for me, one of those secret places on my body only he's ever found, a place that turns me straight to putty in his hands.

His hands slide down my hips to grip my backside, that ever-favored part of my anatomy. I shy, but he holds me still, grasping and kneading while his mouth finds one taut nipple and starts to suck with abandon.

"Ooohhhh." The moan leaves me before I can help it. His lips and tongue busy themselves, nipping and pulling on the sensitive pebble before moving to the other, while his hands continue to massage my ass.

"Fuck," he breathes against me, his breathing growing rougher along with the touch of his hands. I know Nico—it's not in him to be gentle when he gets started, and he's quickly losing control. I love that I can make him do that.

I grasp at his hair and yank his head back. He welcomes my kiss, pulling me to straddle him in the bed, opening his mouth to mine so our tongues can twist together with abandon.

"You sure you can handle this?" he mumbles in between long, intense kisses.

"I...need you," I mutter, gripping his hair even harder as I suck on his bottom lip that drives me crazy.

He nips me back, then flips me over so I'm on my back with a squeal. He quickly rids himself of his underwear, and I'm faced with his naked body in all its glory kneel over mine. He peruses my nake form with the same adoration I'm sure is all over my face.

"God, you're so fuckin' beautiful," he says, tracing his hands over my breasts, my waist, and down between my legs. I arch against his hand as his fingers find my clit, immediately finding that rhythm he has become so good at performing.

"Mmmm," I hum while he watches with darkening eyes. He reaches down with his other hand to massage his erection, rubbing his fist leisurely over it while he helps me build as well. It's incredibly hot watching him, masturbating us both at the same time, in the same rhythm. My hips rise and fall with his movements as if of their own accord, and without thinking, my hands move to my breasts to play with my nipples while he works. Nico growls at the changes; his pupils dilate noticeably.

"Fuck, that's hot," he says as his hands pick up their pace.

Layla's dad reminds her it's Ash Wednesday

I am feeling somewhat better. The headache is still there, as is a hint of a sore throat, but the wooziness is gone, and for the first time in three days, I feel like I can think clearly.

The truth is, since taking this new job I've been burning the candle at both ends, working too long into the evenings, studying too late at night, and then going out too much on the weekends. I study at work when I can, but it's hard to focus with phone calls interrupting every minute or two. So I've been staying up much later at night to keep up with school, often studying until two or three in the morning before getting up for classes at six-thirty. Spending the weekend with Nico was the straw that broke the proverbial camel's back, so to speak—I'm not that surprised my immune system finally collapsed.

I toss the covers aside and yank myself out of bed, doing my best not to disturb Quinn's sleeping form across the room. The girls all have ten-thirty classes, lucky bitches. With a wistful glance at my warm, rumpled comforter, I trudge off to the shower to wash the grime of fever off my body.

There's a bowl of oatmeal cooking in the microwave, and I'm just starting on my first cup of coffee when my phone buzzes angrily at seven. I swipe down to find a message from my calendar reminding me that it's Ash Wednesday. I groan as the phone vibrates again, this time over and over again with an actual call. I sigh. I know exactly who it is. And if I don't pick it up, he'll just keep trying.

"Hi, Dad," I greet my father. "You know it's four in the morning in Seattle, right? That is one God-awful hour."

I'm joking, but it's actually not that surprising. My father, the consummate workaholic, is the kind of man who wakes up at four to go to the gym before performing three back-to-back surgeries and coming home sometime after ten. Apparently sleeping less than six hours a night doesn't make *him* sick.

"Layla, don't take the Lord's name in vain, especially today." My father's accented voice, deep and proud, scolds me through the speaker. Even from three thousand miles away, he has the ability to make me feel like I'm about three feet tall.

I roll my eyes, grateful he can't see me through the phone. Outside it's snowing again. Damn, that means I'll have to wait for the shuttle instead of walking to campus with Vinnie.

"Okay, okay, sorry," I relent. "But do you want to tell me why you're calling me before the crack of dawn on a Wednesday?" The microwave beeps loudly. I pull my steaming oatmeal out and doctor it up with brown sugar and milk, sitting down at the counter. I set the phone next to me and flick it onto speaker. I haven't spoken to my dad in several weeks, so this has the potential to go on for a while.

"What are you eating?"

"What? Dad, seriously, you got up at four in the morning to ask me what I'm eating?"

A heavy silence, the kind only my father can communicate over a telephone, echoes through the kitchen. His disappointment is palpable, and I felt predictably and inexplicably guilty. I know that sigh well. Catholic parents perfected it, and mine have made it an art form.

"What day is it, Layla?"

I frown at my oatmeal. It's Ash Wednesday, I know. Oh...shit. I mean, shoot.

"Don't think that just because you live so far away we don't expect you to observe Lent. I already know you don't go to mass like you're supposed to—"

"Ugh, Dad, you don't know that!" I protest, irritably shoving my bowl away from me on the counter. He's right, of course, but I don't need to confirm it. Part of the conditions of letting me go to school so far away is that I'm supposed to attend Mass at least once a week, but I never do. Usually, he never asks except on special days like this, and if he's annoyed, he usually requires some kind of photographic proof. Usually, it depends on how guilty he's feeling. The fact that he's calling me doesn't bode well.

My father just continues his diatribe as if I said nothing. "Lent is important, and you know it. It's a time to be grateful. You know this. I'm calling to remind you today is a fast day, and I expect to see that you are going to Mass this afternoon. With proof."

"Dad—" I start to protest. I have no time for Mass, especially in the middle of the week. When am I supposed to fit it in? Before work?

As if he's reading my mind, my father promptly says, "I just emailed you a list of churches with afternoon masses and their times. There is one by your new job. You should be able to go before you work at two. And don't forget—only one full meal today. We may not be able to see you there, but Layla, God does."

Ah, God. The man with so many eyes I sometimes wondered growing up if he was a giant insect, like the picture of the flies I would see in my science books. If I have been threatened by his all-seeing presence once, I have been threatened a million times. I sigh and put my bowl of oatmeal into the sink and pour my coffee regretfully down the drain. So much for breakfast.

"Okay. Thanks for the reminder. I have to get going. Class starts in forty-five minutes."

"Your mother says hello. Send your picture tonight."

It's not a picture of my pretty face he wants; it's the proof of the ashes on my forehead. I sigh. Sometimes I really regret the entire existence of smartphones.

"Sure, Dad, I'll text it to you later."

"Goodbye, Layla."

"Bye," I reply, but he's already hung up.

I shove my phone in my messenger bag and toss the oatmeal into the garbage before cleaning my dishes. I grab my water bottle and put a piece of bread in a napkin to take with me on the shuttle bus to campus. Maybe if I pretend hard enough, I can make it taste like a donut. Maybe if I pray hard enough, the big man himself will help me out with that.

***

Layla is even sicker

My slight sore throat has morphed into knives down my esophagus, and I can't seem to get out of bed for more than an hour before feeling weak and needing to get back in again. My roommates make me chicken noodle soup again, but I have a hard time getting any of it down because I still feel nauseous, and anything going down my sensitive throat feels like I'm swallowing knives.

I've gotten a few worried texts from Nico, but I've ignored all of them, letting my phone die completely on the top of my desk. Though I know I should be glad I don't actually have the energy to have strong emotions, let alone fight them, I still fall asleep each night feeling disappointed that he hasn't bribed his way into the building again to check on me or send up another round of comfort food. Maybe he doesn't know I'm not actually at work and thinks that I'm purposefully avoiding him. Maybe he doesn't want to see me anymore either. The thought is painful.

After going to her last class on Friday morning, Quinn marches into my room and finds me collapsed again on top of my bed, in the simultaneous throes of a coughing attack and complete emotional misery.

"That's it," she says, yanking me up roughly by one arm. "You need help, Barros."

"Hey," I protest, weakly batting her hand away without much effect. "I'm fine. I just need to sleep."

In response I have a coat tossed in my face.

"I'm taking you to the doctor, lady," she informs me as I yank it off. "We have an appointment at the Student Health Center at one. Layla, you've been seriously sick for a week, and you're getting worse. You look like you've lost about ten pounds already. It's time to see someone."

When Quinn is like this, I know better than to argue, and I have a fraction of the will power that would normally fuel my irritation.

"Okay," I relent, and follow slowly out of the apartment.

THE STUDENT HEALTH center off Washington Square is housed on the fourth floor of one of the larger NYU buildings. I've been there all of twice before—once to update my immunizations before going to Brazil last summer, and once to get my yearly STI check and stock up on free condoms. Don't judge. Condoms are expensive, and there is a big basket of them up for grabs at the SHC.

The waiting room is reasonably packed with students in various stages of winter viruses when we arrive. I slump gladly into one of the hard plastic seats to wait while Quinn checks me in.

It's getting to the point where it's hard to speak. I'd never had strep throat, but I'm wondering if that's what this is—according to WEBMD, it's the most likely illness for my combination of symptoms. Quinn's nicely catty as we wait for the doctor, making jokes about the interior design of the building and the irritating students who surround us. She's working hard to make me smile, so I try to plaster on a grin or two even though I would rather just go back to sleep. Right now the stained carpeted floor looks like the best bed I've ever seen. Ugh. Being this sick is unbelievably inconvenient right now. I have midterms in two weeks, and I can't really afford to miss any more class.

The thing I really hate about the SHC is the sheep-like mood of the place—it's a very "get 'em in, get 'em out" kind of ethic, and there are hardly any doctors there anyway. I'm glad my dad hasn't seen it—a complete and total snob, he'd be horrified that his daughter's primary health care providers are all nurse practitioners.

Once I'm given a small bed (they don't even have proper exam rooms here, just beds separated by thin blue curtains), I have to wait another thirty minutes. I listen to Quinn making increasingly dumb jokes until eventually I start to doze off while she reads her marketing textbook.

"Layla Barros?"

The voice of a young man jerks me out of my fever-induced stupor, and I sit up from the bed, blinking wildly to look alert.

"Hi," he says. "I'm Aaron Bradford, one of the nurse practitioners here."

See, this is what I'm talking about. Three times I've been here, and I still have yet to see a real doctor. Nurse practitioners are fine and all, but sometimes I'd like to see someone who's actually done a full round of medical school, you know? Plus, this guy looks like he is about twelve.

Apparently I'm a bit of a snob too.

"What seems to be the problem here?" he says affably, taking a seat on the small black stool in front of the hospital bed.

"She's sick," Quinn pipes up behind him. "Sore throat, fever, super tired all the time. And you can't swallow, right, babe?"

Gratefully, I nod at her.

"That's right," I whisper to the nurse. "What she said." Every word feels like someone is sticking a hot iron down my throat.

"Well, let's take a look," says the NP. "Open up your mouth for me?"

He shines a small light and sticks a tongue depressor down the back of my throat as he examines it. Okay, so he might be young, but he's not incompetent. He then runs his hands up and down my neck and under my throat, checking my ears and eyes and taking my temperature.

"One-oh-one," he reads off the thermometer once it beeps. "You're quite hot, Layla."

Sounds familiar. Except for when I'm freezing cold, of course.

"Is it possible it's mono?" Quinn asks from her chair, which she's already edged forward a few inches. "A couple of kids on our floor had it last month."

The NP shakes his head while he takes my blood pressure. "No, I don't think so. You've got pretty clear signs of strep throat,

Layla. Fever and white spots on the back of your tongue and throat. I don't think I'll even have to do a culture."

"Are you sure?" Quinn replies suspiciously. "She's tired all the time. Like, she can't stop sleeping. It's weird. I've had strep, and I never felt like that."

If I had the energy, I would roll my eyes at her. She's so pushy. A year into pre-med and she thinks she knows better than an actual healthcare provider.

"A bad case of strep can make you feel fatigued. People respond to illnesses in all different ways." The NP flips out a white pad and scribbles a prescription on it.

"This is for amoxicillin," he informs me, ripping off the paper and handing it to me. I take it gingerly between my palms. "Swallow the pills with food and drink as much water as you can. You should be better by Monday, but you're still really contagious right now, so try not to be in contact with too many people. If you're on the pill, don't have unprotected sex with your partner when you're on antibiotics, okay?"

So much for bedside manner. Gratefully, I nod him, not wanting to speak if I can avoid it. I'm not actually on the pill, but since I don't have a partner right now, there will be on sex, unprotected or protected.

"Any questions for me?" asks the NP, already slinging his stethoscope back over his shoulder and looking on his clipboard for his next patient.

"No," I croak. Before I can say thank you, he's already left.

THE ANTIBIOTICS WORK QUICKLY. I sleep in on Saturday and wake up around eleven feeling like I can actually function again. My head still aches a bit, and I still feel tired, but my sore throat and fever are all but gone. I emerge from the bedroom to find Jamie and Quinn making orange juice and some kind of breakfast after a spinning class at the gym. I frown. I don't even want to think about how long it's been since I was able to work out.

"Hey, lady!" Jamie bounds over to me and hands me a fresh cup of orange juice. I look at it warily—my throat isn't sore, but the memory of that rawness makes a giant cup of citrus juice look like sulfuric acid. I take a small sip. It tastes good. I take another.

"Thanks," I say, proceeding to gulp down the whole glass. I realize that it's been close to four days since I've eaten a proper meal, and much longer if you don't count Nico's pity takeaway. My pajamas—one of the many pairs of scrubs I stole from my dad —hang even looser than normal from my hips. "What are you guys making?"

"Scrambled egg whites with spinach," Quinn says from her place at the stove. She turns. "Do you want some?"

I smile at Jamie's covert eye roll. "Or you can just have normal eggs and bacon with me," she says. Quinn is the only one of us who eats things like egg whites, living in constant terror of gaining back excess pounds. Her food usually lacks fat, salt, sugar, and also taste.

"Um, that's all right," I say. "I'll have some of Jamie's. Thanks, though."

"One for the yolk lovers," Jamie says, taking my empty glass and walking back to the kitchen.

"How are you feeling, babe?" Quinn asks as she pushes her egg white scramble around the skillet. Even though I know it probably tastes mostly like rabbit food, it still makes my mouth water.

"Better," I say as I sidle up onto a stool at the kitchen table. "Sore throat is gone, and I feel like I can actually move without losing all my juice, so to speak."

"Nice." She flips her eggs onto a plate and moves over so that

Jamie can crack a few into the pan for her and me. Quinn comes to sit at the table next to me. "Did you take your antibiotics this morning?"

I roll my eyes and produce the bottle of pills from the pocket of my scrubs. "Doing it now, Mom."

Jamie helpfully supplies me with a glass of water, and I toss down one of the pills while Quinn watches with a smirk on her face.

"Satisfied?" I ask her.

"Someone has to make sure you take care of yourself, Barros," she tells me through a bite of eggs, her brown eyes gleaming. "I think that's how you got sick in the first place."

"Because I don't have a babysitter? Yeah, well, I'm still contagious, so you bitches are probably going to get it next."

I stretch my arms up overhead with a loud yawn. I've been cooped up in this apartment for the better part of the week (my half-foray to work and glance at the health center don't really count), so I'm starting to get a serious case of cabin fever. Apartments in New York aren't made to be lived in—that's what the city's for.

Jamie sets a plate of eggs and bacon down in front of me, which I immediately inhale. I'm already making plans of what I can do today that will be cheap and get me out of the apartment, despite the cold weather. I desperately need a shower, and I probably need another day's rest before going out with the girls, but I think I can handle a trip to a museum. I realize yesterday was Friday, which means I finally got paid too. I smile. Even though I'm not one hundred percent better, it's going to be a good day.

Layla in Pasadena after *Lost Ones*

"Hey, baby."

His deep, melodic voice plucks at a chord deep in my chest.

"Hey," I reply, not even caring that I sound like a lovesick schoolgirl.

He hums, clearly hearing my tone. "What are you doing?"

"Just finished with Dr. Whelan and heading to work. You?"

"We just ended. I'm beat. Getting some dinner and then home for the night, thank God. My first weekend off in fuckin' months."

We talk like this every night when Nico gets off from the Academy, where he's training to become a member of the FDNY. And then we do it again when I get off from my summer job helping in the childcare center at the YWCA. And often again if he has to work an extra shift checking IDs at one of the clubs around the city. And usually first thing in the morning too, before he leaves for the Academy. It's usually about four a.m. LA time when those calls happen, but I don't even care.

"I like pretending I'm waking you up with me," Nico will say. And then he rumbles, and before I know it, we're engaged in some very explicit phone sex that should not be possible at four a.m. but still very much is with him. Because it's Nico.

"You ready?" he asks me as I get into the car I've been driving all summer—my grandmother's old Lexus that she kept for a few extra months for me after she bought a new one.

I turn on the ignition and the A/C immediately. It's late August in Pasadena, which basically means it's hot and sweaty, and the car is a freaking sauna.

"Yeah," I say.

"You sound thrilled, baby." There's an awkward pause. "You, um, sure you're ready to come back?"

It's a loaded question. Three and a half months ago, I left New

York broken. Literally bruised and battered after suffering an attack by a crazed and, as it turned out, high-as-a-kite boyfriend, I arrived in Pasadena in May only after Nico had physically rescued me from the scene and escorted me to the airport two days later after arranging it with my mother. Since then, she and I have been...reconnecting. Sort of. I'm not sure my mom and I will ever have a truly close relationship, but the look on her face when I got off that plane was at least enough to tell me she still cared.

But after a summer of therapy. Of spending my time helping other battered women and their kids. Of I'm ready to go back.

I think.

"It's hard," I tell him. "I'm...I'm a little nervous, to tell the truth."

There's a pause. My nervousness makes Nico nervous too, I can tell. But I don't want to be anything less than upfront with him.

I am nervous. Three and a half months ago, the love of my life rescued me only to say goodbye with a promise he'd be there waiting when I returned.

But then what?

Despite talking multiple times a day, Nico and I don't really know what we are. I know he's not seeing anyone. I know he loves me. But beyond that...I don't really know what I'm coming back to. Or how yet we'll be able to move on from our own painful past, one I know he still takes the blame for.

Over a year ago now, Nico left for LA himself. After dating me, loving me, making me fall hopelessly in love with him that spring, he left New York, off

I understood why he needed to go. And I also know that it's not the only reason for my disastrous year last year, certainly not the only reason why I ended up with someone like Giancarlo. But it's part of it. And, as Dr. Whelan has helped me identify, there is maybe a small part of me that does hold him a little responsible for what happened to me. Because it's true, what he said. If he had never left...things wouldn't have happened.

Yeah. I'm pretty ready to see him again.

Layla surprises a tired Nico

Her eyes, the color of the ocean around us and just as deep, swirl, full of mischief.

I don't care how tired I am. I don't care that I spent my day crawling around on my hands and knees, running up and down stairs of what feels like a dozen different walk ups in Jackson Heights. I swear to God, the city needs to outlaw curling irons and deep fryers. We'd go on about half the calls we do if those things were done with.

But I don't care that I'm about ready to drop. I'll carry her to the top of the Empire fuckin' State Building if it will make her laugh like that again. The way she still only does here and there since I found her in that apartment last spring. They way I want her to do all the time, if I could just fine a way...

"Hey." She puts a hand on my cheek, and I lean into her touch. "Everything all right?"

Her smile is gone, replaced with worry. Fear. *Coño,* I fucked this up.

I shake my head and push off the couch, then pull her up with me. "Nah, baby. Everything's fine."

Layla frowns. Doubt is written all over her beautiful face—she wants to know why I stopped. No, you asshole. You're not going to ruin the evening by bringing all that shit up again. She thinks about it enough as it is.

"Um, I'll just close the door, I guess," she says, skirting around me.

Fuck. *Fuck.* That skittishness is back, the same as last week, last spring. And it kills me after I finally saw her again, *my* Layla, the one I met before everything went to hell. The person whose smile was free, whose light shone brighter than the sun.

I hate that it's dimmed again. I want my baby back. So I sit back on the sofa and toss my hat on the coffee table along with her purse. Layla glances at me, then shuffles into her room.

"I, um...I'm just going to change," she says and shuts the door behind her.

Sitting alone in the dark, I stare up at the ceiling. *Fuck*, I'm such an idiot. I had a girl—no, I had *the* girl—crawling all over me, laughing, sucking on my lip like a Jolly fuckin' Rancher, and I stopped her. After a month of nothing but my fist, my dick is screaming at me right now. You fuckin' idiot. You just can't leave well enough alone, can you?

I push my hands over my face. "Ahhh," I groan to myself. "You should take your sorry ass back to firehouse. Just go."

"I don't want you to go. Why would you go?"

I turn and find Layla standing there in nothing but a scrap of lace. Half a smile tugs at one side of her mouth, and a flush rises clearly up her neck as she catches my expression. Fuck me, she's so goddamn beautiful.

"You...you like it?" She tugs nervously on the ends of her hair. "I bought it in LA. I...I thought you might want to see it."

She bought this for me. Maybe to some people, this wouldn't be that big of a deal. Another girl. Another lacy whatever-you-call-it. But I'm not the guy women buy this shit for. I'm the guy they sneak into their apartments when their roommates are asleep. The guy drunk girls hit on after a long night at the club. The guy they slum with. Not the one they actually make the effort for.

But not Layla. She's only looked at me the way she is right now. Like I matter. Like I actually deserve this effort of a fancy lace whatever-it's-called. Like I deserve the way she's always just given her whole self to me.

"Do I like it?" I ask, the words sticking in my throat.

Layla needs Nico

I yank his t-shirt out of his waistband, eager to find his skin. I'm naked in front of him—the least he could do is return the favor.

To my regret, Nico steps back, and with another sly smile, reaches behind his neck and pulls his shirt over his head. My mouth drops at the sight of him, but he doesn't noticed, suddenly intent on kicking off his shoes and undoing his pants. When he finally does look up, he still when he catches me staring. Drooling.

He's perfect. It shouldn't surprise me —after all, it's hardly the first time I've seen him like this. But on Monday, we were a fumbling mess in the still-dark morning, too blinded by awkward need to really notice each other. And how long had it been before that? Three, four weeks? It might as well have been an eternity.

He looks the same, and yet somehow different. Still the same smooth brown skin that glides over muscles made from motion, not dead weights. Still the same tattoos—the half-sleeve that winds around his right shoulder and upper arm and the large compass over his heart that now bears my name. The small line of script over his ribs. But the edges of him are a little sharper, the sinewy lines just a little deeper. The broad ridges of his chest and abs ripple as the moonlight catches on their shadows. With his sooty black eyes and slightly overgrown black curls, Nico looks like a marauder, a pirate out of a regency novel, bent on pillaging a maiden.

Except his eyes. Reflected in them is all of the conflicting, complicated emotions I feel. Love. Pain. A wanting so bad it hurts.

But, as I'm finally learning to accept, it doesn't have to anymore.

"Come here," I say softly, reaching out my hand. "I need you."

The white dress

"Nico?"

Layla's voice floats over the barrier.

I jerk around. "Yeah, baby, what's up?"

"Um, nothing. I just wanted to know what you think of this dress. "

She steps out from behind the curtain looking shy in a short, white dress.

"Oh, yeah," I breathe. "That one."

Layla stands up to her dad

"I don't need this." Nico stands up and flips a few bills onto the table. "That should cover Layla's and my dinners, Mr. Barros."

Then, with a quick black look at me, he leaves.

Once I've recovered from my shock at what just happened, I turn back to my father, who's still staring after Nico's receding form.

"What is *wrong* with you?" I demand. "How could you be so insulting!"

My dad shrugs and takes a long sip of his whiskey. "It's not my fault the boy can't take some criticism."

"You just called him a criminal, not to mention a lot of other things."

"He *is* a criminal," Dad cuts out neatly. "He admitted it himself."

"He's a hero," I correct him. "He's a firefighter at the most well-known department in the world. He saves lives *literally* every day. All you do is give women bigger tits!"

"Watch your mouth!" Dad sets his glass on the table a little too hard and gives me a hard look. A few years ago, that look might have shut my mouth, put me in my place. But things are different now. He's not the man I thought he was, no longer someone I idolize, but someone whose flaws have increasingly gotten the better of him. And I, I realize, am not his little girl anymore either. I'm a grown woman who can make her own damn decisions.

I stand up from the table and grab my purse.

"What do you think you're doing?" Dad asks, giving me a sideways look as I brush any errant crumbs off my dress.

"What do you think?" I snap back. "I'm going after the person I love whom you've just offended so badly he had to leave."

"Let him go." Dad waves his hand, a strangely effeminate gesture for a man who prides himself on his masculinity. "If he doesn't care to defend himself, he's not worth my daughter's time anyway."

I just shake my head and start edging around the table.

"Layla," Dad says, a little more sharply. "Sit down."

"No," I say, and start walking around.

Dad grabs my hand, his fingers pinching around my wrist. I glare at it, but he doesn't let go.

"You walk out that door," he says in a voice that's so low I'm the only one in the restaurant who can hear him, despite the fact that a few people are watching us curiously, "you can say goodbye to NYU."

I snatch my hand back, full of fury.

"Then I'll say goodbye to NYU," I state just as evenly. "But I'm not leaving New York, and I'm sure as hell not leaving him."

And without giving my father room to argue with me further, I turn and leave, ignoring the stares of the other restaurant patrons while I sweep through the shop.

A VERY LONG, frustrating hour later (which including two delayed trains and very long wait at the Herald Square station), I'm standing outside Nico's building. I press the buzzer, praying he's there. It's dark, and his street is oddly quiet. It's only ten o'clock, but it's still not the kind of neighborhood where I like to walk around in after dark.

"Yeah?"

My body sags with relief as Nico's deep voice thrums through the scratchy speaker.

"It's me," I say.

There's no answer, but a split second later, the door buzzes open, and I head inside and up to his apartment. I knock on the door, and after a few minutes, I hear the shuffle of feet inside. The door opens, revealing Nico, stripped of his finery of the evening, dressed in a pair of ratty sweatpants and an old white T-shirt.

He looks me up and down and pushes a hand through his hair, which looks like he's been tugging at it a lot. "Hey."

I swallow. "Hey. Can I come in?"

He pauses a second, doesn't meet my eyes. Then he nods, and steps aside for me to enter.

The apartment doesn't look like anyone's home—not even Nico. None of the lights are turned on as I follow him down the long hallway toward his bedroom, which is also dark.

"Were you sleeping?" I ask after he switches on the lights.

He sits on the bed with a thump. "No."

Nico is late

It's already dark by the time I'm standing outside her building, dog-tired after a very, very long day at the Academy. My muscles ache. My bones ache. But I'm almost done with this four-month program, and in just another few weeks, I'll officially be one of New York's Bravest. Sometimes it's hard to believe. A kid like me, knock-down, juvenile delinquent from Hell's Kitchen, just weeks away from being a firefighter. From saving lives for a living instead of screwing them up.

Sometimes it seems too good to be true.

I rub the back of my neck, taking a few moments in the brisk night air. Fall is finally here after a very long, hot summer. Layla's apartment, a six-story walkup on Delancey Park, is on a corner of the city that I wouldn't exactly call quiet, but it's not exactly populated either. Across the street, Delancey Park is deserted, but about two blocks in every direction, once you get past the barrier. I'm not crazy about the idea of her walking around here by herself, but it's a good neighborhood overall.

I'm late. Two hours late, actually, so there's a pretty good chance I'm going to have a very irate girlfriend waiting for me upstairs instead of an excited one.

If that's even what she is. Five days ago I picked her up from the airport, and then it was back to Randall's Island for the rest of the week for me. Five days of up at five, falling into my bed at ten. Rinse, repeat.

But I couldn't not come. Because it's her. And it's been months. No, really, it's been over a year since we were really together. And through all that time.

I press the buzzer. A few moments later, her voices sound, buzzy and faint, through the speaker.

"Hello?"

I clear my throat. "Hey, baby. It's me."

There's a pause. Shit. She's mad. This was supposed to be our night, our big reunion. It was supposed to be special, and here I am, I came straight here as soon as we got off; I didn't want to be anywhere else.

Then the buzzer goes off and the door clicks open. With relief, I enter the building and start up the six flights of stairs.

THE AFTER PARTY

A BAD IDEA STORY

A lot has changed in the nearly ten years since Shama Sandhu and K.C. Ortiz crossed paths via their best friends, Nico and Layla Soltero. Enough that when Shama is forced to produce DJ Cairo's latest music video, she doesn't actually recognize him. All she knows is that he's the latest arrogant musician she has to work with...and he wants her to be on his newest single.

ONE

Shama

The walls are shaking.

No, not those kinds, you dirty bird. I mean, the *actual* walls of my hotel room are shaking. The windows rattle in their frames, the big platform bed shuffles on the carpet, and the big brass mirror over the vanity claps against the plaster.

"Don't drop, don't drop, you fucker," I mutter without even opening my eyes. How many earthquakes have I experienced in five years of living in LA? Ten? Twelve? Twenty?

I don't even know. This thing is barely a tremor, hardly even audible over the noise bubbling up from Santa Monica Boulevard. The only reason I can feel the damn thing is because I'm flat on my back. And, no, not in that way either. Jeez, you guys really are perverts.

Three. Two. One. The shaking stops. The mirror is crooked but has the good sense not to fall. No seven years of bad luck. I exhale. I need coffee. But to do that, I need to get up.

Seven years I've lived in LA. Five since I took the job with Capitol Records as a video production assistant. I did the job, and I did it well. Worked steadily up the ladder until I was eventually producing music videos on my own.

Two days since I left my apartment and officially began my ten-years-coming vacation here at the Santa Monica Marriott, not four blocks from my old studio.

You think you know how hard the music business is? No one tells you about the behind-the-scenes. No one tells you about the boys clubs. The way they treat women like playthings. No one tells you just how hard you have to fight to make *any* of them listen to you. They hear a name like Shama Sandhu and assume I'm there to provide the "catering," usually to one of the talents' trailers, not be the damn boss.

But now I'm finished. No more producing. No more music industry. No more of these assholes who, starting with my DJ boyfriend from college, can't seem to keep their dicks in their pants for more than five minutes.

You want to know something crazy? I originally wanted to be a video journalist. I started at NYU thinking I'd travel the world making docu-shorts and video essays for places like *The New Yorker* or *The Atlantic*. Instead, it's been seven years of telling people how best to "back that ass up."

But I'm done. I saved my money. I paid off my bills. And now I have enough to take a full year off with my camera and return to the dream. I just have to tie up loose ends.

My cell phone blares its sickly-sweet tinkle on the floor. The bed frame squeals as I grab the phone.

"What up, bitch?"

"Hey, girl. Just wanted to make sure you were still alive before your trip. Are you ready to go?"

I smiled. My best friend, Layla Soltero, is seriously one of the sweetest people on the planet. Maybe too sweet. We lived together for three years in college, and she's been a rock ever since. Unlike most, she's never put off by my, ah, "harsher" moments. She's one of the few people who loves me for exactly who I am.

"Dude. I am more than ready. We just had an earthquake. I think this city is literally trying to throw me out."

"An earthquake? Oh my God, Shams, are you okay?!" A clamor sounds on the other side of the phone, like dishes jumbling on a table, followed by the squirrely voices of two small children. I smile.

"Mami, is Auntie Shama okay?"

I grin, shoving my hair back from my face. Mateo, Layla and Nico's son, is the cutest damn kid in the world. Their three-year-old daughter, Camila, better known as Coco, is a close second.

"Tell Mattie I'm fine," I say as I haul myself out of bed.

"He wants to know when you're coming for a visit."

I study myself in the mirror, drawing a finger over the dark circles under my eyes. "Lay, I was just out there at Christmas."

"That was six months ago. You're really not going to come back before your year-long travel extravaganza? What if you die over there, Shams? What if you get eaten by a crocodile?"

I smile into the mirror. "She perished by way of crocodile" isn't a bad thing to have in your obituary.

"This is the beauty of FaceTime, my friend," I say. "God bless smartphones. And the fact that there are no crocodiles in New Delhi. At least, I don't think."

There's a long sigh. I don't tease her more, because I know it's partly jealousy. Well, I'm jealous too. Layla might now get to travel, but she's got the rest of her life buttoned up. Two adorable kids. A job she loves as a city social worker. And a sexy-as-sin, firefighting husband. Yeah, I'm not going to feel so sorry for Little Miss Domestic.

"So, what's your plan before you leave?"

"I give the keys to the landlord at eleven, and then I get to check into the hotel. Two days as a tourist in LA. I never thought I'd see the day, but I don't want to leave the City of Angels on bad terms, you know?"

"Stupid city. I'm glad you're leaving. They don't deserve you."

I have to grin. Layla has a personal vendetta against LA after Nico, her husband, moved here for a year when they first met. They actually come out sometimes because her mother lives in Pasadena, but in general, neither one of them like it. Honestly...I don't blame them.

"Eh, it's not that bad. I'll miss Huckleberry for one. Oh my *God*, those lemon croissants...I should go there today for breakfast." I smack my lips, imagining the butter-soaked pastry that only me and about two other women in this stupid city are willing to enjoy. Only the people behind the cameras in LA ever eat. Whatever. More for me.

"Yum. Have one for me."

"And me!" Mateo's little voice chirps behind her, and soon after that, Coco's lisped drawl follows. Damn. I will miss seeing those kids for a whole year.

"One year, babe. And then it's back to New York. Or London. Or wherever else I happen to land."

She tuts at the idea, but internally, I'm thrilling. I love the idea of not knowing the future. I love the idea of the adventure ahead of me.

"Maybe I should come visit you..." Layla says just as another call rings through.

I frown at the number. Why is the head of A&R at Capitol calling? The guy spoke to me maybe once in seven years.

"Hello?"

"Shama, this is Gary Clayburn. How are you?"

I sit down on the edge of the mattress and frown into the mirror before I get up to straighten it. "Ah, fine, thanks."

"I hear we're losing you to...a private project. Is that right?"

My frown intensifies. Damn, I really should have cut my hair before leaving. Maybe a trip to the salon is in order...

"Yes," I say as I hold my hair up, trying out a mock bob. Yeah, no. I need my long hair. "I'm leaving on Monday, actually. Taking a little downtime before my flight to Delhi." I meander over to the closet and shrug on the back maxi dress I'm planning to wear for the next two days when I'm not on the beach.

"Good, good, so we haven't lost you yet. Any chance you're available this weekend for an emergency? We lost the producer on the DJ Cairo video. Apparently, Cairo didn't like the final mix and refuses to appear in the video until it's fixed."

"He's back in the *studio*?"

But Gary just sighs. "He's an EP. And apparently his agent got him final cut."

The irritation in his voice is palpable. I don't blame him. Final cut makes for tyrants. I've heard of DJ Cairo, of course—everyone has. He's one of the most talented music producers in the business, the next Dr. Luke. He was the most recent get for Capitol, and they bought his entire album, which, rumor has it, he recorded in his own apartment two years ago. I haven't heard this single, but I do know this is the first time he's stepping out as a performer, and the studio is putting everything they have behind it.

So sure, maybe the guy has first-time jitters, but that's no reason to hijack an entire production and cost the studio thousands of dollars a day just to redo some auto-tuning.

"We need someone to step in, Shama. Take the reins. Make sure everything gets done. We need you."

Now my frown is an all-out scowl. I quit this job precisely because I was done babysitting all the narcissists in LA. The last thing I want to do on my mini-vacation is to chase some prima donna beat boy into performing like a trained monkey. No. I want the beach. I want sunshine. I want margaritas.

Then Gary offers exactly five times what I've ever gotten paid for one of these projects. It's more than I usually make in six months. More than I made in my first two years as an assistant producer. It's enough to fund my entire year long project on top of the money I've saved.

I cough.

"Everything okay, there?"

"Sorry," I said. "I just didn't quite hear what you said."

So he says it again. And this time, I'm sure.

"Wow." The word pops out before I can stop it.

"So you'll do it?"

"Um, well. I only have three days before I leave LA. How involved is the project?" I'm not staying past Sunday. Absolutely not.

"Not too bad. They've already started filming," Gary replies. "The director has a pretty clear vision for the video too. Beach party. They're doing it mostly on location in Redondo Beach. You know Jeff de Soto?"

I nod, though he can't see me. "Oh, sure. Jeff and I have worked together a few times." I glance at my maxi. So much for vacation. "All right. I'll do it."

Whatever. It's a music video on a beach, right? Of all the types of videos to shoot in LA, that's pretty much the easiest. Oil up the girls. Catch the right sunset. Have people jump around a little, *Baywatch*-style. Extras galore. Simple.

"Well, first things first," Gary says. "We need to get Cairo out of the studio and back on set."

TWO

K.C.

"It's still not right."

I flip off the track and sit back in my chair, tapping my lips for a second while the studio stops shaking. The motion makes the big watch on my wrist slide forward, a gift from my agent after she signed me to this deal with Capitol. Funny thing...we were so excited at the time. I could have never realized how the transition from producer to performer would have turned out.

"I think it sounds dope," says Joaquin, my personal assistant. "That bass is hot."

I just roll my eyes at the soundboard. I like Joaquin. I do. One of my cousins from New York, he's been my body man since he graduated high school five years ago. He's loyal, trustworthy, and doesn't snort half his paycheck like half the people in this industry. And more than that, he always has yeses when I need to hear them. But right now I don't need a yes man. I need someone who's going to tell me what the fuck is wrong with this track.

Problem is, when you're the producer on top of the talent, everyone expects *you* to have that answer. Today, though...the magic is not happening.

"Here." I pull off the two fat chains around my neck, the diamond-encrusted ring on my pinky, and the watch and hand them over my shoulder. "This shit is weighing me down. Take it back to the hotel and have them put it in the safe, all right?"

Joaquin whips out a velvet cloth to take the jewelry. He knows I don't like my ice getting his fingerprints on it. Or getting scratches neither. And this happens often enough that he's usually ready for it when I've had it with the hardware around my neck. The funny thing is, I don't even like it that much. When I'm by myself, I keep it simple. T-shirt. Jeans. That's about it. But when you don't come from much, you feel like you need to insulate yourself once you have something. Maybe to convince yourself it's real.

I remember that feeling when I started making a little money. First came a record with my first job at The Hit Factory. Then someone picked up my mixes. They started hiring me to mix at bars. Clubs. Festivals. More records. More gigs. They just kept coming and coming.

But the numbers didn't seem real until I saw what they could buy. Nothing—*nothing*—will ever compare to that feeling of handing my mother the title to her very own two-bedroom condo on the West Side of Manhattan, four blocks from the falling-down building in Hell's Kitchen where I grew up. From there, she could look over New York like the queen she was, not the servant she'd always been forced to be.

I turn to Barry, the sound technician. "What do you think?"

"Needs more bass," he says, directly contradicting Joaquin. "You knew I was going to say that. It needs bounce."

I turn back to the console like it's going to give me all the answers. I did know that. Barry's in-house here at Capitol—a good guy who's worked on some other projects with me. Old school, though, and very LA. He wants to make my shit sound like Dr. Dre. I'm not having that. I'm from New York City, not Compton. *Boricua*, not Crenshaw.

"Joaquin. Phone. Call Nico." I hold out my hand behind me, and like magic, my phone appears, the number to my best friend already ringing.

"Yo, *mano*. Where the fuck you been? I tried to call you, what, five times last week?"

I grin as the voice of Nico Soltero, my best friend, echoes through the room. Joaquin grins too. He loves Nico. Everyone loves Nico.

Me most of all, though. Because out of everyone in my life, especially once it blew up, my boy is the only one who keeps it real. He tells me when I'm being a jackass. He tells me when I'm getting too big for my head. And it tells me when I'm getting shit right too.

"Where else, man?" I reply. "I'm in the studio."

"Don't you have that video shoot today? I thought today was the day you become a real rap star!"

He's messing with me, but to be real, my friend was almost as happy as I was when Capitol picked up my record last year. He knows what it means. Since I was a kid, I've been mixing beats for other people. Making music from other people's creativity. This thing...it's mine. And I need it to be perfect.

I grimace into my reflection in the window. "Yeah, the video's on hold."

Behind me, Joaquin snorts. Okay, fine. So I ran off set to fix the damn track and tell the producer where to shove it. What the fuck is the point of doing a video if the track's not right?

"Layla good?" I ask, deflecting. "Family good?"

I can practically hear my man's grin over the phone when I

mention his wife. Cha-*ching*, if there was ever a man whipped by his woman, it's my best friend. But I don't blame him. She's fine as hell, and really fuckin' good for him, to boot. Nah, if Nico's the brother I never had, Layla's basically my sister too.

"Yeah, man, she's good. Got a promotion at work last week. She's director of the whole damn office now. You believe that?"

I nod. "Yeah, yeah. I can believe that. How about you? How does it feel to be a fuckin' FDNY lieutenant now, *mano*?"

There's another deep chuckle before he launches into some updates. He probably thinks I'm humoring him with these questions. But really, who's doing better things for the world, huh? A firefighter and a social worker with two beautiful kids? Or an asshole making records about shaking ass and popping tags?

I don't know what. Maybe it's this business. I've been at this shit for close to fifteen years now. Same tired beats. Same tired talent.

Something's gotta give.

"Yo, man. I need you to listen to this track," I say. "You got a minute?"

"Ah...sure, I guess. But you know I don't know anything about music, bro."

"Just tell me if you like it," I say. I don't have time for this song and dance. Nico isn't a musical talent, but he knows good shit. If anyone else has an ear for the vibe I want, it's him.

"I'm trying to make it sound like home," I clarify.

Before he can ask any other questions, I flip on the song, hold the phone up to a speaker, and let it play for a solid minute before turning it off.

"Okay, what do you think?"

There's a long pause. Shit.

"I mean, it's nice...I'm sure it would play well with the younger crowd these days...they seem to like that auto-tuned business that got so popular."

I groan into my palm. I knew sampling that shitty pop star was the wrong way to go. Capitol demanded fuckin' "synergy" on this project, and they gave me straight-up shit.

"It's weak," I translate. "And Katie Derek sounds weak on it."

"Well...yeah. *Claro*, man. I'mma be real, I'd probably change the station. The beat is tight, but you need a better voice with it, you know? If you're gonna use that rhythm, you need a hook to match. Maybe...shit, Kayce, I'm not a producer."

I groan again, this time loud enough to make Joaquin jump behind me. "Nico, cut the shit. I asked for your help, so just tell me what you're thinking of."

"*Coño*, calm the fuck down all right. God, you're such a sensitive fuckin' artist, you know that?"

I snort. "Shut the fuck up."

"*You* shut up. You want my opinion or not?"

I sigh. I do want his opinion. Honest to God, Nico and I are probably...what's the word...codependent. "Hit me."

There's a long pause while he thinks. "All right...I hear the lyrics...and I hear that beat you got going. It's a rumba, right?"

"Right."

"It reminds me of those Sunday mornings, you remember? Remember our moms, they used to hang laundry out the fire escape while they listened to that Ghetto Brothers album?"

My eyes pop open. "Oh *shit*. I forgot about that album. The one with those licks like Dusty Springfield? Like it's echoing in a glass goblet? *Viva Puerto Rico Libre...*"

"Ah...I guess? But yeah, that song. That's the one I mean."

I can already hear it. Sultry harmonies, a lazy hum liquid as the ocean. In a flash I'm back on the fire escape in Hell's Kitchen, watching the sway of my mother's skirt while she sings along and pins my shirts to the clothesline in the summer heat. She'd stay in the hot summer breeze flying off the Hudson, and in those moments, I could tell she was back in Santiago, sitting under the palm trees, watching the ocean as blue as the sky.

"Tell Layla I said what's up," I say in a hurry. "I gotta go." I hang up—Nico knows there's no more time for goodbyes, not when I got *the sound* locked in my head now. I swing around to Barry. "Yo, we need a guitarist. "

Barry nods—he's been listening to my end of the conversation to know what I'm thinking. "You want me to call Danny, the cat who worked on Drake's last album?"

"How about Elian Ramirez? I think he's in town. He could do it."

I'm rocking now to an unheard melody. Ba-da-da-dahhhh. I can hear it clearly now, swimming over the beat I already wrote, but with a different voice, not with the auto-tuned pop shit the studio threw at us. I shake my head. We need a new singer too.

"Who, Barry, who? Goddammit, who's available right the fuck now? Deeper voice, kind of husky, but Latin? *Coño*, who'm I thinking of? I need to get this shit down before it flies."

Barry taps a long finger on his thick lips while Joaquin's expression ping-pongs between us. "I don't know, man. Capitol ain't gonna like it you ax Katie Derek..."

I wave it away. "They're gonna like it fine when I give them a platinum record. She doesn't work with this, and you know it."

"Ariana can do it the way you're saying—"

"Nah, she's touring in Australia with Katie Derek right now," I said. "Who else?"

I'm snapping my fingers, like a guy who needs his fix. I haven't done that stuff in more than ten years, never really got into it, unlike a lot of people in this industry. You wouldn't either if you grew up in a neighborhood full of junkies. My level head is what got me out of that mess—why would I want to fuck that up?

Barry opens his mouth and rattles off a few more names, but none of them work. Fuck, *fuck*. I'm sitting there racking my brains, trying to think of someone, *anyone*, who can sing this fucking hook for me.

And then, before I can name anyone else, the studio door opens, and *the voice* enters.

"All right, where's the bastard who delayed a production to adjust a few fucking beats? Where's the prima donna who thinks the entire fucking industry revolves around him? Which one of you assholes is DJ Cairo?""

I swear to God, I don't even remember what she said after my stage name came out of her mouth. She practically sang it, like she was making fun of a singer, but it was melodic, and the deep, husky tone shot through my bones.

Without even turning around, I raise my hand. "That would be me, sweetheart."

"Damn," Barry murmurs behind me. He bats me on the shoulder. Then he does it again.

Finally, I swing in, wondering what he's on about and ready to get this intruder into the sound booth so we can finish this shit. Then I look up, and I can't think at all.

THREE

Shama

He's just...staring at me.

I won't lie. I stare too for a second. But I did it the nice appropriate way through the tiny window on the studio door. Because it was a shock—a *shock*, I tell you—to walk in here and see world famous, yet oddly reclusive producer DJ Cairo sitting there with no jewelry, no flashy clothes, no posse, brow furrowed while he listened to a track over and over again. Lost in the zone. Totally floating away on his music.

Look. It's not like I've never seen a hot musician before. Shit, I've been brushing these assholes aside like flies since I started this business. Get it done, get it done. The number one rule of being a producer, and I'm the best at this.

But this...somehow this is different.

I stride over and snap my finger in front of his face. "Hey! Rapper boy! You there?"

Finally, he blinks and bats my hand away. "*Coño*! Yeah, I'm here! No need to get into my face, damn!

"*You're* DJ Cairo?" I let the name slide off my tongue with disdain so thick it's practically molasses.

I don't know why, but he doesn't look like what I would expect a Puerto Rican rapper to look like. Pale enough to blend with the clouds, with close-cut hair that's even blacker than mine, deep-set eyes with tiny green freckles in the dark brown, and a full mouth that seems to be set in a never-ending smirk.

I must have seen his picture before somewhere. Of course I have. That must be why he looks somewhat familiar.

At that, he blinks, then gives me a lazy smile and raises his hand. "*Claro*, sweetheart, that's me. But I'm going to need you to say that one more time, sweetheart. This time, into the mic, *por favor*." He points toward the studio, and the other guy, whom I'm guessing is the technician, is already standing up, ready to escort me inside.

I push his hands off me. "Hey! What's the big idea? I'm not a back-up singer, you asshole."

"Then who are you?" Cairo grabs a red Yankees hat off the soundboard and claps it on backward, then absently toys with the one small chain around his neck, pulling out a small medallion of what looks like a Catholic saint while he scowls up at me. Ah, there's the rapper I was expecting.

I cross my arms. "I'm Shama Sandhu, asshole. I'm your new producer. The studio ruined my first vacation in seven years to get your entitled ass back on set. Do you have any idea how much time you're costing them by tinkering with the auto-tune?"

The scowl deepens, which might be hot if I wasn't so fired up about the fact that I have to be here at all.

"No use making excuses," I say. "You might be a hit-making veteran, but you're a virgin performer. In this economy, you're lucky the studio gave you any kind of video budget for your first single, but if you squander it making the crew wait, you won't get another."

"Oh, really?" he says. "According to who?"

"Says *me*," I retort. "Plus my seven years wrangling idiots like you. Do you want to do this or not?"

He taps his lip again. It's distracting. And then that smile reappears, and for a second, I have to balance myself against the walls.

"Fine," he says. "You want me on set?"

I nod sharply. "What's it gonna take?"

A wide, slow smile spreads across Cairo's face. "Your voice."

FOUR

K.C.

It takes us less than two hours to finish the track. For real, I don't know if I've ever made any music that quickly. It wasn't just because Shama was a damn natural, purring into the mic like she wanted to make out with it later. No, it was that with her, every-thing just *worked*. She might have scowled at me the entire time I asked for another take, but damn if her husky, somewhat imperious vocals didn't add exactly what this track needed.

When I first asked, she stared at me like I was crazy. Who the fuck knows. Maybe I am. But there's a part of me that turns on, like a button, at the weirdest fuckin' things. A tone. A new pitch.

And then I can hear it. Not just that one sound, but I can hear how it fits in a whole fuckin' symphony in my mind.

This track, it was missing something. And the second she said my name, like a woman who's pissed and turned the fuck on all at once, the syllables dripping off her tongue like honey, I knew *that* was the exact thing we needed. Sultry and stubborn, right where it belongs, like a call and response to the lilt of my rhymes.

Porque eres mi gatita (*DJ Cairo*)
Porque eres mi mamita (*DJ Cairo*)

Pop star out, cranky producer in. Add the extra riffs from the guitarist Barry wrangled, and we were on our way back to the video set by noon. And, apparently, not a moment too soon.

"Finally!" shouts Cary, the director, as Shama practically drags me across the beach toward the section off the Santa Monica pier the studio blockaded for the next two days.

"I know, I know," Shama says, accepting a hug from the director. He kisses her on the cheek, and I have to fight not to be jealous. I just spent the last two hours with no one but her, me, Barry, and the guitarist. Now, standing here on a beach full of extras and crew, I'm feeling a little invaded. I want our privacy back.

And why would that be, mano? Nico's laughing on my shoulder. That motherfucker. He knows what's up. Whatever, I'm a professional. And this pain-in-the-ass chick is my boss. At least for the next two days.

I accept a slap on the hand from Cary.

"We done?" he asks. "You got the new track?"

I nod. "Joaquin?"

My body man holds out his phone with headphones for Cary to listen. "Here you go. It's so hot, man. You're gonna love it."

Cary just rolls his eyes but puts in the earbuds and starts bobbing his head almost immediately. "Yeah. Yeah, that is much better. Damn, that's a hit." His eyes pop open right when the hook thumps through the tiny speakers. "Who's the girl?"

"That would be me."

Shama looks bored, but I can already tell she's kind of proud.

She knows the goods as well as I do. *"Porque"* is going to be the song of the summer. It's gonna be her voice bumping through every open window between LA and New York. How many people can say that?

Cary gives the headphones back to me. "Ah...you know we don't have a model for this. Shit, I know it's good, but she's all over this track, and I can't do a whole new shot list. And we didn't hire anyone to lip sync..."

"Nah, Shama's gonna be in it," I say, only just realizing I mean it. "Just add her to my shots during the hook. That's all you gotta do."

At that, Shama swings around, her soft-looking lips open. "Um, *excuse me?*"

Behind me, Joaquin chuckles, but already Cary is sizing her up. I want to tell him not to bother. Shama's just as gorgeous as any of the girls we got out here. Tall and slim, with an ass that doesn't quit hiding under that giant dress she's wearing. Yeah, I was looking on the way out to the car. And on the walk down the beach. No shame in that. The fabric clings and wasn't nobody doing any harm, all right?

But it's not just the body. Shama is fuckin' gorgeous in a way that's a hell of a lot more real than most of the bimbos crowding the sand around us. Her hair is blacker than mine, if that's even possible, and her skin is deep brown and glows like she's been out in the sun a little too long recently. But it's her eyes, which sparkle like black diamonds and are glaring right at me, that will really make the video come alive. The push and pull that was in every utterance of my name—that's going to fuckin' *jump* out of the screen. I know it.

"Yeah." Cary nods appraisingly, and I can tell he sees what I see. "Shama, you got it, baby. We need you."

Another thick scowl. "Cary, I am here as a producer, not a

performer. You need me here to keep this on track not to get off course!" She tugs at her hair, which is falling over her shoulders in thick waves. For a second, I imagine what it would look like spread across a white sheet. While I cage her under my body, undulating in time to the rhythm.

Whoa there, you horny motherfucker. One look at this girl, and suddenly you're a Backstreet Boy? What the fuck is going on?

"Come on, Sparks," I say, cuffing her lightly on the shoulder.

"Sparks?" She whirls to me, and Cary covers a smile. "Who the hell is Sparks?" she demands.

But the fire I see only makes me like the nickname more. Not caring whether or not anyone is watching, I reach out and tug the end of her hair.

"You are," I say, enjoying the feel of the silky strands between my fingers and the fire that rises in her eyes. "All we need are these lips"—I drag a finger over the bottom one—"saying my name"—I smile, and I swear to God, I think she shudders—"into that camera." I wink. She stills. "You think you can do that for me, sweetheart?"

For a second, it's like the hustle and bustle of the beach fade away. It's just her and me standing there, my finger poised over her mouth while I'm wondering what the inside looks like. Her tongue sneaks out to one side.

She stares at me for a long second, and just then, I wonder if she can see through more than just my bravado. Shama's eyes are dangerous. They pierce right through you.

Yeah. Sparks, for real.

"But I'm not a video girl!" Shama suddenly bursts out. "Look at me. Do I look like these bitches over there?"

She gestures wildly toward the models and extras milling around the set, all of them in the smallest of small bikinis, asses oiled, done up to the nines. They're hot, yeah. A few of them I've probably hooked up with at some point. But so is Shama, with her jet-black hair and skin that looks dipped in gold. And she's got one thing none of those girls have: spark.

"Shama," I say. "You want me to get this video done today, right?"

She opens her mouth, then presses it shut again and nods succinctly.

I shrug and hold my hands out. "Well, you better get to makeup, sweetheart. Because we ain't got time to run new auditions, right?" I tap the watch on my wrist. "Chop, chop."

Shama opens her mouth like she wants to argue all over again. But instead, she turns toward the tent set up for wardrobe.

"Fine!" she shouts as she stumbles over the sand. "But I am *not* parading around in my underwear. And under no circumstances will I *twerk*!"

FIVE

Shama

Two seconds into this shoot, and I'm already regretting it. It's chaos on the beach; we've got about two hours to get a party together that will last for five hours, and now I'm letting the makeup and wardrobe people fit me.

At least I get to choose my own damn clothes instead of wearing the dental floss the models and extras consider bikinis. Both Cary and the creative director tried to convince me otherwise, but Cairo insisted that I stay clothed. If, by some chance, my parents stumble upon this video, I'd rather not horrify them more than I have to by my association with someone like DJ Cairo.

And so, we found ourselves sitting in makeup at the same time; me getting rubbed all over with gold shimmery body makeup under the magenta cover-up they gave me; him getting smeared with an oil and water substance that makes him look like he just walked out of the ocean.

"She's a class act," he keeps muttering to himself, winking at me when he catches me looking at him.

It would be easier to do this if he wasn't so damn good-looking. Most musicians aren't, really. People love them because of their talent, their glamor, but when you're up close, nine out of ten of them look like regular people.

Not Cairo. I see now why the studio courted him so hard. The second the guy takes off his shirt so the makeup girls can oil him up for the shoot, it's clear he either has a *really* good metabolism or a hell of a trainer. Abs for days. Coated in a light sheen of oil, just enough that he looks like he's been diving into the ocean recently.

Curiously, he cringes when they settle a few of the thick gold ropes around his neck and give him a pair of diamond-encrusted sunglasses sent over from Gucci. This is basic stuff. A music video is just a marketing tool, and you have to speak to your audience. Reggaeton lovers are looking for the next Daddy Yankee, even if the guy looks more like Enrique Iglesias.

"Come on, Cairo," I jeer from my chair, where another hair-stylist is putting the finishing touches of beachy waves into my hair. "Can't you handle a little bling?"

I hold up my own wrists, which are loaded with gold bangles to match the diamond-laced hoops the costume designer assigned me.

Can you imagine if you brought him home, Shams? Layla's voice giggles in the back of my mind. I chuckle with her. I can imagine perfectly the expressions on my stolid Indian parents' faces if their daughter brought home a Puerto Rican rapper.

"Carlos," Cairo says quietly as he stares at his newly ringed fingers. He looks up, and his eyes pierce, even through the sunglasses. "That's my name. Not Cairo. I used to be DJ Carlos when I first started mixing. But I did this tour opening for Abel Rodriguez in Europe when I was maybe twenty, twenty-one. Still a nobody, right? And the German announcer couldn't read my name or something and pronounced it Cairo." He shrugs. "My manager thought it was hot, so we kept it. It's dumb, but I can't lose it now."

I can't deny its appeal. DJ Cairo is a much better stage name than DJ Carlos, which just sounds like some kid messing around on turntables in his dad's basement. But his voice lacks the bravado it had ten seconds ago, and when he looks up, his eyes are pleading with mine. I've been a bystander to this industry for years, but still I forget how lonely it can be. When everyone thinks they know some version of you, eventually no one knows you at all.

Time to put on the nice producer hat. Sometimes talent needs their ass kicked. But sometimes they need a little coaxing to get the job done too.

"Hey," I say, sliding off my chair and padding across the tatami mats to where he stands. "Are you...okay there, slugger?"

All right, so empathy isn't really my best face.

Carlos tips the aviators down and examines me over the rims with a sardonic expression. The sun hits the silver edge of one, gleaming like a giant sparkle in his eye. "Why, you gonna cheer me up, pretty?"

All vulnerability is gone—the cocky musician is back.

I scowl. "I just need to make sure you can perform. I'm not your fluffer, asshole. I'm the producer."

"No, *I'm* the producer," he corrects me.

"Not on this video, you're not."

This time he takes off his glasses completely, and I'm struck once more by just how penetrating his gaze is. "Do you always talk to talent this way?" he asks.

I snort. "Did you just refer to yourself as the *talent*?"

His gaze doesn't waver, but before he can answer, Cary pops up between us.

"Okay," he says. "We're about ready to film the first sequence. The original plan was to juxtapose three separate parties, back and forth between them, so the audience can see how Cairo rolls. The pre-party, the beach party, and the one at night. Make sense, Shama?"

I nod, smirking a little that I'm the one he asks, not the illustrious DJ. Well, I'm the professional here, buddy. I'm the one who knows whether not things are going to look good. Not you.

"I like it," I said. "What comes first?"

"First, we need to do the pre-party. The set up. Just a few friends, hanging out at the beach. Cairo starts rapping. It's chill, everyone is drinking, laughing, having a good time, and as the beat heats up, so does the party. We've already done a lot of the basic shots of the beach crap—hot bodies, volleyball, you know. But we need you two. This is where you meet."

Carlos grins at me, his teeth bright white. "You should give me a dirty look like you did in the studio, pretty."

I glare at him.

"Yeah," he says. "Just like that."

Cary smirks.

I just shake my head. "Okay, so after that, then what?"

"Then we'll do some work with the group as the sun starts to go down," Cary says. "That's got to move the fastest so we can get the light. I'll be working with Cairo while the other cameras are on the crowd."

"Show me," I said, beckoning for the shot list. It's pretty simple. There are five cameras rolling at the same time to get as much as possible to edit later. I've seen Cary's videos before. His work tends to be on the spontaneous side.

"The end is at night. After everyone goes home." He looks to Carlos. "Originally we were going to shoot you by yourself, but since you added Shama's voice to the hook, I'm thinking it should be with her too."

Carlos nods. "Yeah, I like that. Sort of what happens when the lights go out?" Again, he shoots me his cheeky grin. "The after party, right?"

The way his voice slides over the words leaves no doubt what kind of party he's envisioning.

I scowl.

"Just like that," Carlos says again.

I hand the shot list back to Cary. "Everything else ready?"

He nods.

"Good," I say. "Because thanks to this asshole, we don't have any time to lose." I yank on Cairo's arm, ignoring the way his slick, oiled skin feels warm and *very* hard under my hand. "Come on, you. Let's get this over with."

SIX

Shama

Two days later, I'm hot, tired, and cranky. Unfortunately, it turns out Cary is as much of a perfectionist with his videos as Carlos is with his songs. Shot after shot after shot after shot, which meant that when I wasn't actually being filmed myself, I was working double duty trying to wrangle the extras so they wouldn't wander off.

So I'm sick of the beach, sick of this song, sick of baby sundresses, sick of being covered with gold body paint, and *really* sick of watching silicon-lipped models gyrate all over Carlos. It's not because I've spent approximately forty-eight hours with the man staring into my eyes like I'm the only person he sees. It's not because we had to pretend to almost-kiss for almost an hour and I can still remember exactly what his cologne smells like. It has *nothing* to do with the fact that I fell asleep last night in my hotel room with my vibrator because I could not get the asshole out of my head.

And he knows it. He has to fucking know it. Because every time he catches me scowling at one of the girls, he smiles. Every time he sees me staring at his finely-formed ass or those should-be-illegal arms of his, he smirks.

It's getting harder and harder to keep everyone on task when I'm losing my focus every ten seconds. *That*'s what's making me cranky.

But finally, *finally*, it's Saturday night. It's the last scene of the video, the one where it's just me and Carlos, alone on the beach at night. The "after party."

"You two can rest on the blanket for a while if you want," Cary says, gesturing toward the giant setup at the top of one dune. "Just don't move, okay? Otherwise we'll have to do Shama's makeup all over again."

Carlos and I sink down onto the rug in the middle of the night set. The designer basically created any woman's dream date, with a giant kilim rug dotted with cushions, candles, scattered fruit, and tiki torches all around us. It's basically a sex pad in the middle of the beach, and if we weren't surrounded by a crew, it would probably be doing the trick.

We sit there for a long time while the lighting crew works to get things right. No one tells you how much time you have to wait on a video set. These things take time.

Carlos lies back on the rug, and eventually, his eyes close. Not for the first time, I notice how thick his eyelashes are, resting against his pale skin. In the moonlight, he looks almost ghostly, like a pirate from the days of old. It's not a bad look.

His eyes open, and slowly, he gives me a lazy grin. "You checkin' me out over there, pretty?"

I snort. "Just making sure you don't pass out."

He smirks. "Whatever. You've been staring a hole at me for two days, *mami*. How long has it been? One year? Two?"

My jaw drops. "Um, excuse *me*, Mr. Sexual Harassment. That is none of your goddamn business."

He shrugs, lying back again and closing his eyes. "You gonna tell Cary on me? Report me for a couple of jokes when you've been throwing shit at me for days?"

Finally, I lie down too. I'd rather look at the stars than at his smug face. "I just want to finish this crap tonight so I can start my vacation properly."

"Vacation? What vacation? Don't you live here?"

I shake my head. "Not anymore, no. I was staying in the Marriott for a few days on the beach when Gary called. I'm leaving tomorrow."

Carlos turns. "Leaving for where?"

I toy with the hem of my skirt. "Delhi. I'm taking a year off to do some documentary work."

I wait for that familiar "how nice" or something equally trite. It's the response I always get when I tell people my plans. They look at me like I'm a child who wants to play make believe, not a grown woman with her own dreams. I might as well say I'm leaving LA to find a frog to kiss.

"Passion project?"

I turn. There is not a drop of patronizing anything on Carlos's face. In fact, he's watching me intently, no trace of taunts or flirtation on his face. Just pure interest.

I nod. "Yeah. Yeah, it is. I'm just really tired of producing."

"Well, it's not your work, is it? It's managing someone else's."

I perk up more, surprised that he gets it. "That's right."

He sits up and balances his arms over his knees. I sit back up too.

"It was like that with this album. I worked on it in secret for... shit, two years? Maybe more?" He draws a line in the sand with his finger, tracing a box and then a circle inside it. A turntable. "Ten years I made music for other people. Wrote their beats. Mixed their shit. Charted artist after artist."

"Don't make it sound all that bad. You did win a couple of Grammys."

That sly smile makes another appearance, though it's tinged with an adorable shyness instead of the cockiness that comes out around others. "You knew about those? I was a producer, like you. I wasn't on stage or nothin'."

I shrug. "The crew talks. It's still an impressive achievement, especially considering how much the voters don't like hip-hop."

"Impressive, maybe." Carlos shrugs, his big shoulders rippling under the moon. "But those songs were never really mine. A real artist has their own voice. They need to speak their own truth."

His words echo my own truth, the truth that's driving this whole crazy trip I'm about to begin. "So what's the documentary about?" Carlos asks.

"I...I don't know yet." I stare at the weave of the kilim rug, wondering who made it. If it's authentic, lifted from a souk in Marrakech, or if it's a knock-off from a Bangladeshi factory. Both places sounded worth exploring with my camera. "I'll have to see what I find."

The other truth is, I want to create my own art, but I don't know if I'm really an artist. I wouldn't know if I have a real voice, a real truth, until I try to speak at all.

The idea is terrifying.

Carlos sighs and looks up at the stars. "I'll never get tired of this."

I look up too, welcoming the change of subject. "The stars?"

He nods. "You can't see them in New York. It's the only thing I like about LA better."

I nod. After spending four years at NYU, I remember yearning for my parents' house in New Jersey. The glow of Manhattan obscures everything but its own corona.

"So where'd you grow up, Sparks?"

"Montclair," I say. "Not far from the city, but close enough."

He whistles. "Montclair is nice."

I nod. "Yeah, it is. I was lucky." I consider my parents, who still live in the same split-level house where I grew up. Still have the same La-Z-Boy furniture that smells faintly of cardamom and coriander. Every day, my mother cooks and cleans, tending an empty nest while my dad goes to work. In another few years, maybe he'll retire. But I doubt it.

"What about you?" I asked. "You're from the Bronx, right?"

He shakes his head. "Nah, the Kitchen. Forty-Ninth Street."

"Really? That's funny." I smile. "I actually have a friend who grew up on that street too. Well, he's my best friend's husband. You don't know a Nico Soltero, do you?"

For a second, Carlos gives me a funny look. "Ah, I've heard the name. It's a big city."

"He and Layla are the best," I continue. "They live in Riverdale now with their kids. Tiny happy little family."

"You sound a little jealous." Carlos lies back on the rug.

I sigh and lie back again too. Above me, Cassiopeia spreads her arms wide like she wants to give me a hug.

"Maybe I am a little," I admit. "I don't know. I'm not in a hurry to get married or anything, but I think it would be pretty amazing to have the kind of partnership they have. It's hard to explain if you don't know them, but from both accounts, it was love at first sight. They had their hard times, but I have never met a couple more dedicated to each other."

My parents suddenly spring to mind with their quiet dedication. Not all love is passionate—they are a good example, an arranged marriage that evolved into a quiet partnership over the years. But that's not something I could ever do. Be obedient. Live my life alongside my husband's. That's the whole point of this adventure I'm supposed to begin, right? To be on my own.

"It would be pretty amazing," Carlos agrees. "Ambition has its own price. It's tough being alone."

I turn. "Are you really alone? It seems like there are always people with you. Or who want to be."

Carlos just shrugs. "You can be with all sorts of people and still feel alone."

I ponder that for a moment, considering who has been around him. Video girls. Techs. I definitely spotted a few people trying to slip him tapes. To DJ Cairo, the hitmaker.

I wonder if anyone knows his real name.

"Yeah," I said. "I can see that."

For a few more minutes, we gaze up at the stars, and it's like the crew bustling around us doesn't exist. All I can feel is Carlos's warm shoulder against mine, sense the gentle shift of skin on skin as our breath causes our bodies to move.

For a moment, I don't want to leave LA at all. Not if I could stay on the beach with him.

Whoa. Where in the hell did that come from?

"All right, guys, ready?"

We sit up to find Cary poised with a couple of camera guys. The hair and makeup team come in to fluff my hair and straighten my dress (blue this time) after we both stand up.

Carlos gives me another shy smile. "Ready to finish this thing, Sparks?"

Unaccountably shy myself, I nod.

"All right, guys, this is the seduction scene. Third verse, Cairo," Cary calls out.

"I'm sorry I ruined your vacation," Carlos says, reaching out for my hand. He pulls me close while the lilting beat of the song we've all come to know so well starts. "I...I didn't mean it to be like this. But I didn't know I needed you until you walked into the room."

I open my mouth to respond but find I don't know what to say. I'm caught in the depth of his dark eyes, drawn to him like a moth to a flame. But I need to leave LA. I can't afford to be burned by someone like him again.

"I—"

"Let's go!" Cary shouts from behind one of the cameras.

And I watch as Carlos launches into another lip sync, moving his lips while sound emits from speakers next to the camera. It reminds me that this is fake. None of these moments are designed for anything but performance. And this world is something that after tonight, I'll be leaving behind forever.

Still, Carlos's deep eyes never leave mine. And as I watch his mouth move silently in time with the music, I find myself wondering how I'm going to feel, knowing he might never look at me like this again either.

SEVEN

K.C.

"Room 714."

That was what she whispered after Cary called, "That's a wrap" to the crew's delight. Right before she pressed a piece of plastic into my palm and slipped into the wardrobe tent to change out of the slinky blue dress she wore for the last few shots.

"For what?" I ask, just before she disappears.

She turns and grins, looking almost devious under the remnants of the moonlight. "For the after party, of course."

Shocked the fuck out of me, lemme tell you. Two days ago, this woman hated me. Two days, I couldn't help staring at her while I wasn't looking at the camera. Wondering why I dreamed about her nagging voice at night, threaded with the husky sound of my name coming through her lips.

But now I know.

Because she's not a strange woman. She's a someone.

Layla. Nico. Pretty little family in Riverdale.

It wasn't until she mentioned their names that I realized why Shama seemed so familiar. It's because we've met before, at my mother's freaking apartment, no less. Thanksgiving. Almost ten years ago.

She clearly didn't remember me either, but I don't blame her. I look a hell of a lot different. I was still just a skinny, pale-faced asshole with a goofy grin and some corny-ass game. It's amazing what a trainer and a few extra years will do for you. I was using the name DJ Cairo back then, but mostly I was playing clubs in New York and LA and producing. I had no major name for myself yet. Money was coming, but fame was a long ways off. How could she know?

And Shama...damn...yeah, she looked different back then too. Her hair was shorter, she had a little more baby fat, like girls do at that age. But she was still beautiful. And she still had that attitude.

I was just too much of a douchebag to know a good thing when I saw it.

I palm the card back and forth in my palm before sliding it into the back pocket of my jeans. She wants one night before she leaves. A game with an about-to-be famous musician. Take advantage of this cat-and-mouse game we've been playing for three days before she takes off.

I'm undecided on the ride back to my own hotel on Wilshire. Undecided while I shower off the residue of the video and change into a pair of simple black pants and a black T-shirt, keeping just the chain my mother gave me, and then I stay undecided after I tell Joaquin that he's done for the next two days. After I sneak back downstairs to grab a taxi. Stop at a supermarket for a bouquet of cheap pink roses, champagne, and some strawberries, like I do for a lot of the girls I meet at events.

I'm still undecided when I find myself standing on the seventh floor of the Marriott, turning the card key over and over in my palm while I stare at the numbers next to the door.

714.

Then, before I can make a decision, the door opens anyway.

Shama stands there, looking about ten times more gorgeous than she has on the beach. Gone is the makeup, the jewelry, the glitzy fuckin' dresses. She's in nothing but a T-shirt and these little shorts that ride up her smooth brown thighs. Her hair is tossed over her shoulder, wavy and slightly wet after a shower. A drop of real water, not makeup, still glistens on her cheek. After two days of work, she looks tired. But also relaxed. Back on vacation.

I blink. I know what this is. I might have the feeling like once we cross the line we've literally been dancing around for days, the earth is going to shatter, but the reality is, Shama has a flight tomorrow morning. She's leaving LA, maybe for good, off to find herself in this big, ugly world of ours.

And I'm leaving too. After this video is done, the tour starts. The promotional blitz. I've got real money to make, a project to finish, and it's not going to help if I'm pining after this girl.

But there's no doubt in my mind anymore.

We have one night.

And the fuck if I'm not going to make the most of it.

Suddenly, the roses, the champagne, the strawberries—all of it seems cheap, fake. How many times have I done this, for how many girls? More than I can count, and for the first time in my life, I'm actually kind of disgusted by it.

I consider the painting that hangs in my apartment in New York—the picture of a woman's nipple that I thought was a sex magnet when I was twenty-three. Nico still teases me about that thing. Apparently, when he brought Layla to the apartment one weekend, she took one look at that thing and ran in the opposite direction.

Smart girl.

I wonder if that's when he knew she was worth the trouble of settling down. A woman who knows her worth is a woman worth having.

Who said that?

Papito, please. Ah. Ma. Yeah, I should have known.

I press the St. Cecilia medallion to my lips, the only thing around my neck I haven't taken off, not since my first communion. A gift from my mother, who knew I had my own gifts to share with the world. The patron saint of music, to guide me through this crazy life that maybe she knew I was going to have before I did.

A woman who knows her worth, papi, is a woman worth having.

Goddamn. If I've heard that once, I've heard it a hundred times.

"Ahem."

Shama's husky voice pulls me out of my daze. A woman who knows every inch of her worth, from the top of her shiny black head to the tips of her perfectly painted toes. Shama knows she's worth the fuckin' world. I knew it the second I heard her voice. *That*'s what I needed on the record. That worth.

"H-hi," she says, sounding anything but certain. But then she straightens. That confidence—it's so much more than swagger—is back. "Are you coming in?"

But I don't answer. I just stare for a few seconds longer, taking in this beauty in front of me.

And then I kiss her.

EIGHT

Shama

His kiss begins suddenly, and at first, I'm frozen, stunned by the sudden grasp of his hands, the feel of his body fully pressed on mine.

It's not like I didn't know what I was doing, inviting him up here.

What was the harm in giving into a fantasy for once in my life? Especially when I was leaving the very next morning?

But then he walks me into the room. The door slams shut behind him, the bottle and flowers he carries fall to the carpet, and my body springs to life.

"Oof!"

"Fuck," he hisses as my hands slide into his thick, cropped hair.

My mouth opened to his, accepting his tongue, his full lips, his bites and licks. He tastes like caramel and Hennessy.

Only one word runs through my mind, fast and hurried, like an electrical current.

Carlos.

"Get this off," I mutter, yanking his shirt over his shoulders, revealing the finely toned chest and delicious set of abs that have been taunting me for the last two days. Only this time I can actually touch them.

"Play fair," he says before he steals another kiss. His hands reach down to take ample handfuls of my ass, and he groans against my mouth as he squeezes. "Goddamn, I've been wanting to do that for fuckin' days, Shama. You know that? *Days.*"

"Is that right?"

I smile against his mouth before nipping his lower lip. He captures my mouth with his, and I sink into it. Because holy *hell*, the man can kiss. His tongue is hypnotic, twisting me into a daze, so within seconds, I barely know where I am.

"You drive me crazy, you know that?" he growls as his hands travel up and down my sides, squeezing here and there, mapping the terrain of my body as he peels my clothes off. Soon I'm standing in front of him in nothing but my underwear and bra. He takes a step back, like he's examining a piece of art.

"You look like you're examining a piece of art of something," I remark.

His eyes travel back up to meet mine, and that wicked grin makes another appearance as he reaches down lazily and unbuckles his pants. "Well...I am."

I try and fail to ignore the way my heart gives an extra thump when he says it. But before I can say anything else, he backs me up against the wall, reaching down to lift me against it before fusing our mouths together and grinding between my legs. I mean...wow. That's not just a belt buckle down there, if you know what I mean.

"What?" I ask as he pulls my panties to the side. "Am I not good enough for the bedroom?"

He stills. Shit. If I had a dollar for every time I killed a guy's mojo after opening my big mouth, I'd...well, I wouldn't have had to work quite as long as I did.

But Carlos doesn't move away. Instead, he smiles again. It's not the same smile as before. There's no swagger there, no game. This is charming, almost shy. It brings out a dimple in his left cheek I didn't see before, and his full lips purse together while his dark eyes twinkle, like he's trying to figure out exactly what to say.

"You're *too* good for the bedroom, if that makes any sense," he says, then drops my feet to the floor, takes my hand, and leads me to through the bedroom and out to the balcony.

We're on a corner, looking out to the beach. Maybe people could see us if they really wanted, but there are no lights here other than the moon slicing through a few clouds in the summer sky. Carlos pulls me close and kisses me again, kisses me until I'm dizzy and can't breathe right. Whoa. Those lips. Fucking hell, that shouldn't be legal.

"Sit," he says, gesturing at the big lounge chair. "I'll be right back."

He disappears into the bedroom, and I wait curiously, wondering what he's rustling up in my little hotel room. I'm just starting to wonder if I should go in there after him when the doors reopen, and Carlos emerges carrying my comforter and at least three of the massive pillows from the bed. I get up to help him, but he sets the pillows by my feet and proceeds to spread the comforter onto the balcony floor.

"You know they don't clean these things regularly after use, right?" I ask him.

"They do at this chain," he said with a smirk. "Ma was a hotel maid for a long time, and she worked for this hotel in New York. I used to help her for extra money when I was younger."

The idea of him cleaning rooms is...charming. And disarming. Though I know theoretically that Carlos, like a lot of similar artists, didn't come from much, it's hard to imagine when he pretty much drips with wealth now.

"They are not going to be happy about cleaning that," I say.

Carlos stands and shimmies out of his black pants, revealing his arousal, that hasn't faded under a pair of plaid boxers. "Send me the bill, pretty," he said. "Just get down here with me."

Slowly, I slide down to lie next to him and allow him to gather me into his arms.

"You make me...you make me..." he says again and again, in between kisses that smear across my shoulder, neck, between my breasts.

I clasp his head to my breasts, urging him on. "I make you what."

His mouth finds mine again. "You make me want to be better. Live better," he says in between an avalanche of kisses. "I want to be good enough for a woman like you."

Oh, hell. This is going to be one hell of a night if he keeps saying things like that.

You have to leave, Shama. You're on a plane in the morning.

"You *are* good enough," I manage to get out as I slide my hands over his strong, defined arms, then reach down for the waistband of his boxers. "You're perfect."

He groans as my hand wraps around him, then presses me backward so he cages me against the ground. The roar of the ocean sounds below us, and the stars twinkle over his shoulders, but all I can sense is him.

"Please," he gasps as I guide him between my legs. "Please. Fuck, Shama. I need you so bad. I—fuck!" he exclaims as he finds the entry he desires. He fills me in one deep thrust. "Tell me," he orders. "Tell me again. Tell me you need it too."

He's long, but not too long. Big, but not too big. I arch against his movements, my legs wrapping around his waist of their own accord.

"I...need...it." The rhythm he's setting makes it hard to speak at all, but I manage it for him. I have this strange feeling I'd manage just about anything. If he would just ask.

He sits up, takes hold of my thighs, and spreads them wide so he can watch himself pound into me. "Fuck, that's hot."

My eyes shut tightly as I take every rough pound, every harsh lunge he has to give. This isn't what you'd call making love—it's not sweet and soft; it's not gentle and slow. But it doesn't feel easy either, the way a fling should. It's intense and furious, like the waves pounding on the sand. Like we both know there isn't a moment to lose.

When I look up at him again, his eyes are bright, then they pop open wider, two hazel stars as a supernova flashes through us both.

His thumb slips between us, brushes lightly over my clit. And in that moment, that's all I need.

We split apart together in cries of desperation that neither of us expected. But above, the stars just twinkle on, like they expected this the whole time.

NINE

K.C.

I didn't sleep. Not after she climbed on top of me about five minutes after we finished together the first time. Not after I spent an extra ten minutes tasting her *everywhere*, until she shouted my name for the whole city to hear it. Not after she conked out on my chest right there on the balcony, then woke up and surprised me with the best fuckin' BJ of my life. And definitely not after we fell into this crazy daze; a new song still ringing in my ears. Music. Our music. This crazy melody that seems to be her.

Santa Monica twinkles below us, the ocean a black, dark space beyond the promenade. For the first time since I was a kid, I'm sleeping on the floor, wrapping up this incredible, irreplaceable woman and staring at the ocean she's about to cross. Wishing to God I was going with her.

Absently, I pull the St. Cecilia medallion to my lips and kiss it for good luck.

I've worked too hard for this day to leave it all for some girl.

And even if it was a good idea, I'm still contractually bound. To a tour. Promotions. Appearances.

Too much to leave without paying a massive price.

But...

"When's your flight?" I wonder as I watch the sun peeking over the horizon.

Shama stirs on my chest. I watch the elegant lines of her shoulders ripple a little as she stretches to check her watch. "In about five hours," she replies. "We have some time."

Time.

"You really want to go all the way over there?" I'm a dick for asking, but I can't help it. "Seems...hot."

Hot. In India. Way to fuckin' go, Captain Obvious.

Shama just chuckles. "Yes. It will be hot."

"What are you going to film? In Delhi, I mean?"

She sighs. "I honestly don't know. I need to see what I see first. See what speaks to me. I'll stay with some family first while I get my bearings. And then I'll go where inspiration leads, I guess."

"What if..." I toy with her hair, combing out some of the tangles I put there. *No, you can't say it.* I shouldn't. She's doing her own thing, and I'm doing mine. I don't have more than one night. I'm about to spend the next year on the fuckin' road, and I won't have time for myself, let alone most people.

Most people ain't her, mano. There's Nico again, telling me what's what. And you know, he's right.

I open my mouth to tell her that I knew her before. But instead, something else comes out.

"Come with me instead." I blink, shocked by the words, but also by how much I mean them. Quickly, I recover. "You could do your documentary everywhere we go. Do it on the tour or something else. But we'll be on the move. And Shama, we'll just keep going until you're ready to stop, not me. It might be my tour we're on, but it will be *your* schedule that runs it. *Te prometo.* I promise."

The words become babble, a ridiculous string of nothings, everythings. Anything to get her to reconsider her plans and come with me instead. Because I can't be the only one feeling what I'm feeling. I can't be the only one who sees beyond just tonight.

Shama makes me feel like I'm not alone anymore. And right then, I know I'd beg her to stay if I thought it would do the trick.

Shama sits up, unabashed, as the blanket falls from her shoulders. But I'm too distracted by her face to be distracted by her curves or the beautiful shadows of her body. I could go another round or four with her. But everything I need right now is on her face.

And it's going to break my head.

She cups my cheek and runs her thumb over my lips.

"Carlos," she whispers, and her eyes glimmer, almost like she's about to cry. "Carlos, I know. I so, so want to..."

I swallow. "But the answer is no."

Slowly, she nods, and I watch as a tear slides down her cheek. Sadly, she shakes her head. "I've been waiting years to do this," she says, her voice cracking over the words. "*Years.* I can't...I can't just back out now, you know? This is the first time I've ever done something...for me."

I get it. Fucking hell, do I get it. How many people did I leave behind in New York every time I flew out to LA for months, even years, to get my career going? How many hearts have I broken, never willing to settle down because if I did, I would have ended up just another bodega owner or janitor in New York, working two or three jobs just to get by.

You only get so many chances in this life to be yourself. I'm not about to take hers.

"Don't cry, Sparks," I whisper, though the words only bring more tears. "Not for me, pretty. I don't deserve your tears."

She hiccups back a choked sob and gives me a grim smile. "You deserve anyone's tears, Carlos," she says. "Least of all mine. I hope you believe that."

I press a kiss to her lips and pull her close so she's lying on top of me. "I believe it now, Sparks. I think you could get me to do just about anything. That's what you've been doing all weekend too."

She laughs, then lets me pull her down for another kiss that turns into something more than just a peck. I keep doing it, let her slide down, feel how much I want her *again*. She guides me inside her, wincing slightly as she lowers herself onto me, then tips her head up with pleasure.

"Don't hurt yourself," I whisper, though I'm already starting to thrust from underneath her.

Another tear falls. She doesn't fight them because we both know what this is. Goodbye.

"Shut up and take it, Carlos," she mutters, laughing and crying all at once.

I slip a hand around her neck and pull her down for another kiss. If these are our last moments, I'm going to make them good. "Whatever you say, Sparks. Whatever you need."

EPILOGUE

ONE YEAR LATER

Shama

The cab pulls up to the townhouse in Riverdale, a shabby, yet spacious home in the Bronx that houses two of my best friends.

I'm tired. Exhausted, actually. Not just from the multi-day flight that somehow got me back to New York from the tiny town in Bali, where I finished my documentary on South Asian indigenous music. From the entire year I spent documenting tiny communities all over that part of the world, capturing their music on camera for a docu-series that was commissioned by none other than HBO halfway through the year.

Thank you, Gary, I suppose. I never wanted to produce that last video, but it changed my life in multiple ways. One call from the A&R executive kicked off the career I'd always wanted as a music documentary filmmaker.

The other way, of course, was Carlos.

It's not like I never heard from him again. I had a cell phone, after all, and when I returned to the city here and there to send my films back to New York, I'd always be cheered by the sudden flurry of texts and emails. Carlos would send me the news, of course, along with pictorial reminders of just what I was missing out on. Carlos on stage, usually shirtless, while he gave the crowd what they wanted. Carlos standing next to his certified gold, then platinum record. Carlos at the Grammys, accepting his first-ever award as a performer, not just a producer. "*Porque*" won Song of the Year. And I won't lie. I cried a little when I watched him thank me on a scratchy broadcast I managed to track down in Hanoi.

"I'll hold on to this until we meet again, Sparks," he said, holding up the shiny gold statue and blowing a kiss to the camera just before the music played him off.

But the texts, just like everything else, eventually petered off. I spent a month riding a bike around Indonesia while "DJ Cairo" was back in the studio. Naturally, we were both relegated to a memory, a lark at the beginning of a vacation, at the end of both of our previous lives. One magical night that might have ruined me forever, but which I wouldn't give up for anything.

I knocked on the door and waited eagerly as the sounds of tiny feet pitter-patted to the door. It swung open, and almost immediately, I'm bowled over by Mateo, my godson.

"Auntie Shama!" he cries as he wraps his thin arms around my waist.

"Hey, you!" I love this kid so damn much. Even though he's almost seven, he's never too big for hugs.

"Shamashamashamashamashama!" The tiny voice of Mateo's sister, Coco, squeals behind him, and like a flea, the doll-like three-year-old plasters herself to my legs. "Did you get me a present?" she asks.

"Coco!" The deep voice of Nico, the kids' father, bounds through the hallway as he comes to collect his kids. He scoops the little girl up and sets her on her hip. "*Mija*, you got better manners than that."

"What's up, special delivery?" I say as I accept Nico's kiss to my cheek.

He just scowls at the old nickname, a remnant of his days at FedEx. "Trouble," he says as he stands back to let me into the house. "Always giving me shit, girl."

"Where is she? Where's my best friend?"

I look up to see Layla running down the stairs, and a few seconds later, I'm tackled by *my* best friend.

"Ahh!" she cries as she rocks me back and forth. "Look at you! You look amazing!"

"Thanks, dude," I say, squeezing her back just as hard. "I also look like I haven't slept in two days, which I haven't. I'm going to bed forever, but I wasn't going to miss your birthday. Speaking of." I pull out a little box from my purse and hand it to her.

Layla opens it and lifts the delicate gold bracelet. "Oh my God, Shams," she murmurs. "This is too much."

"I got it from this amazing artist in Bangalore. Hold out your wrist. I'll help you put it on."

She obeys while Nico shepherds the kids out the back door to the deck, where a bunch of other party attendees are mingling. As Layla admires the gift, I spot some familiar faces from college, a few others I remember from Nico's family. There's another man standing with his back to the door whose shoulders in his Giants jersey look very familiar.

I shake my head and turn back to Layla. It's been way too long since that night in Santa Monica. One whole year of nothing but me. I need a drink. And a bed. And eventually, a date.

"I see you checking out K.C.," Layla says slyly.

"Who?" I ask.

"Nico's best friend," she says, nodding toward the deck. "He's back in town. You remember him, I'm sure."

"No, I was just...remembering someone else," I say.

Layla frowns. "Remembering who?"

"Oh, you know. That guy just kind of looks like Carlos."

Layla looks back and forth between me and the guests. "Carlos...You mean Cairo?" Her eyes widen as she considers the story I told her last year.. "Oh, my God, Shama. You mean you didn't... you didn't know that—"

I frown. What is she talking about? I told her all about my little tryst with Carlos. What else is there to say? "Know what?"

Her mouth opens and closes a few times before she stands up straight and grabs my hand. "You know what? Let's just join the party."

But I'm stuck on the guy, and suddenly, I don't want to go out there. I don't want to meet some new guy who looks from behind, just like the one I haven't been able to get out of my mind for twelve months. I'm too tired for a poor substitute. Especially when it's for someone I can never have.

"I'm just going to get a glass of water," I say, but my friend isn't having it.

"Don't be rude," she says. "It's my birthday. You have to do what I say."

She leads me to the tiny backyard, and then, to my horror, reaches out and taps the Giants fan on the shoulder. "Shams, you remember K.C., don't you?"

But I can't answer. My throat is caught in my chest as the man turns around.

And it's him..

DJ Cairo.

Carlos.

A complete and total stranger, but also someone I know...*very well.*

"K—K.C.?" I choke.

His dark eyes are diamonds, the way they sparkle under the lights. The dimple in his left cheek appears. The one I still see almost every time I close my eyes.

Carlos smiles, warm and bright, but without surprise. He knew I'd be here tonight.

"Kevin...Carlos," he says softly. "How you doing, Sparks?"

"Why didn't you tell me?" I hiss at Layla, who is just grinning..

She shrugs. "Honestly? I thought you knew."

"Almost everyone important to me calls me K.C." Carlos tells me.

"Almost everyone," I whispered.

He takes a step closer. "Except one."

I blink. But now that night is coming back to me. An awkward Thanksgiving where Nico's little brother and player-looking best friend spent the evening hitting on me before I escaped to my parents' house. We were just in college. It was eons ago.

But how couldn't I have known him?

"Shama."

Our friends fall back into the party, but all I can see is him.

"Where...where did you go?" I ask. "I stopped hearing from you. Over a month ago now. After the Grammys, you stopped— you forgot about me."

"My tour ended," he said, taking a step closer, his broad shoulders lumbering. "I went back into the studio. I had all these rhymes. Beats in my head. Sounds like the ocean." Another step forward. "Like us."

He holds out a flash drive, and I know without asking what it contains. Songs, rhythms. New music this incredibly talented man has made. Just for me.

I don't want to tell him that he's been in my ears for the last year. That after I left LA, I downloaded every artist he's ever worked with, not to mention his own album. I listened to our song, "*Porque,*" on repeat every night. No music I recorded could erase the rhythms that we had made together.

His hand touches mine, and by instinct, our fingers entwine. In the periphery, I can see people watching us curiously, but Carlos's gaze doesn't waver.

"Sparks?" he asks.

My bottom lip quivers. "What?"

One last step, and he's only a few inches from my face. His hand cups my chin, and his thumb gently brushes over my cheek.

"I could *never* forget you, sweetheart," he whispers. "I came back to New York to wait. Because I knew when you got back from whatever you needed to do, I needed to be here for you. I spent a year apart from you, Sparks. I'm not doing it again."

I looked around, though my vision couldn't focus. Carlos just watches, clearly entertained.

"But...but what if—"

"Shama, who are you kidding?" he asks. "Even when you left the business, you were still in love with music. Your whole docu-series is about it."

I blink, now genuinely shocked. "How did you know that? I haven't even edited everything yet. It doesn't start airing for another three months."

That smirk returns, the one that makes me want to punch him and kiss him at the same time. But mostly, I realize the latter.

"I haven't missed *anything* you've been doing, Shama," Carlos says. "A few phone calls from my agent made sure I was always in the know. It's beautiful work, Sparks. It really is." He slips a hand around my waist. "I'm so fuckin' proud of you."

It's not until he says it that I realize how much I needed to hear it. That I needed to have *someone* validate this long journey I've been on to find myself.

"So what do you say, Sparks?" Carlos whispers. "You ready to continue this journey together, or what? I'll be recording for another three or so months...and then I'm going to need someone to film my next tour. Netflix is calling for it."

I open my mouth to argue but find I can't. He's right. Music calls me. Film calls me. *He* calls me. And all the questions I ever had about him melt away as I realize that his arms are where I'm supposed to be.

I press a kiss to his lips, and his hand slips around my head to hold me close and deepen it. A few whistles sound in the background, but he doesn't release me until he's good and ready.

"So what do you say, Sparks?" he asks again, this time when we are both out of breath.

"What else, you idiot?" I'm grinning so hard that tears are about to fall. "I say yes."

Thank you for reading The After Party!

You can check out how these two met in Nico and Layla's story, Bad Idea. Read it here: www.nicole frenchromance.com/badidea

THE DISCREET DUET

For Maggie and Will, their peace on Newman Lake is the most valuable thing in their lives. Will they risk it for Maggie's career? Can they grow their family without threatening their sanctuary at the lake?

The Discreet collection includes:

- The Discreet Duet extended epilogue
- A brand new excerpt from Hollywood Touch, the upcoming prequel
- Extra scenes and snippets

EXTENDED EPILOGUE

Two more years later

"What's the aurora, Daddy? And why do we need to go see it?"

My daughter and I rock with on the swell of the lake as we watch the stars come out. The murky white of the Milky Way spreads across the sky like it's being painted with a brush. The cat is a great boat for nights like these—soundless and light enough so that when you're lying on the trampoline stretched between the hulls, you can almost feel the earth turning.

"Daddy?"

I smile. Mickey's more like me than her mother this way. Maggie will give me a second to think things through, even though she won't let a question go. But she's a little more patient than me. Mickey, on the other hand, has my patience, or lack thereof. It's answer or perish with this one.

"*Daddy!*"

"It's the northern lights, bug," I reply with a chuckle. "It's a light show the North Pole puts on when a bunch of particles collide."

"Okay," Mickey says, like she knows exactly what that means, even though she's not even five yet. Who knows? It's possible. This kid is smart—a hell of a lot smarter than I was at her age. "But why do *we* need to see it? It's late. I'm a'pposed to be sleeping."

I smile up at the stars. "Because it's special, bug," I say. "It's not something you see every day."

"Like you?"

I turn my head. "Way more special than me, bug."

Mickey pushes a thick spiral of hair out of her face. In the moonlight, she looks so much like her mother. Other than the color of her hair, which is an even brighter blond than mine, she's basically Maggie's clone. Just like how Kip, her younger brother, is mine, except for his mop of black and the copper-colored skin. I love the way our kids are basically a blend of Maggie and me. They got the best of both of us.

A tiny fist slams into my shoulder. "Daddy!"

Okay, maybe not *all* the best. My daughter definitely has my temper too.

I blink. "Michaela, what did we tell you about punching people?"

She scoffs. "Daddy, you were ignoring me again. I had to get your attention!"

I just press my lips together and wait. Mickey might give me a run for my money in the stubbornness department, but I have a lot more practice.

Her big brown eyes open wide, just like Maggie's, and for a second, I falter, ready to forgive. But only just.

"Michaela."

"What?"

I sit up, looming over her little body. But the wide-eyed look on her face tells me she's not the slightest bit scared. She knows exactly what she's doing, the little scamp.

"Michaela, I don't care if this is a special night. If you don't apologize right now, you're going to be watching the aurora with the fishes in three...two..."

"Okayokay*okay*, I'm *sorry*Daddypleasedon'tthrowmeinthewaterPLEASE!"

Her words emit in a stream of squeaks, and almost immediately, I tackle her onto the net and tickle her sides until she's laughing so hard, she's almost crying. I love that sound. I had so many years where I never laughed, and now I just want to listen to my kids do it all the time.

"No! Stop!" she squeals, her voice cut with giggles as I tickle her tiny neck with my scratchy face, and her laugh bounces off the water, out to the hills.

But I do stop. I stop because even though I love to hear my daughter's laugh, I want her to believe in the importance of her consent more.

Almost immediately, she shouts, "Again!" And the whole thing starts over until we're both breathless.

"Apology accepted," I say as I settle onto my back again, Mickey splayed over my chest, her little body heaving. "And I'm sorry for ignoring you. What were you asking again?"

"I was...oh, yeah, I was asking if Mommy is as special as the aurora."

I chuckle and stroke her hair out of my face. "Oh, bug. Mommy is *way* more special than the aurora."

"Is it prettier than Mommy?"

This is a game Mickey plays. Trying to find things that I think are more beautiful than her mom. She has yet to discover one.

"No way," I say, and she relaxes further into me at the

response. My adoration of her mom is one of the things she depends on. Hell, it's one of the things *I* depend on.

"Even when you and Mommy got married?"

I smile into her hair. "Especially not then."

"Daddy! Look!"

Mickey sits up straight, and I follow her pointed finger toward the far north end of the lake. Sure enough, just above the tree line in the deep black of the night, there's a slight glimmering of light green, seeping ghostly out of the horizon, licked by a few touches of purple.

"You are right," Mickey whispers, entranced by the sudden lights. "Mommy's definitely more special than this."

I smile, though my attention is taken with my daughter, not with the sudden lights. "So are you, bug. So are you."

A light flashes from the dock—Jenna Forster, telling me it's time to come back in. She babysits for us here and there, and she agreed to come for a few hours so I could take Mickey out. Most of the time these nights are just me and the kids, and usually that's fine. But there's nothing like a night sail, and at one and a half, Kip's not quite old enough to go out on the water after dark.

I sit up and help Mickey back into her life jacket. "Come on, bug. Time to go in."

An hour or so later, I wake up, almost falling off Mickey's twin bed. I don't usually stay in there with her that long when she's going to sleep, but tonight it was hard to let go. Somehow, tonight feels precious. Sometimes I think about everything I've gained in the last five years—my kids, my wife, a life where I don't live in secret anymore—and I can't help feeling like it's all just a dream. Like one of these days, I'm going to be all alone again, constantly watching my back and sneaking in and out of my driveway like a thief for fear that someone will recognize me. Or, even worse, that I'll wake up and I'll never be alone, lost in a haze of pills and drink to block out all the people who thought they knew me but never did.

I brush Mickey's hair back from her face, then tiptoe out of the room. I check on Kip, my brick of a son. Kid's snoring up a storm like he always does, out cold until seven a.m., when he'll be running around the house at a million miles a minute until his next nap time. My boy. My crazy, perpetually moving, full-of-energy son.

After I've satisfied my fear and remembered again that this is actually my life, I go downstairs, grab a seltzer, and watch the stars again from one of the outdoor lounges on the deck. We kept the trees around the house to shelter us, but if you look up, you can see the light blinking through the tops of the tall pines. The stars here at the lake are one of my safe images—what Dr. Blanchard taught me to visualize when I feel myself starting to panic.

It still happens from time to time. We go to LA or New York a few times a year, and occasionally, a paparazzo will take interest, or a bunch of people will flock for autographs. Even here, when we have to run into the grocery store or make a random trip into town, I might get recognized. And yeah, sometimes I still snap.

Sometimes I wouldn't mind a drink or two to take the edge off. But when I think of the stars here, especially in a big city where the lights block them all out, the urge lessens, maybe even disappears. I see the stars. I see the lilies. I see home. And I'm usually all right again.

The rumble of an engine announces an arrival down the driveway. My heartbeat picks up a few beats, but I don't move as I listen to each consecutive movement. The crunch of gravel under the tires. The open and shut of a car door. The knock of boots on the now-paved walkway leading to the house. There's a silence as she enters the house, followed by the whisper of the sliding glass door opening. Her footsteps, light and bare now on the deck wood.

And then her smell. A blend of fresh greens, a hint of steel from the guitar strings, overlaid with the sweet scent of her perfume.

Lily pad.

"Hey, you." She lays a hand on my shoulder and peers out at the lake, which is still. The moon's face dances off the surface.

I look up at her. I don't say anything, just enjoy her pure, simple beauty. She's kitted out a little more than normal in a short black dress, hair down around her shoulders, her only jewelry the engagement and wedding rings I bought her. She's not much for flash, my Lil. Our wedding was little more than a quick "I do" on Moon Rock, followed by a barbecue at the Forsters', just a few months after we both won our Oscars and Kip was born. I smile. Yeah. That was a banner year.

I've tried, over the years, to give her a little ice, mostly on Benny's recommendation. A new guitar? That'll make her light up. But any bauble I give her goes straight into the safe, only to be brought out for the occasional awards show.

"Cavern" was just the start for her. After Rob Reinquist took her under his wing, she quickly became one of the most sought out composers in Hollywood. She's gotten an Emmy and two other Oscar nominations the last two years. I've gotten a few other SAG nominations for my screenplays, and I'm considering taking a shot at directing. We'll see. Actors, junkets, press. It's a little too close to the world I worked so hard to leave. Still, the idea of being behind that camera, bringing my words to life...yeah, it sounds *really* good.

"How was the show?" I ask as I pull her onto my lap.

She sighs, burying her face into my hair for a moment before she starts playing with it, as is her habit. I need a haircut, but I won't get one until she talks about it. There isn't much more I love than my wife cutting my hair for me.

"It was good," she says. "We did a couple new ones. Dad really has such an amazing voice."

It took a long time, but in the last five years, Maggie's grown really close to her father, Jim Edelman. It was a hard road. After meeting him at her mother's funeral, Maggie kept him at arm's length while she processed her own grief. It was too much, she said, to bring someone else into her life when she was mourning the absence of others. At that point, we were both so fragile. She was pregnant with Mickey, and the only thing we wanted was some peace for the six months or so until I had to leave for the *Green Lantern* promo tour. She was wary of the fact that he was a recovering alcoholic, particularly since I was only just acknowledging my own addiction issues at that point too. My girl shoulders everyone's burdens along with her own. She needed structure and stability—if not for ourselves, than for the family we had coming.

But Jim, to his credit, didn't quit. He'd call each week like clockwork, just to check in on Maggie, see how she was doing, make sure she was okay. And when she was finally ready to talk, he did it on her timeline. A coffee here and there. Eventually, a dinner at the house.

He never seemed to give a shit that his daughter was married to a famous person, since he had more than enough stories of his own to impress. Jim's is a life well traveled, and as Sunday dinners became a regular thing, we'd listen as he regaled his daughter of the life she'd missed. His years on the rodeo circuit. The time he spent in the Marines. There were even a few about Ellie, before her drinking turned really bad.

Maggie doesn't say it, but I think in the beginning, Ellie tried to be a good mother. Jim was pretty frank about the fact that he was a fall-down drunk at the time, and she cut him out because of it. She fell off the wagon too, but she tried, for Maggie's sake. I think remembering that will be how Maggie finds peace with her death. One day.

We learned about James's family on the reservation too, the extended network that always made him come home from his travels. Just before Mickey was born, Maggie accepted an invitation to visit them. We drove out to Wellpinit for dinner with Jim's sister, all five of her kids, and his mom and too many cousins to count. I played basketball with the kids outside while Maggie got a chance to know her relatives, and then we stuffed ourselves silly while Kim, James's sister, showed us all the old photo albums. Sat around a fire pit outside while James brought out his old guitar and started singing old country songs. In the middle of a rendition of Johnny Cash's "Walk the Line," Maggie joined him.

After we came home, she crawled onto my lap and cried for an hour. Tears of joy for what she'd gained. Tears of anger for what she'd missed out on. But after that night, she never looked back. And neither, thank God, did her dad. Every Sunday, they teach a music class together on the reservation, and afterward, they play at a coffee shop downtown together before she has dinner with her family. Usually the kids and I go, but every now and then, like tonight, we let them have their time.

I stroke her shoulder while she curls her small shape into my lap. I wrap my arms around her, slipping a hand naturally up her thigh, under the cotton hem of her skirt, to feel her smooth, taut skin.

"You ready for the race?" I ask. "Do we need to get anything before Friday?"

"Just your butt, ready to get handed to me."

It's become a tradition, competing in the Newman Lake triathlon together. Last year I actually beat Maggie, which was surprising, since she's a much better swimmer than I am. I doubt

I'll get her this year, though. She's been training a lot more, and I'm guessing her times are a lot better than mine right now.

"We'll see about that," I murmur, tracing my lips around her ear. "I might tire you out before then."

She shivers in my arms. "Is that so?"

"Yes, Mrs. Baker. That's so."

Yeah. I like calling her that way too much. Lil might have kept her name for her career, but legally, she's a Baker all the way.

My hand on her thigh moves a little farther up her skirt, and when she turns her face up to me with a retort, I capture her lips with mine. Soft. Sweet. Always pliable. Kissing her has always made me feel like I'm drowning and breathing at the same time. And by the way her body responds, I'm pretty sure she feels the same way.

My mouth releases hers, and she's out of breath while I drift down her long neck, pressing kisses into the divot between her clavicle, the hollow between her breasts. I can barely breathe myself. Two minutes with her taste in my mouth, and I'm harder than a fucking schoolboy.

"Oh!" she squeaks, as I pull aside her underwear. "Don't you... don't you want to go inside?"

"We'll wake up the kids," I say as I pull the fabric of her skirt all the way up her thighs. With quick, practiced movements, I settle my hands around her impossibly small waist, pick her up, and settle her back so she's straddling me.

"Will," she breathes as I lick a trail up her neck and suck at that sensitive spot below her ear. Her hands sink into my hair, holding me in place, urging me on. "Oh...babe. D-don't you think we need some p-privacy?"

That stutter. I used to hate it, but now the only time it comes out is when she's like this, caught on that line between control and ecstasy. It makes my pursuit of her pleasure that much hotter.

"Lil, I have fucked you all over this house," I say as I run my lips back across her face, dipping my tongue in for a kiss that steals her words. My hands slide down her ribs, enjoying the way she arches into my touch. "Blinds up, doors open. The whole fucking lake knows what you sound like when you come, baby."

For that, I get a sock on my shoulder, but I quickly capture her smile with my lips. And because she can't help it when I suck on the bottom on, she moans, grinding into me below.

Fuck. I *really* can't keep control of myself when she moves like that, with her head thrown back, her tits thrust in my face, nipples poking through the cotton. Fuck. Me. She didn't wear a bra tonight. Did she look like this all through her set? Her perky, round tits covered with nothing but this thin cotton dress, while she's swaying back and forth in front of the mic?

I'm not stupid. There's a reason why the music lessons she and Jim do attract a bunch of thirteen-year-old boys. God knows if I were that age, I wouldn't be able to stop staring.

Seriously, though? Jim couldn't have told his daughter to cover the fuck up?

I swallow back my jealousy as the hands in my hair yank me back to the present, back to a place where I'm just fucking grateful I get to call this goddess my own. Quickly, I pluck the column of buttons of her dress down to her waist, then spread the fabric so her breasts are bare in the night. I'd love to bury my face in them, but for a moment, I just look, enjoy the gleam of her skin and the pucker of her nipples in the moonlight.

Maggie's hands slide to the nape of my neck, and she tips my face to look at her.

"Baker," she says, her voice husky from singing all night, and also, I think, with want. "What are you waiting for?"

And in a second, I'm taken back to the early days when we first met. Those terrible, torturous moments, when I had to try every minute of every day to convince myself that we were wrong, when I did just about everything I could think of to hold myself back from doing what every animal instinct in me screamed at me to do. Hold her. Kiss her. Fuck her. Love her.

"Fuck it," I say softly, recalling our first kiss. "I don't fucking know."

She smiles, lighting up my chest and the night all at once. I watch, rapt as her small hands drift down, opening my flannel shirt, running over my chest, my abs, and down to the buttons of my jeans, which are pretty much ready to burst anyway. She takes me out, holding my cock in her small hands for a few seconds, her thumb drifting over the head. I do my best to hold still, but I'm fucking shaking. I need to be in her. Now.

"Lil," I whisper. Some nights I'll just take what I want. Some nights I'll flip her over the deck railing and fuck her silly, make her hold on for dear life.

But tonight, I need to know she wants it as bad as me. Tonight, I want *her* to be the one to take charge.

"Sometimes," she whispers as she continues that maddening touch, "I can't believe this is my life. That I live here with you. That we have this family. All of it." Her eyes, deep, dark pools of fear and desire, find mine. "Do you ever feel that way?"

I slip a hand around her head and pull her close for a kiss, the kind that I hope shows her everything I feel, everything I want to say, and everything I can't. When I release her, her eyes are shining like the water below.

"Baby," I say. "I feel that way every damn day with you."

She takes hold of me again, strokes lightly. It feels good, but right now, it's not what I want. Right now, I want *her*.

"I went to the doctor this morning," she said as she watched the movement of her hand, mesmerized.

"I know," I reply, wondering where she's going with this. My hands are drifting over her too, feeling her shape, her curves, touching her everywhere. I want her so badly, I can barely register what she's trying to tell me.

"I told her I didn't want another shot."

Her eyes drag up to mine again, and slowly, the gravity of what she's saying lands. After her IUD failed—twice—she switched to getting a shot in her arm every three months to make sure we didn't have any more "surprises" while she was getting her career going. I offered to get snipped after Kip's birth—I swear I did—but every time I tried to make an appointment, my cell phone magically went missing. It was fate, my wife, or both. You tell me.

I swallow, hard, as I realize what she's trying to tell me. "You—you sure?"

Her lips tug outward in a sweet smile. "I thought you wanted more babies with me, Baker."

"I want all the babies in the world with you, Lily pad," I say as I land kiss after kiss on her mouth, her jaw, her neck, her chest. "I just want to make sure it's what *you* want too."

Again, my face is tipped up, and I see in her eyes all the love and adoration I feel reflected right back at me. She kisses me, slow and long, her tongue slipping around mine, stealing my thoughts right out of my head.

"They do say three's a magic number," she purrs even as I'm lunging forward for more. "I want one more, Will. Please."

She doesn't have to ask again. I'd make ten babies with this woman, because having this family with her has never done anything but make this godforsaken world a better place. But instead of answering directly, I lift her up again, angling her hips so if she comes back down, it will be with me inside her.

"I'm all yours," I tell her.

But it's got to be her choice.

She braces her hands on my shoulders and slowly inches

herself downward. Her eyes shut for a second as she accommodates herself. If anything, having kids made this part easier, but she's always been small. She bites her lip as she takes me completely, and I can't help it. I groan.

"*Fuck.*" The word escapes me before I can stop it. I shouldn't cuss so much, not with kids, not when we're actively trying to make another. But Lil has always had that effect on me. Total loss of control.

And then we move. Her hips rock in tandem with mine, up and down, back and forth, and she arches back, giving me free rein to feast on her naked breasts, hold her waist, her ass, revel in every part of her until she clenches around me.

It doesn't take long tonight. Like she was primed for it the second she stepped onto the deck. I slip my hand downward and press my thumb over her clit, moving in the counterclockwise rotation that never fails to get her to where I've been for the last ten minutes—right on the fucking edge of oblivion.

"*Will.*" My name slips out of her mouth and onto the wind, my favorite song of hers.

"Do it," I order, pummeling up from beneath her now. This won't take long. But I want her to find this release with me. "Let go, baby. Feel it. Feel me. Feel *us*, Lil."

"Ahhhhh!"

Her sudden echo flies skyward, and wrapped up in my arms, my girl, my *woman* falls apart completely. Her orgasm jumpstarts mine, and for a few blissful seconds, we come together, shaking, shouting, moaning, breathing. We find that instant when the boundaries between us disappear, that place where the lines between Maggie and Will are gone, and only this nameless, beautiful entity exists. Together.

Sometime later, after we've come down from that high and many others, our thoughts drift as much as our clothes, scattered all around the deck. Maggie sits between my legs, lying against my chest in the chair. Still on the deck, we're covered with one of the stash of blankets she keeps out here in the summer months. I keep one arm wrapped around her waist, my other hand playing lightly up and down her arm. We'll pay for this night tomorrow, with tired minds, traded naps, and way too much coffee needed to deal with the kids when they wake up in a few more hours. But right now, I'm just enjoying it.

Because in the end, this is all that matters. One day, the kids will be gone. Our friends will come and go, and so might our health, our money, our looks, and everything else. But this crazy energy that's always been between us, that continues to inspire us both, will persist. Something nameless.

Her and me.

Maggie and Will.

Us.

Thank you for reading the extended epilogue for the Discreet Duet. If you haven't already, check out their original stories, beginning with Hollywood Secret. Get it here: www.nicolefrenchromance.com/hollywoodsecret

If you've already read those, there's more to come! Hollywood Touch, the Discreet prequel, releases January 2023! Preorder here: www.nicolefrenchromance.com/hollywoodtouch

FROM HOLLYWOOD TOUCH

A DISCREET PREQUEL COMING JANUARY
2022

EXTRA SCENES & SNIPPETS

Maggie runs off

With that, I turn on my heel and march back down the dock, leaving Will sitting on the grass, dumbfounded.

"Maggie!" he calls, but I just wave a hand in his direction.

"I gotta go!" I shout over my shoulder. "Got some freeloading to do!" And before I listen to another self-righteous retort of his, I dive back into the wave and start the swim back. It's funny. Five minutes ago, I was about ready to pass out, right there on that dock. But Will does something to me, something that gives me more energy than I've felt in years.

Hate, I decide as I stroke through the water. That's what it is. Hate.

That spark

"Promise me you'll try," he said. "Even if it's here, promise me you'll keep playing, keep sharing your voice. Talent like yours shouldn't be wasted, Maggie."

We stared at each other for a few seconds, and for once, he doesn't I open my mouth to speak, but instead, I kissed him.

I didn't mean to do it. We were inches apart, and I was leaning in, drawn like a magnet, intending only brush his lips lightly.

But the spark, of course, the one that's always there, said otherwise.

Maggie's hair

"Your hair," Will said. "It's getting curlier."

I turned over, pulling the strands out of his fingers. He frowned and pulled a few back to examine.

"What are you doing?" I said irritably, pulling them back.

"What are *you* doing?" he replied. "Why can't I play with your hair?"

"Because it's not a toy," I snapped.

Tickling Will

He looked down. "What are you doing?"

I deflated. "What does it look like? I'm trying to tickle you."

That crooked smile I was seriously beginning to love reappeared. "Tickle me? Am I five?"

I huffed. "One day I'm going to get you to laugh, Baker. I've made it my life's goal now. I don't give up."

The words, though they started lightly, fell heavily between us. I swallowed, suddenly wanting to look at anything else but him. Because I had given up. That's exactly what I was doing here instead of making music in New York. Giving up.

Will cleared his throat and took my hand.

A birthday present

"Shit," he mumbled into my lips. "I need to get you a birthday present, don't I? I feel bad. I don't even know what you want. What you like."

Suddenly, I grinned. "I know what you can get me."

Will brightened with relief. "Name it, Lily pad. Please."

"Keep shaving your beard?"

Will blinked. Then he tipped his head back and laughed. Really, really laughed. It wasn't a chuckle or a snort, but a genuine laugh, the kind that came from deep down in his chest.

"Oh, baby. Oh, *shit!*"

When he calmed himself down, he slumped into the sheets still grinning like a fool. I had never found him more attractive.

"Does that mean you're going to do it?!" I asked, trying not to sound completely like I was begging.

"Not a fucking chance," he said.

Will "marks" Maggie

He groaned as he spilled all over my chest and stomach, marking me as his in the most visceral way possible. His forehead was traced with lines. And in the end, when he opened his eyes, raw, primal satisfaction painted across his features, he smiled like a cat who'd finally caught its prey, reached down, and I watched, mouth open, as Will proceeded to smear himself all over my skin.

"I can't believe you just did that," I said as he finally stood up and grabbed a towel off the floor to clean himself up.

He turned back around with an almost dangerous look on his face. "Mine," he mouthed, and then left for the bathroom.

"You'll come, won't you?"

"I have two more months of this before filming wraps. They haven't set a release date, but I'm guessing it'll be either Christmas or late spring to kick off blockbuster season, depending on how it ends up looking."

I mulled on that for a second. "So that means…"

"I'll have to promote, yeah. It's part of my contract." His entire body shuddered, like a wave had hit him.

"Is it that bad?" I wondered.

Will held up a hand and started counting off on each finger as he spoke. "Press junket. Five days straight of mindless interviews. Talk shows. Radio spots—especially with Seacrest. And the premieres—the endless fucking premieres with all the goddamn cameras." He turned to me. "You'll go, won't you?"

I balked. "What, to your premiere?"

Will's face screwed up adorably. "Well, yeah. Lil, you will, won't you?"

"Don't people get really dressed up for those things?" The images from the magazine, and several others I'd seen just like it, flashed through my mind.

"The studio will hire a stylist," Will said. "They'll get all sorts of free shit thrown at them. You don't have to worry about that."

Interrupted by the trainer

Will was just getting into the kiss, and getting into things a bit lower down, when a loud knock sounded at the door. Will pressed his forehead into my neck and groaned.

"Who's that?" I asked.

With a scowl, he pushed himself up, brushed off his still-wrinkled shirt, and glared in the direction of the front door when the knock sounded again. "That's Cliff. My trainer."

I followed him into the living room, but hung back when, after Will opened the door, a short, bouncy man with the energy of a typhoon practically bounced in.

Will freaks out

"Rise and shine!"

"Get. The fuck. Out of my house."

"Oh, it's *fine*! The studio sent me over here with your week's worth of food! Aren't you lucky that principal photography will start here in LA?"

"Get out!" Will roared. He reached over, took the man's shoulders, and bodily moved him to the door. By the time he had slammed it shut again and turned around, he was shaking.

"Fuck," he whispered. "Oh, *fuck*. I can't do this without you, Lily," he said. His eyes squeezed shut as he pressed his forehead to mine. "You're the only thing good in my life. The only thing that's real."

Lucas fights for Maggie

"He's right for me."

"He lied to you."

"For good reason."

"You could do better."

"What, like you?"

There was a long pause, and immediately, I felt terrible. Lucas had never done anything but support me and my mother when no one else would. He was a genuinely good man, and even if there had been a time or two where he'd struggled to take no for an answer, there was a part of me who would always love him. He didn't deserve this.

"I'm sorry," I said. "Lucas, really, I am. It's just that—"

"I get it." His voice was tight. "I'm not going to pretend that I wanted a second shot, Mags, but I get that it's not in the cards for us. I do. But that doesn't mean I stop caring about you. I just don't want to see you get hurt."

ROSE GOLD

Matthew and Nina's wedding day is here at last! But will these two lovers overcome their fears and nerves to make their happily ever after at last?

The Rose Gold collection includes:

- "The Italian Wedding"
- Extra scenes and snippets from the original series

THE ITALIAN WEDDING

Nina

"You look fabulous," Jane pronounced from the floor. "Better than fabulous. Spectacular. Magnificent. Mythologically gorgeous, Nina. I'm not kidding. You could be Helen of Troy in this thing. I half expect Paris to bust his way through the doors and start a war on your behalf."

"Well, let's not get ahead of ourselves," I said superstitiously. I'd had enough fighting around my marital status to last a lifetime. "There's only one man I'm interested in marrying, and he's waiting for me at the church."

Jane made a sound of agreement as she continued to arrange the paper-thin Italian lace over my shoes. "Fair enough. I don't think it would matter, though. That man would fight a thousand Greek armies to marry you."

"Well, army or not, I really do think they pulled it off," I said as I looked at myself in the mirror hanging from the *pensione's* ancient stone walls. "And Matthew is going to love it."

The dress was perfect, both as a reflection of my own tastes and also for marrying my Italian-Catholic husband in a seven-hundred-year-old church. Today was all about tradition, and as daring as Matthew could be in *some* ways, I sensed that our wedding was not one of them.

At first, the idea had felt...constraining, to say the least. After all, I'd already had a "traditional" wedding, just over eleven years earlier. And it had felt like a farce. Like this one, it had been arranged in a matter of weeks, not months or years. Like this one, I had been masking an early pregnancy.

But that was where the similarities ended. On that day, I had shoved myself into an enormous wedding dress modeled after Grace of Monaco, fully covered from neck to wrist, a skirt that kept my horrible husband at arm's length simply by virtue of its eight-foot diameter. I was a walking pincushion, a pathetic actress, heavy with the weight of my despair and lies.

I hadn't known how much I dreaded the recurrence of that feeling until I looked at myself in the mirror now and felt it all float away.

The woman in the mirror stood tall and graceful in the sleek column of Italian lace with a demure boat neck and cap sleeves. Her antique engagement ring, which had been worn proudly by her future grandmother-in-law for more than fifty years, gleamed on her left hand, matching the sunlight bouncing off blond waves smoothed into a delicate chignon. A touch of color painted her lips, which couldn't stop smiling—a joyful scarlet red that matched the bouquet of roses on the table by the sofa.

I looked myself in the eye and smiled. I had never felt more true than I did in this dress. This was *exactly* where I was meant to be. And there was no doubt in my mind about what I was meant to do.

"My *wife*," Matthew had whispered in awe over the last month, night after night as we lay in bed together in our new home in Boston. Cupping my face gently before kissing me breathless. "You're going to be my *wife*, Nina."

As much as he liked to call himself a sinner, I knew the truth. My beloved was eager to make an honest woman of me, especially now that we were expecting. And now that I stood here in my lace finery, I had to admit...I felt the same.

"I still can't believe they found me a dress this short notice," I said as I turned around to inspect the long line of buttons trailing down my spine.

I honestly hadn't expected to wear anything better than off-the-rack after Matthew and I had decided to elope only a month ago. He was making do with the Givenchy tuxedo I had gifted him last spring for the Met gala, but as a couture piece, it was hardly skimping. Considering the way Matthew made most suits look better than anyone had any right to, in couture he was as much a work of art as any of the Renaissance masterpieces Italy had to offer.

Now, being a longtime client of the house of Valentino had paid off in one way when the creative director offered me a dress right off the fall runway.

"There will be photographs, no?" he had asked when we spoke on the phone. "You will promise?"

"*Vogue Italia* has asked," I told him. "I suppose we could oblige."

It was fate. Because the moment I had seen the gorgeous lace frock, I knew it was the perfect dress for marrying Matthew Luca Zola.

"Well, it certainly helps that you're a sample size," Jane remarked dryly as she clambered awkwardly to her feet. She was in one of her own designs, a pretty safe green piece altered to fit her five-months' pregnant form. "Or were, until this weekend. Did Isabella get over the last-minute alterations after you ate too many *cornetti* this week?"

The senior seamstress from Valentino had only put up a minor fit when he had discovered that my bust size had expanded another inch in the last three weeks.

I smiled, turning from side to side to check that nothing more had changed visibly. My body was growing by the hour, it seemed, especially in the bust. While Matthew certainly noticed (and appreciated) my new curves, I wasn't particularly fond of them. I drifted a hand over my mostly flat stomach.

"You really can't tell too much, can you?" I murmured to myself.

"Tell what?"

My eyes popped open as I realized my mistake. "Nothing. It's nothing."

"Wait a second..." Jane said as she came to stand next to me. "Are you..."

Her gaze shot to where my hand lay flat over my abdomen. I dropped it like the dress was burning.

But Jane's eyes, bright hazel through thick black glasses, popped open with sudden recognition. "I *knew* it!"

I rolled my eyes and stepped off the small pedestal. "Oh, Jane, you did not. You had no idea."

"I *did*. I had a hunch—those are real, you know. First, you wouldn't eat any of the soft cheese last night. And when you gave Zola your wine, I knew something was up. Oh my God, does he know?"

"Shh!" I glanced over her shoulder at the sound of footsteps coming down the hallway outside the door. "For God's sake, Jane, keep your voice down! We're not advertising this to anyone yet, for obvious reasons. But, of course, he knows. He is the father, after all."

Jane's eyes glimmered with joy.

"Holy crap!" She pushed up her glasses and dabbed at her eyes. "I—shit, pregnancy really makes you cry at everything, you know. I saw a homeless kitten yesterday and started bawling. But God, Nina, you guys just really, *really* deserve all the happiness. And Zola's going to be a great dad. You know that, don't you?"

"Jane, stop. I'm going to have to redo my makeup."

Suddenly, I found I needed my own handkerchief. I wiped away the tear that had appeared—as it almost always did whenever I imagined Matthew cradling our child in his lean, strong arms. Sometimes I yearned to see it so badly, I couldn't breathe.

Before I could say as much, the door to the room burst open, and two girls skittered in—my daughter, Olivia, followed by Sofia, Matthew's niece.

"See, I *told* you they were here!" Sofia said triumphantly. She turned to me, then frowned adorably. "Aunt Nina, where's your crown? I thought you would have one since you're a princess today."

For the first time in my life, the term didn't hurt. I had been called a princess since I was born—one of two heirs of a family dynasty, then by the man who had pretended to love me and left me only with a daughter, and then later in tones of derision and hatred from the first man I married.

But now, in the simple admiration of a four-year-old's kind voice, I didn't mind it. Not at all.

"Sorry, Mama," Olivia said. "I tried to tell her you were getting ready, but she wouldn't listen."

I smiled at both of them. "There's no need to apologize, darling."

I bent down to look at Sofia, who, as the flower girl, was

dressed in the blush-colored silk that matched Olivia's bridesmaid dress.

"Not all princesses have to wear crowns," I told her kindly. "Sometimes we wear veils. Would you like to see mine?"

Sofia nodded eagerly, so I picked up the floor-length veil trimmed with lace to match my dress. I turned back to the mirror, and Jane helped me affix it securely over my chignon.

"There," I said, turning around. "What do you think, ladies? Is this princess-like enough for you, Miss Sofia?"

The little girl nodded eagerly, causing her thick black curls to bounce up and down. Olivia smiled, but her face didn't glow in the same way.

"Jane," I said as I watched my daughter. "Would you mind taking Sofia downstairs to her mother? I'd like a moment with Olivia."

"Sure thing. Come on, jelly bean. I bet if we're *really* nice, we can talk your mom into another gelato after the ceremony."

"More ice cream!" shrieked Sofia, as if she were already on a preemptive sugar high. Matthew's niece and nephews had all been *really* enjoying that aspect of Italy since they had arrived.

They left, and I turned to Olivia, who was sitting on the sofa in her wedding day finery, gazing quietly at her hands. Her expression was unreadable, which only reminded me for what felt like the millionth time over the last month or so how much more I had to learn about this lovely, quiet girl who was my own flesh and blood. Because the last month hadn't only been about building a home with the man I loved. It had been about getting to know my daughter again too.

Olivia had attended boarding school since she was five years old, when I had sent her away in order to protect her from the monster she believed was her father. In hindsight, I wondered if on some level she knew our home wasn't safe, though I had taken pains to shield her from the worst horrors. Instead of fighting boarding school, like most children would, she had accepted it readily, even at such a young age. It had killed me every year to say goodbye to her. Now, for the first time, she was attending Andover Preparatory Academy as a day student only, coming home each evening to her own bedroom in our Newton house instead of a dorm room she shared with another girl.

She was still quiet and unsure, still paused before asking for the things she needed, still stopped at every door to check it was safe before entering. But over the last month, I had watched my shy, quiet daughter blossoming in ways I had never thought possible. I had watched her learn to smile unguarded, especially at Matthew's jokes, and ask questions more often as fear of rebuke slowly left her. It almost made up for the guilt I felt about the first ten years of her life.

Almost.

"Hello, darling," I said as I sat beside her.

She looked up, her dark brown eyes nearly black. So different from mine. So like her father's. Her *real* father's, long dead. "Hi, Mama."

I took her small hand and sandwiched it between mine. Her shoulders relaxed. This was something else I had learned—like me, Olivia was affected more by a friendly touch than any words. And just like me, she would almost never ask for it.

She smiled. "You look so pretty, Mama."

I smiled back and touched her cheek. "Thank you, my love. So do you."

Olivia's face pinkened at the compliment as she looked down at her silk dress. Matthew and I had chosen to keep our bridal party small—one of his nephews was playing the ring bearer, Sofia was the flower girl, and Olivia was my one and only bridesmaid, and then we had asked Jane and Matthew's best friend,

Jamie, to stand at the altar with us. Eric would walk me down the aisle.

"Darling, are you okay with everything?" I asked. "With the wedding? Are you happy that I'm marrying Matthew?"

Olivia bit her lip with the same nervous tic I recognized as my own.

"You can say no," I assured her, though my heart thumped in quiet panic. What if she did say no? What if I was wrong and secretly she hated Matthew? What would I do then?

You'd help her through it, and so would I, doll. Matthew's voice was sweet, patient, and confident, like it always was when I voiced such fears. After all, I'd never had a real family like this, whereas he had grown up with it in various iterations all his life. *A real family takes time, duchess. And now we got all the time in the world.*

"I won't be angry," I told her honestly. "And neither will Matthew. I would understand. It's a lot of change."

Olivia looked up with mild panic. "Would that mean—would Matthew leave?"

I frowned. "No, my love. He wouldn't leave. Matthew would never leave us." I tipped my head. "Why? Do you not care for him?"

There was that fear again, though in my heart, it didn't make sense. I had watched Matthew bring my daughter further out of her shell than I had ever seen her. From helping her with her homework to taking her out to dinner in Boston's North End to kicking a soccer ball with her in the backyard, he had been nothing but a thoughtful and supportive future step-parent. And if Olivia's sweet giggles were any indication, she was just as smitten with him as he was with her.

"My daddy—um, your hus—Calv—" she stuttered, clearly unsure of what exactly to call Calvin. "*He* left," she said finally.

"He didn't say anything to me when he—when he went to jail. Even though he was allowed."

My heart twisted. Though I hadn't been privvy to any of the grief counseling she had been going through, I knew the summer couldn't have been easy for my daughter, after discovering that the man she believed was her father was most definitely not. When Calvin was sentenced, Olivia had asked to visit him in the prison. To say goodbye, I thought, though a part of me also wondered whether she wanted him to be her father still. To demonstrate that while his relationship with me had been an utter farce, perhaps he had loved her a little, at least.

But his answer had been clear when he had refused even her as a visitor. And our own relationship had been strained, as it would when you discover your mother has been lying to you for most of your life, even if it was out of love. I wasn't sure I'd ever forgive myself for it. But in the meantime, I had to earn her trust right along with Matthew.

"I see," I said quietly. "And you're afraid that Matthew will leave too."

Her silence was simply an acknowledgment.

And so, I made a decision. "Would you like to know a secret, my love? Will you keep it?"

Dread filled her face. "More secrets, Mama?"

"No, no, darling, it's a good secret. It's only...we can't tell anyone for another month or so. Only Jane and Eric know. And Matthew. Just to be safe."

Olivia frowned. "What is it?"

I took a deep breath. "Well, did you notice that I haven't been drinking any wine on this trip?"

Olivia nodded. "Yes. But I thought it's just because you're kind of picky, Mama."

I held back a smile. "Perhaps. But it's not that." I took a deep breath. "Sweetheart, I'm pregnant. It's very new, which is why you can't really tell yet. And it's a little out of order. But you deserve to know that our family is going to grow even more. You're going to have a little brother or sister sometime next spring."

Her dark eyes grew progressively wider the longer I spoke. "You're—you're going to have a baby? You and Matthew?"

I nodded. "Yes. We are."

For a moment, I thought I might have made things worse. For all the time we had spent apart, Olivia and I had a special bond. Matthew might be my soon-to-be husband, but she was my one and only child. And though I knew nothing would ever break that bond, perhaps she didn't. Her world was still so tenuous.

But I needn't have worried.

"So you and me and Matthew...we're going to have a *real* family?" she asked, now only sounding incredulous. Her eyes shone with eagerness. "All together?"

"Well, if you ask him, we already have one," I told her, just as Matthew had assured me so often himself. "But it's another way for you to know that Matthew is *always* going to be a part of this family. Because family is the most important thing in the world to him. He would never, ever leave his children, and as of today, my love, you are one of them."

Olivia was quiet for a long time, digesting my words. Then she slowly nodded and scrunched up her little brow. "Should I—do you think I should call him something different besides Matthew? So he knows he's in our family too? And so, you know...so the baby doesn't feel left out, I mean."

She was searching, poor thing, for a name, a label, one that would appropriately solidify the relationship in her heart as well as her mind. Calvin had been "Daddy," which was clearly tainted for her now. After meeting her sisters, Giuseppe was now also her *Babbo*, though she didn't speak of him often. I could understand the desire to bless Matthew with something more as well.

For a moment, I considered telling her that Matthew had already raised the idea of officially adopting Olivia as his own. To hear him tell it, he had fallen in love with her at first sight in the same way he had with me. I had no doubt of his intentions, but for my daughter's sake, it wasn't something I was willing to rush into. One day, though. And maybe sooner than I thought.

"I think that's something you and Matthew can figure out together," I told her honestly. "But I do know he loves you very much."

Again, that curious, shy pleasure crossed Olivia's face as she nodded to herself. "Me too," she whispered, more to herself than to me.

"Can I teach the baby to ride?" she asked, eyes brightened all over again. "When it's old enough, I mean? Can I show it the stables and the horses?"

"You can teach it a great many things, my love," I said as I pulled my daughter close. "I know you'll be a wonderful big sister. You're already the best daughter anyone could hope for."

Matthew

"Let perpetual light shine on him. May he rest in peace."

My voice was a murmur as I finished lighting a candle for *Nonno* at a small stand of candles just behind the altar of the church of Santa Margherita d'Antiochia. On the other side, the people were quickly filling the small wooden pews in the nave, their voices echoing around the ancient stones as they waited for the ceremony to start.

It was still technically an elopement, but it looked pretty damn close to a full wedding to me. Nothing like the big affair I'd attended back home, banquet halls with sixteen-member wedding parties and a reception line a mile long. This was just family and close friends, like Nina and I had discussed when we had decided one month ago to get married in Vernazza.

But the people who insisted on witnessing our union turned out to be more than just Jane and Eric, my sisters, and my grandmother. Lea brought all three of her kids and Mike for the honeymoon she never got (Atlantic City, she said, didn't count). Skylar and Brandon had carted their entire family across the ocean for an impromptu European vacation. Nina's mother arrived two days ago with a bunch of her cousins and Eric's mom, to boot. And several of Nina's socialite friends were taking up the better part of one row with their hats alone. Even Derek, Jamie, and a few other friends from the DA's office and the service also flew out for the big day, plus at least fifty of my cousins, second cousins, great-aunts and uncles, and all their kids from Rome and Naples wanted see me, the only grandson of Mattias Zola, tie the knot to a legitimate heiress.

To my surprise, Nina had just shrugged with every additional attendee and said, "the more the merrier," then made a quick call to the wedding planner. It was amazing what a little de Vries cash could do to open doors that usually remained strictly shut with so little notice. Really, though, it was just humbling, really, to see how many people wanted to honor the love Nina and I had. Especially after we had to hide it for so long.

"You ready?"

I finished my prayer, then crossed myself before turning to Brandon, who was hovering just behind me.

If you had told me seven years ago that one of my best friends would end up being a hot shot billionaire from Boston, I would have told you to have another, why don't you. If you'd told me I'd be living there instead of my beloved hometown of New York, I'd have told you to get moving, or I'd kick your ass out the door myself. And if you'd have told me I'd be happy, I'd have told you to fuck off and have a nice life.

And yet here I was, and all three were true. Sure, I missed my family, but in some ways, I wondered if the change wasn't good for all of us. I hadn't realized until now how codependent all of us were. So much of my life was bound up by being needed by my sisters and my grandmother, and so much of theirs. In turn, Frankie had been afraid, at first, when I had told her my plans to leave. But once I had finally allowed Nina to pay off the town-house so that she and Sofia could stay there without any worries, she had surprised me by refusing a free ride, insisting on at least paying the same rent as Pete, the basement tenant. Over the last month, my sister was learning to thrive on her own. Meanwhile, I was thriving too. Brandon and Skylar had both taken my arrival as their personal mission to acclimate Nina and me to Boston. Nina had re-enrolled at Wellesley to finish her art history degree at last, and I was getting settled in as a defense attorney at Skylar's firm, which I was happy to discover donated nearly fifty percent of their time to pro bono cases in Boston. I couldn't lie—a part of me still missed the public service, and Boston had enough organized crime to keep me plenty busy. Skylar assured me that a few years with her would only give me an edge once I decided to dip my toe back into that particular pond.

"A few years more, I wouldn't be surprised if you were asked to run," Brandon had said over one late dinner on our newly painted back deck.

"Run for what?" I asked.

He shrugged. "I know some people, if you're interested."

"Are you?" Nina had asked curiously as she brought out a tray of antipasti, some of my favorites she often picked up for me in town. "Interested in politics, Matthew?"

At the time, I had shrugged. "I don't know."

And I still didn't. But the seed was planted, and something deep inside was germinating. Maybe even growing.

One thing was true. By leaving New York, I'd assumed I was closing a bunch of doors. But to my surprise, so many others were busting wide open.

For now, though, I was here. And there was no place else I'd rather be.

I straightened my black bow tie and the pocket square. "I was born ready to marry this woman," I said to my friend.

Brandon smiled. "I can see that."

"Zo, you need anything?" Jamie asked behind him. "A shot of vodka? Or a getaway car?"

I snorted. "Very funny. What are you doing out here? You're supposed to be getting ready to do the catwalk."

It wasn't a strictly typical wedding ceremony, but then again, nothing Nina and I did together was ever typical. We had decided to forgo the typical procession of both of us, simplifying it to just a few key people: the kids with Olivia, then Jane as the matron of honor and Jamie, my best man, and then, Nina, escorted by Eric. No bench for a Mass since Nina wasn't actually Catholic. She had attended catechism classes all summer but had yet to make the leap to conversion. I honestly couldn't care less if she did, but she insisted it was because she wanted to understand me better. Just a quick blessing from the priest, an exchange of consent and vows, and then the kiss, because even if it wasn't *strictly* necessary, I'd be damned if I was going to give up that particular rite of passage.

"Yeah, yeah," Jamie answered. "But what kind of best man would I be if I didn't take care of the groom?"

"The kind who freaks out my soon-to-be *wife* by going missing?" I answered. "Listen, Quinn, you want to take care of me? Take care of her."

"Go," Brandon urged him. "I got him."

"I'm good, man," I told him. "No nerves here. Just ready to finish the job."

Jamie laughed, clapped me on the shoulder, then returned to the wedding party waiting just outside the church. The priest signaled from the altar that he was ready to get started—after all, there was another Mass after this short affair. Brandon returned to his seat with his kids and Skylar, who was beaming at me with the pride of a sister, as if I didn't have five others making moon eyes at me in the front row.

A few rows back, I spotted Olivia's half-sisters, Rosina and Lucrezia Bianchi, who were chatting with some of my cousins from Naples. They had been understandably stiff at first, but my nosey family had loosened them up considerably. I might not have had much love for Giuseppe Bianchi, but his daughters were definitely willing to roll with the punches. After meeting their little sister for the first time over the summer, they had finally agreed to allow Nina to finance their olive farm's regeneration and expansion in Olivia's name so that it would become a property all three sisters would share in equally.

Nina knew what she was doing. She understood the power of the birthright, but she used it not to manipulate people, but to bring them together.

She was more like her grandmother than she thought. In the best possible ways, of course.

The organ in the front of the church began the wedding march, the doors flew open, and the procession started.

Sofia led the way, followed by Tommy, who was trying to be a good cousin for once, and hold Sofia's hand. Sofia, however, kept slapping it away so she could hurl handfuls of red rose petals onto the floor of the ancient church with the same gusto she used to pelt old bread at the Central Park ducks.

"*Sofia*," Tommy whispered as he tried to guide her to sit next to Frankie in the front row. "Come on, we're supposed to sit down."

"Stop telling me what to do, you hooligan!" she hissed back before tossing a bunch of petals into his face.

"Ma!" Tommy whispered at Lea, who just made a frantic gesture for the two of them to keep walking.

"Hi, *Zio*," Sofia said, walking straight up to me to chat like the aisle wasn't currently full of the rest of the procession. "Did I do good?"

"You did great, baby girl," I told her with a wink. "Think you can go sit with your ma now?"

Sofia nodded, then stuck her tongue out at Tommy on her way back to Frankie's lap. The tremor of laughter through the church told me no one was particularly put off by the interruption. Even the old Italian priest looked amused, and he had been nothing but bored since we had arrived last week.

"I tried to keep her under control, *Zio*," Tommy said as he came to stand beside me, rings in hand. "But she won't listen."

"She's a Zola," I said with a shrug. "You did fine."

Tommy's little chest swelled proudly as he stood beside me and watched as Olivia continued down the aisle, followed by Jane and Jamie.

Olivia made her way nervously down the aisle, smiling at her sisters, then at me. I winked at her, and her smile turned into a grin. Little by little, I'd been working on that girl, with a solid bit of help from Skylar and Brandon's kids, as well as my own niece and nephews. But I wasn't lying when I told Nina I felt almost as fated to be in her daughter's life as I was in her mother's. And it wasn't just because she was practically Nina's clone. She was something special all on her own.

"Hi," she murmured as she took her place next to the altar.

"Heya, kiddo," I replied. "You look like a dream, sweetheart."

Her flush deepened. "Thanks, Matthew." Her flush deepened. "Wait until you see Mama, though."

I grinned. "I can't wait."

The piano in the back of the church abruptly shifted to a different tune, and as the priest gestured, the entire group stood as the back doors opened wide.

Light poured in through the ancient wood frame.

Then she stepped into the light, and I couldn't breathe.

The first time I'd ever seen her, I had thought I was looking at an angel. Swathed in white.

But it was nothing compared to how she looked now.

She was dressed head to toe in lace, a conservative affair that draped across her shoulders and over her slim curves with the grace you could mostly find only on the silver screen. But here she was, very much in color, lips curved in a smile meant only for me. And red, a deep scarlet that matched the huge bouquet of roses. Red. The color of passion to some. The color of sin to others. But for Nina and me, it was the color of fire, of life when sometimes everything else seemed doomed. It was the color of hope.

As she approached the altar, her eyes shone with love. For me. This sorry, rough-edged, jaded sinner from the Bronx. But if I was a sinner, she was my salvation. Just like I was hers.

Thank you, God, I prayed without even thinking. *Thank you for this woman. Thank you for her love.*

"Are you ready?" she asked as she came to stand next to me in front of the priest, echoing the same question.

"Since a cold night last January, doll," I told her honestly.

She bit her lip, cheeks red with pleasure.

"Oh, Matthew," she whispered. "Me too."

I squeezed her hand, then we turned to face the priest, who began the ceremony.

It passed in a blaze, but at the same time, I knew I'd never forget it. I'd remember every word, Italian or not, that bound me to Nina de Vries. But it was the look on her face that caught me more. The pure, adulterated joy when she whispered the words "*sì, lo voglio.*"

How long had I waited to see that expression, without its mask of cool, calm, that holding back she had practiced all her life? Her openness blinded me with its beauty. I was the luckiest bastard on the planet.

"And now," said the priest in slightly less bored Italian, "I pronounce you husband and wife. *Signore*, you may kiss your bride."

I grinned as I slipped a hand around Nina's waist. "With pleasure."

But before I could kiss her, her lips found mine in a hurry. Nina Evelyn Astor de Vries, ever in control, the iciest princess of the Upper East Side, was a living flame as she wound her arms around my neck and crushed her lips to mine with the fury and eagerness of ten years of misery, suddenly let go. And church or no church, I took her willingly, kissed her back in a way that made my aunties murmur in shock and my sisters jeer and the kids moan while everyone else clapped with delight.

"Did you get enough, there, duchess?" I asked her once she finally let go, stumbling a little, as if I were drunk myself.

"Never," she said with evident delight as she touched her nose to mine. "But lucky for us, my love, we've got a lifetime."

Thank you for reading! You can check out the rest of Nina and Matthew story here: www.nicolefrenchro mance.com/rosegold

Already read it? Read Frankie and Xavier's story here: www.nicolefrenchromance.com/firstcomeslove

EXTRA SCENES & SNIPPETS

Matthew makes *Page Six*

"What?" she demanded, "is *this*?"

All five of my sisters gathered around the kitchen table when Kate slapped a copy of the *New York Post* on the worn oak. It was *Page Six*, the infamous gossip column that tracked celebrities as well as local socialites in the New York. I never bothered with that kind of claptrap myself, but my sisters clearly did. And today, apparently, there was something special.

"What the hell?" I bent closer. "Shit."

"That's *you*!" Joni squealed. "Oh my God, oh my *God*, that's my *brother* on *Page Six*!"

"No, it's not." Lea snatched the paper away from me to look at the picture herself. "Who would be interested in Matthew?"

"I think they're more interested in who he's with," Kate remarked as she examined her nails.

"Who is Nina Gardner?" Joni asked, now bouncing like rabbit over Lea's shoulder. "She's pretty, Mattie. Is she a natural blonde?"

"How should I know?" I snapped, although I immediately realized I *did* know, because five months ago, just before she stripped naked in front of me, she had told me.

"She looks rich, too," Marie remarked as she joined the other two peering at the paper. "Like those rich ladies on Park Avenue who've never heard of color."

"See?" Kate said. "What did I tell you about beige?"

"Stop," I snapped all of them.

"Oooh, look at her nails," Joni said. "And those shoes! She's so graceful, Mattie! Where did you meet her?"

"Nowhere!"

"She also looks married," Lea added.

"Who's married?"

We all looked up to find Frankie entering the kitchen with her hands on Sofia's little shoulders.

"Zi-zo!" she squealed as she made a beeline for my lap.

"Hey, monkey."

I swung the little girl up and shamelessly used a three-year-old's snuggles as a shield against the five pairs of dark green eyes currently trained on me like a bunch of bloodhounds. Jesus *Christ*, my sisters never knew when to let up. And Frankie was the worst of all. When she was around, the others naturally deferred to her.

"Who's this?" She plucked the paper out of Lea's hand and examined it as she walked to the table and sat in front of me. Her eyes widened as she caught sight of the picture. "Nina Gardner?"

"It's to do with a case I'm working on," I said, shifting Sofia on my lap. "A potential witness."

"Do you usually take potential witnesses to cute little bistros in the Village?"

"I take them wherever I think they might tell me something useful." The fact that my tone was a little too sharp didn't help.

The temptation of Nina

She took two steps toward me. "Matthew."

I sucked in a breath. That name. From her mouth. *Damn.* "What?"

"John Carson has done nothing but hurt this family," she said. "He is responsible for kidnapping my cousin, his wife and my friend, her mother, and who knows how many other people."

Her voice quavered as she listed all of Carson's faults. And for once, I didn't have a retort. The truth was, I didn't usually get this close to people who were affected by the crimes. I was a prosecutor, not a personal lawyer. I followed the bad guys, took depositions from witnesses. Rarely did a case ever get this personal.

In another world, Nina gets sick, and Zola finds out

I looked around. "Where's Nina? I thought she was supposed to be here."

Jane looked up from her sketches. "Oh, she got chicken pox, poor thing. Sounds like Olivia brought it home during spring break." She shook her head. "It's rough."

I blinked. Both Eric and Jane just stood there in the kitchen, going over their plans like no one was ill. "And neither of you has been over there?"

Both of them finally looked up, plainly surprised. Jesus Christ, was this really what people were like in this world? Eric, I might have expected it, but Jane was from a middle-class Chicago family.

The Upper East Side was more foreign t her than to me. Did it do this to people? Swallow them whole and at up their empathy?

"What are you saying?" Eric said, his voice slightly steely.

"Calm down," Jane cut in with a hand on her husband's wrist. "Zola, neither Eric nor I have had it."

"But chicken pox is actually dangerous for adults."

"Yeah, we know," Eric replied. "That's why she told us not to come."

"Are you serious?"

They just blinked at me.

"Is *anyone* taking care of her?" I finally demanded.

I wasn't totally sure, but I was pretty sure that Jane took a long drink of tea to hide a smile. She didn't ever say anything, but I was pretty sure she knew exactly how I felt about Nina.

"She has a housekeeper," Eric said blithely.

"Zola, come on," Jane called me back, but it was too late. I had already turned on my heel.

"One day this family is going to owe me big time for everything I've done for them," I said as I put my coat back on. "Never thought I'd turn out being your nursemaid, but here we are."

"I got it when I was six," I called over my shoulder. "It's done."

Zola takes care of Nina

"Look at me. I'm covered in spots."

"Well, good for you, I've always had a think for polka dots." I leaned in with a spoonful of soup. "And you just about make the prettiest damn hospital case I've ever seen."

"Matthew." Again, that whisper. That mewl. I'd never met a

woman who could jump from tigress to kitten and back again so quickly.

"Open up, beautiful," I said holding out the spoon.

Her mouth opened, and I watched, entranced as the spoon disappeared

She swallowed and cleared her throat. "I, um, I think I have it."

"No kidding, duchess. The sky is blue too, did you know that?"

Nina misses her grandmother

Nina shook her head. She had been hard on her grandmother when she was alive, but now that she was gone, she missed her terribly. Celeste de Vries hadn't been a woman of much praise— criticism was more her style, to the point where it sometimes bordered on abuse. Nina couldn't remember a single day as a girl where she wasn't criticized. Her hair was out of place. How could she possibly wear a white skirt after Labor Day? What could she possibly be thinking with those shoes?

But the worst treatment was if she ignored you completely. Grandmother never suffered the presence of fools, nor did waste time on people she deemed incompetent. And so, when she did turn her critiques this way, Nina had eaten them all up like candy. Combed her hair until it shone.

"Dance?"

"Dance?"

Nina looked up, her mouth open slightly with surprise, then looked back at my extended hand. "I..."

I hated the doubt that was written so clearly across her face, warring with the desire that was undoubtedly written across mine.

"It's just a dance, doll. No harm, no foul."

"So you say."

Her thin blonde brow arched wryly. *There's my girl*, I thought to myself. I couldn't help it. I loved bringing this side out of her.

She shook her head slightly in the same way *Nonna* did whenever I was teasing her about serving day-old amaretti. *Scamp*, she'd call me. And she was right.

Nina knew it too.

But instead of shooing me away, she called my bluff and took my hand. And there was that electric spark again, the one that never failed to skip through our fingers when we touched. The one we both tried and failed to ignore every time. Nina rose from the sofa with the grace of a trained debutante, looking for all the world like she had a book perched atop her head. I guided her to the center of the living room, where two of my sisters were swaying in time to Frank.

"You'd better be careful," she said. "I've been taking lessons since I was three. Do you even know how to dance properly?"

In response, I yanked hard on her hand, snapping her around so she was flush against me and I could catch her in my other arm.

"Oh!" Nina gasped.

"You'd better shut that pretty mouth of yours, beautiful," I growled. "Now, just let me lead."

Messy

"Do you ever get messy?"

It was an inane question. Simple. But something about the way she said it made me want to kiss her.

I swallowed. "So you're going to make the mess, huh?"

She smirked. Her seamless features twisted adorably. Nina de Vries...had some *attitude*. "What are you going to do about it, Mr. Zola?"

Swearing

"You don't swear, do you?" I asked.

Nina blanched. "It's coarse."

"Unrefined?" I prompted.

Her lashes, dark brown and lush compared to the rest of her, swept across her upper cheek. "Something like that."

I stepped forward. "Say it."

"Fuck," she whispered, and her tongue slipped out, touching the top of her lower lip like she was licking some remaining sugar off the top.

Matthew on Kate's couch

"Mattie, get up. Mass starts in an hour."

I yawned. After having a drink with a few friends last night after confession, I'd decided to stay on my sister's couch instead of going all the way back to Brooklyn.

Who are you kidding? I asked myself. I was avoiding Manhattan. Because I knew there was a very good chance that I'd just *happen* to opt for the four instead of the D line. And if I did that, I just might *happen* to get off on 96th Street.

I should have never taken her home. I should have never seen where she lived.

I should have never seen that little girl, the one with the gold braids, who looked curiously at the strange man who walked her mother home.

So instead of going out and trying to douse my temptations with work or alcohol, I opted instead for the most sexless thing I could think of: my sister's house for dinner.

"Mattie, get up!" Kate's husky voice rolled out from the kitchen, just off the small living room of her apartment. "There's coffee in here, but I need to get to work."

"I'm up, I'm up." I pushed a hand over my face, grimacing at the stubble that scraped my palm. I'd pressed my suit the night before and slept in my undershirt and boxers, but without a razor, I'd still look like I'd rolled out of a dumpster.

Nina's guilt

"It's such a mess," she moaned into my shoulder. "Oh, God, an absolute disaster."

My hands floated over her back, her shoulder, her perfectly smooth skin. And under my breath, I said a prayer of thanks, because I might have been the only man alive who really knew that this kind of beauty Nina wasn't plastic like most of the other women in her station

"You don't understand." Her voice was a jagged whisper. "He'll...my husband...Calvin would *ruin* you, darling. He would." She shook her head. "He can't ever know. For your safety."

I hated that she thought that way. Like I was some pitiful commoner, not a senior prosecutor at one of the most powerful district attorney's offices in the country. Maybe I wasn't a senator or a cabinet member or whoever the fuck Nina thought had real power, but I had the ear of Juan Ramirez and sometimes even the New York City mayor. I was very good friends with one of the most powerful families in Boston. I was no slouch. And I sure as fuck wasn't scared of a weasel like Calvin Gardner.

"Nina," I tried to say gently. "You don't need to—"

"Promise me you'll stay away," she whispered, her voice shaking like the trees outside my window.

Frankie accuses Zola of homewrecking

"Nina's husband is *nothing* like Pop," I said, maybe a little too vehemently.

Frankie looked at me like she didn't believe me either. "Matthew, come on. You don't know these people. All you know is what she tells you. For all you know, her husband could be a perfectly nice man and a wonderful father. He could be home right now, waiting for his wife to come home to him and his...what did you say, her daughter? And how old is she?"

I swallowed tightly. "Eight. No, nine."

Frankie nodded. "Nine. Nine years old, and probably wondering where the hell her mother is instead of tucking her in."

Nonna considers moving back to Italy

"I'm going home," she said. "And I don't know if I will come back."

I frowned, plainly stunned. "You're moving back to Italy?"

"What? *No.* Of course, I'm not moving back to Italy. I only want to visit my sister. See my mother before she dies. But, you know, I'm an old woman. You never know what might happen." Viciously, she crossed herself, as if even the mention of death might bring the Grim Reaper himself through the window to whisk her away.

At that, I had to roll my eyes. *Nonna* had been using her impending death to guilt us into doing whatever she wanted since we were little. "Matthew, help your dying grandmother and take out the garbage." "Matthew, don't shout at the TV, you'll give your old grandmother a heart attack." But despite the fact that she was in her early eighties, the woman had never shown any signs of slowing down. She still moved with quick, sharp steps up and down the stairs of her house, walked to and from Mass daily, made a full Sunday dinner for her nest of grand- and great-grandchildren every week, and still had the sharpest tongue this side of the river.

"Oh, is that all," I said. "I think it's nice you're going back to see your sister and *Bisnonna*. It's been a while, hasn't it?"

"Six years." She sighed. "Too long."

"Well, maybe the girls and I can put together a little upgrade for you. Let you fly first class, go to the old country in style."

She didn't answer, even when I called my sisters pigeons in that way that usually made her smile. I watched as she moved around the jewelry quietly. There was something off about this moment. Something I couldn't quite put my finger on. She was old, even if she was probably healthier than I was. Was she worried about something?

"*Nonna*," I said gently. "Is something the matter? Did your doctor tell you something?"

As just the thought of something truly wrong with her, my heart gave a thump. I still missed my grandfather terribly, but a world without Nonna wasn't one I could totally imagine, even if I knew it was coming one day.

She turned. "What? No, of course not."

I shook my head. "Jesus, *Nonna*, then why are you worrying me like this?"

"Matthew, your mouth!"

"*Nonna*! What's with the theatrics, huh? You bring me up here, walk me through a mountain of *Nonno's* things and act like you're dying. What the hell is going on?"

QUICKSILVER

After years of trying, Eric and Jane are about to have the family they've always wanted together—just in time for Christmas. Will disparate forces get in the way of their family blessing? Or will they get they finally get the happily ever after they've tried to find for so long?

The Quicksilver collection includes:

- The original extended epilogue
- "Marry Me," a chapter from Eric's POV
- "The Not-So-Silent Night," an all-new second epilogue
- Several extra scenes and snippets

QUICKSILVER EXTENDED EPILOGUE

"Holy shit, Lefferts. You guys really topped yourself this year."

Eric turned for the fourth time around the De Vries Gallery, a brand-new section of the Met's Costume Institute that was unveiled at this year's gala. Despite my reticence to work on the event again, Cora Spring, the editor-in-chief at *Vogue,* had talked me into it. I couldn't say no. This year's theme, "Athens," called for homages to the Greco-Roman influence on fashion. As much of a distaste for Hellenistic history as I'd developed recently, it still felt fitting that I should help organize. A way of putting that past behind me, so to speak.

To that end, Nina and I had decided to donate some of Celeste's personal holdings into opening a wing in her honor. We both felt it was what she would have wanted—a lasting mark on a part of the city the de Vries family matriarch had truly cared for. It would highlight the contributions of independent designers who had formed their own houses or labels without being consumed by large conglomerates. Like the de Vrieses had been, once upon a time.

After making our way through the press line and showing off the clothes I had designed for both of us—on my *own*, I might add, rather than with the help of another designer—Eric and I meandered around the new wing while he took in the fruits of my labor. This was my baby, where nearly every bit of my waking energy had gone when I wasn't waiting for my graduate school applications to come through or figuring out what the hell I was going to do if they didn't.

They had, however. I was starting my MFA at the Fashion Institute in September.

"Thanks, Petri dish," I said.

He darted a dark look at me. "Jane."

I smirked. He knew exactly what I was doing. I only trotted out that name when I was in the mood for something in particular. Or when I was really mad at him, which, yes, happened, but not as often as I would have imagined. Overall, I was pretty damn happy being an old married lady to this guy.

I brushed my lips against his ear. "I saw those new clamps you bought last week. You can't hide anything from me...*Petri dish.*"

His deep gray eyes sparked while his jaw tightened deliciously. Without breaking eye contact, he pulled slightly at his collar. Holy crap. Who knew a minor adjustment could be that smoking hot?

"In the middle of your benefit, pretty girl?" he asked in a disturbingly low voice. "Is that what you're looking for?"

I tipped my head, which currently had about fifty bobby pins and three gold bands keeping my waves haphazardly piled with only a few tendrils falling over my shoulders. I was rocking an ombré dye job that matched the same progression of my one-shouldered toga-style dress. The color started with my natural black-brown, fading into a silvery gray. The exact same shade as Eric's penetrating eyes. The only bit of color I wore was on my lips—that trademark red that my husband loved so much.

I blew him a kiss.

Eric stared, transfixed, then shook his head like he was chasing away a fly. "You're looking for trouble. You better be careful, or you're going to get it."

I bit my upper lip. "Promise?"

Before he could answer, we were interrupted by a familiar voice.

"Eric! Jane!"

Nina weaved her way through the mass of celebrities, public figures, and donors that made up the majority of the exclusive guest list. Nina had surprised me six months ago by asking me to design her dress too. It was another Grecian-inspired number (like many of the attendees), but a bit more subdued than my ombré concoction. Instead, she was in an icy blue so faint as to be nearly white, and the combined look with her sleek blond updo and glittering eye makeup made her look like a marble statue—not unlike the many loaned by the museum for the party.

"Oh my God," I said. "Nina, you look amazing. And so *tall!*"

I hadn't realized it before, but my cousin-in-law rarely wore heels. Yes, I had dressed her, but she'd hired a stylist to do the rest.

She flushed a pretty pale pink and nodded shyly.

"Hey!"

Behind her, Calvin Gardner was rudely pushing through the crowd to catch up with his wife. Not for the first time, I was struck by what an odd couple they were. Calvin may have once been a middlingly attractive fellow in his youth, but as he entered middle age, he looked like something that had been left too long in the sun —expanded, half-melted, and browned in weird places. The white rings around his eyes suggested a lot of time spent in tanning beds, while redness marring his cheeks and nose spoke to a long-term drinking habit. He sort of resembled a hobbit who had just emerged from the Mountain of Doom.

"Nina!" he barked, ignoring several people who turned around. "We weren't done. I want to know who the hell has been texting you, and I want to know *now*."

It wasn't until Nina straightened that I also realized she usually slumped around her husband—probably to protect his ego. She was actually about an inch or two taller than me, which meant that in heels over three inches, she topped Calvin handily.

"Calvin, don't." She looked down her extremely straight nose at him. "This is not the time nor the place. I beg of you, just let it go. It's only a friend. I promise."

Calvin, however, bristled until the stubby end of his very round nose turned even redder than normal. "'Just a friend.' It's that Italian who showed up at the house the other night, isn't it? What was his name? Mark? Michael?"

"Matthew. His name was Matthew." Her voice was so quiet I could barely hear it, but the intensity—almost longing?—ingrained in each syllable of Zola's given name sent a shiver up my spine.

Whoa.

I glanced at Eric, who looked equally puzzled.

"What was that?" I mouthed at him.

He just shrugged.

"You think you're going to get away with this?" Calvin growled. "Well, *you're not.* I'll—"

"Calvin." Eric's voice cut through the argument like a blade. "Let it go."

Calvin was barely able to hide his sneer. The two men engaged in a stare-off that could have cracked a window before the shorter one turned away. Though they managed to tolerate each other for the sake of Olivia, Nina and Calvin's daughter, Eric and Calvin mutually despised each other. You don't tend to forget when someone steps in to take the fortune you thought was yours. And you also don't forget when a man enables a psychopath to go after you and your wife.

Yeah. I doubted either issue would be water under the bridge anytime soon.

Nina sighed. "I need a cocktail."

Calvin scowled. "Now, just wait a minute," he started again, but his wife was already disappearing into the crowd with the grace of a wood nymph.

Eric sighed. "I should probably go with them. Calvin looks like he's going to cause a scene."

"Hurry back," I urged.

For that, I received a bright grin and a thorough kiss. "Always."

"IT'S FUNNY," Eric said as he returned with our drinks. "Zola asked me about her just yesterday."

I accepted my club soda. No PBR at the Met, and on top of that, I needed to be sober to deal with any mishaps that might occur. "Don't tell me you and Zola are getting all buddy-buddy."

Beyond requesting our presence once for a campaign event for his boss, Matthew Zola had generally kept his distance since successfully convicting Jude Letour a few months prior. It had been a bit abrupt, but not all that strange. After all, he and Eric were always more reluctant allies than friends. I, however, sort of missed the suave Italian's random drop-ins. The man had presence. And it was kind of fun to see Eric get riled up.

Eric pressed his lips into a tight line. "Ah, no. It was strange, actually. He said he was calling on behalf of DA Ramirez to see if we'd come to another fundraiser, even though Ramirez should know full-well we've already donated the maximum."

I nodded. We hadn't hesitated to give money to the man who had been one of our only true political allies last year. Ramirez's help (via Zola) had ensured our continued safety against the wrath of John Carson's associates. Even though the kingpin of the munitions world had died in our living room, it was incredible how many names came out of the woodwork once the DA began his investigation in earnest. Eric and I never knew how many enemies we really had until, one by one, they ended up in a medium-security prison, with new indictments still cropping up.

"So, he just randomly brought up Nina?"

She was across the room now, chatting with one of tonight's co-hosting celebrities while her grouchy pancake of a husband sulked into his highball. I made a face. Calvin really was the worst. I hated to think about what he was like behind closed doors.

"Yeah. He wondered if she would be willing to come instead. When I said I didn't know, he started asking about her. How she was. What she's up to. Even her favorite color. That's when I wondered what the hell was going on." Eric shook his head, looking extremely uncomfortable. He never liked getting involved in other people's personal lives.

I, however, was unrepentantly fascinated. "Looks like someone still has a bit of a crush. Poor guy. Nina's about as off-limits as it gets. If there was ever anyone who needed a good bang, though, it's her."

"Jane."

I looked back at Eric. "What? It's true."

"Just let it alone, all right?" He sipped his drink thoughtfully as we both watched Nina. His gaze fell on Calvin and hardened substantially. Then it floated elsewhere, and suddenly, Eric handed me his drink. "Can you find our table, gorgeous? I just spotted the McClintocks. That asshole keeps dodging my calls. He won't give up his property on the east side without some serious *quid pro quo.* I'll be right back, okay?"

I accepted my husband's kiss on the cheek and watched him stride away, broad back straightened with purpose. Several heads turned as he passed. I smiled. Even in a roomful of celebrities, Eric cut quite the figure, and it wasn't just the heather-gray suit I'd designed.

The transformation he had gone through over the last year was notable. He was fully adjusted to his position as the Chair and now CEO of De Vries Shipping. After the last CEO had stepped down, Eric had transitioned into the most active role his family had had in their eponymous company in several generations. Immediately, he had jump-started new plans to innovate the DVS fleet and diversify their holdings. Leadership fit him. For the first time in years, DVS wasn't just making a profit. It was soaring.

He was a little...harder...too. Part of the change was obviously rising to the challenge of the cut-throat business world. But it was also just the bearing of a man who had been through some serious shit and survived. Rumors over what exactly had happened that night one year ago in our apartment still danced around the city. I had been asked to confirm at least a dozen versions, but the key elements were always the same. Now everyone in New York—in the world, actually—knew one basic truth. Eric de Vries wasn't just a businessman; he was a warrior. And he wouldn't hesitate to kill to protect what was his.

"You lucky bitch," I murmured to myself. And I was. I really, really was.

I found our table near the back of the room. Cora had asked us to babysit our tablemates—specifically one celebrity couple who needed to be treated with kid gloves.

I had heard of Fitz Baker, of course. The fact that he was even here was a major coup. Everyone knew of the actor who had been discovered in the mountains years after he disappeared, looking to escape his fame. He had returned to acting in some superhero movie that had just come out, but according to Cora, the man hate-hate-*hated* press. But when Cora extended an invite to one of the biggest events of the year, it was obviously something his studio wouldn't let him get out of.

I found Baker and his girlfriend already seated, huddled together in conversation. Jeez, they must have flown past the press line.

"Hello," I greeted them pleasantly. "I'm Jane, one of the event coordinators."

The couple turned, and the woman smiled warmly. She was very pretty, with caramel-colored skin that gleamed and a mass of thick, almost black curly hair. Shit, what was her name again?

"Maggie Sharp," she answered for me as she shook my hand. "You did an amazing job. I can hardly believe we are actually here!"

She had that same starstruck look that probably mirrored mine last year. Okay, and probably this year too. I doubted being a part of the Met freaking Gala was ever going to get old.

"And holy moly, your dress is incredible. Your whole look," she said. "I loved the little accents in your husband's tux too. I told this guy that, didn't I, babe?"

Baker just grunted, his chin-length hair falling in front of his face while he stared at his hands. Real charmer over here.

"Who's your designer?" Maggie was asking.

I smoothed the gathered bodice. "Actually, me. I'm a designer. Well, almost. I'm actually starting at FIT this fall."

I was finally getting used to saying that now. Even Cora had said she was impressed, and that was just the cherry on top of every other compliment I'd received this evening.

Maggie's big eyes popped open. "What? That's *amazing*! Are you starting a line or anything?"

I shrugged. "It's a goal, one day. I need to do the program first, but I would love to start a label at some point."

"Have you ever considered doing anything custom right now?" she pressed. "The regular fashion people drive me nuts. They are *so* pretentious. As someone who only recently started working in this industry, I only get a look-see because of this guy. Most wouldn't want to touch me with a ten-foot-pole, especially this month."

"That's because they don't know shit," Baker growled.

I stared, but Maggie just smiled and reached down to take his hand. It was a weird dynamic. He held it tightly, like despite being the more famous of the two, he was actually nervous about being here.

He wasn't wrong, though. Maggie really was beautiful, and already I could imagine what sorts of designs I could make for someone like her.

"I *love* doing custom work," I said honestly. "As long as you don't mind that I've only really done it for family and friends. I have some patterns that might fit you guys, though. My husband is about the same size as you, Mr. Baker. I make things for him all the time. They wouldn't be hard to alter."

Maggie nudged Baker. "Babe, we should give her name to Robin for your next blitz. Her style is so different, and you're always complaining about the usual people."

The actor just grumbled unintelligibly and took a long drink of his water, looking like he really wanted it to be something harder. There was an open bottle of wine on the table, though, and he hadn't touched it.

"Don't mind him. He hates these things." She elbowed him again. "Hey, be nice. Introduce yourself."

Baker wrinkled his long nose into his water glass, then finally looked up with a pair of arrow-sharp green eyes. Wow, he was really, *really* good-looking. But also, really, really grouchy.

"I'm Will," he said gruffly.

"Will? I thought your name was Fitz. Shit, did we get the seating wrong?" I looked around frantically at the cards.

"Oh, don't worry about that," Maggie said. "He's just being difficult. His given name is Fitzwilliam, but he only uses Fitz as a stage name. He kind of hates it."

If the glare the actor was giving me right now was any indication, she was one hundred percent right. Holy crap, he could murder someone with that scowl.

"Then Will it is. I don't like it when people call me the wrong name either."

"Does that happen a lot with Jane?" *Will* asked snarkily.

"Be nice," Maggie murmured again. "For me? Please?"

He did soften a little as he looked at her. Okay, maybe the guy wasn't all bad. "Sorry. Maggie's right. I, ah, don't really like red carpets. But this was sort of a necessary evil since I had to cancel the rest of the press tour."

"Because *The Green Lantern* just came out, right?" Eric said as he appeared beside me. "Record-breaking opening weekend too."

The actor turned to him in surprise. Actually, we all did.

"I'm sorry, Mr. *Variety*," I joked. "I didn't realize you were following the Hollywood release calendar this year."

"I do when I invest in the film." He sat down smugly. "I'm Eric de Vries, Jane's husband."

At the sound of that name, both Maggie and Will sat up straight. I frowned. I shouldn't have been surprised. I knew that Eric had his own financial advisor who helped him find interesting projects in which to reinvest our newly expanded personal portfolio. I just hadn't realized that extended all the way to Hollywood.

He just shrugged, clearly reading my bemusement. "It was for fun."

Right. Because that's the sort of thing people do for fun. Throw millions of dollars at a movie budget like it's a dive bar dartboard.

That's what happens when you marry a billionaire, Jane Brain.

I just rolled my eyes, like my dad was sitting right there with me. "Any other little ventures I should be aware of, Mr. de Vries?"

Eric's gray eyes sparked at the name. "Well, I've been thinking about investing in a clothing label. Know of any good designers?"

"Oh, you should!" Maggie agreed. "I was just telling her, she's so talented."

"I don't know why anyone wouldn't want to dress you," I told her. "You're gorgeous."

"Oh my God, you're so nice," she replied. "I feel like a cow. Still trying to lose that last ten pounds of baby weight, you know?"

"Are you serious?" I demanded. "You just had a baby?"

Maggie looked down at herself like she was assessing whether or not that was true. "Lord, yes. About six weeks ago. Can't you see my muffin top?" She giggled and pressed her soft stomach, which looked pretty damn thin to me in the sleek white gown she was wearing. She must have been in incredibly good shape if that was a muffin top. "I should probably be at the gym, but this is our first night out since the baby was born. I couldn't resist."

"Lil." Will's voice immediately commanded the entire table. "Stop. You're fucking gorgeous. End of story."

My mouth dropped. I didn't even like this guy, but I was turned on by his intensity for his girl. It reminded me of the look Eric got in his eyes when he was about to—

"Ahem."

I found Eric staring at me with *exactly* that look. Shit. He knew what was going through my admittedly dirty mind.

With one finger, he tipped my mouth shut. "Save it for tonight, pretty girl," he grumbled into my ear. "Otherwise, I'm going to have to wipe that look off your face behind one of the columns in the exhibit."

I reddened, then glanced back at Will and Maggie, who were engaged in a stare-off that threatened to burn up the entire room. The whole damn table was on fire.

But then Will's hand floated down to Maggie's flattish stomach, like he was cupping the bump of the child who used to be there. The gesture was small, but so heart-achingly intimate. And familiar, though for different reasons.

And I really couldn't deal with it.

I stood. Maggie and Will didn't even seem to notice.

"Come on," I said to Eric, pulling him out of his seat.

"And where are we going?" He took one last sip of his drink, then allowed me to tow him out of the ballroom.

"To make good on your promise."

IT DIDN'T TAKE LONG. While I would have liked to have defiled one of the gorgeous exhibits at the Met, instead I led Eric into the bowels of the building, past the room where the staff from *Vogue* was manning their computers and partying in their own finery, past the rooms where stylists and designers were touching up their celebrities every so often, and to the service stairwell.

"You know what they say about the Met?" I asked as we descended, down, down, down to the point where no sound followed us. "The best stuff in the museum is in the basement."

"So that includes us now?"

I turned on a landing. "Well, it definitely includes you, Mr. de Vries."

Eric didn't reply, just kissed me. His full mouth engulfed mine, twisting his tongue in an urgent dance that made us both breathless in a matter of seconds.

He knew. He always knew. He knew when I couldn't take the loss anymore, when I desperately needed something else to distract me. He would chase away my demons with a different intensity, engaging in a battle that he would always win.

"Pull this up," he said, pawing at my voluminous skirts. "Can you?"

His teeth found my neck, and I gasped at the sudden bite. "Ah!"

But I did as he asked, yanking up my skirt so my legs were bared, so he could spread my thighs and hook my ankles around his waist as he shoved me against the cement bricks. He'd already unbuttoned his pants, and his erection fell against me, a solid reminder of the way this man could possess me whenever he wanted.

"I don't want fast," he murmured as he rocked his hips forward and back. Not entering. Just creating...friction. The kind that would have me moaning into his shirt in no time.

I gasped as the tip slid in, then out to continue that delicious teasing. Good Lord, I was basically a running faucet down there in maybe ten seconds, especially with the voodoo his fingers were working on my breasts, even through a structured bodice.

"But...but it has to be fast," I managed. "We're..."

One hand clasped my jaw, stilling me. "We're going to do it however I say we're going to do it, pretty girl."

I never did understand how I, someone who was toddler-level defiant, enjoyed being commanded like this when it came to sex. A "switch," said my therapist. Apparently, it was a common thing. But that didn't mean it made sense.

"Beg for it," Eric ordered, slipping in just an inch before pulling out again.

I moaned. His thumb found my clit, and an orgasm was already approaching, like I was on a current headed for a waterfall. It wasn't about if. Just when.

Fuck slow. I wanted to tumble over as quickly as I could.

"Please," I whispered. "Eric, *please*. I need it so bad. I need it *right now*."

He exhaled, a shuddering, pained breath. If I liked being ordered around, then that moment of capitulation, the moment when I gave myself up to him completely—that was Eric's kryptonite.

He kissed me again, just a light brush of lip on lip. More teasing. More exquisite torture.

"Good girl," he murmured, and then shoved inside.

I came almost instantly. The hand at my clit pinched the sensitive bundle of nerves, and I arched against the wall as my husband held me up, pounding mercilessly until, a few moments later, he emptied himself as well, growling into my neck instead of emitting harsh groans the way he would normally. We were both holding back. After all, we couldn't risk being caught.

"Jesus," he breathed as he finally let me go. "That was..." He held my chin, this time stroking it gently. "You always surprise, you know that?"

I stood on my tiptoes to kiss him again. His face bore no trace of that mask—just open, honest, and totally in love. With me.

I no longer thought that a miracle. But I sure as hell appreciated it.

"Come on," I told him. "We'd better get back. And I need to clean up before someone realizes how you defiled me in the basement of the Met."

Eric smirked, and a dimple appeared above that glass-cut jaw.

"It was only a matter of time, pretty girl. Pretty sure it's going to happen again too."

I quirked an eyebrow. "Promise?"

FIFTEEN MINUTES LATER, after we had used the custodial lounge room to clean up, I found myself on the dance floor in the arms of my husband, a few couples away from Maggie and Will, who seemed as engrossed in each other as ever. Having the benefit of years of childhood ballroom dance lessons, Eric was a much better dancer than I was. My legs essentially flopped around like a marionette's, but he was such a good lead, it didn't matter.

"Stop," Eric said as he caught me watching the actor and his girlfriend.

I looked up. "Stop what?"

"Being jealous. You know you have no reason."

I sighed. "Don't I?"

I couldn't lie. The resentment was back. Why was it so much easier for some couples to have children than the ones who really wanted them? Why would the universe be so cruel?

"No," Eric said. "You *don't.*"

I screwed up my face, completely confused.

He pulled me closer as he turned us around. "It's going to be like last time, isn't it? You couldn't stop thinking about it. Except this time, I won't be in the fucking slammer." He closed his eye at the memory. "Fucking hell."

"What do you mean, 'like last time'?"

Eric looked at me like I was an idiot, then turned me under his arm. "Seriously? We're going to play that game?"

"What game?" I honestly had no clue what he was talking about.

"Jane," Eric said. "Come on. You're late. Almost three weeks now. Did you think I wouldn't notice?"

He fixed my gaze with his, then arched a brow. It took me a second to catch up with his implications.

I blinked. "Wait...no..."

Now he was the one who looked surprised. "You mean you really didn't know?"

I swallowed. The truth is, I hadn't. Not until right this moment. I'd ignored the delay in my cycle, told myself it was stress. After all, I'd been irregular before. Nothing had been normal since Korea, and we had been trying to conceive again for nearly a year. Nothing. I had long suspected that something had been damaged permanently.

Eric cocked his head. "Come on, gorgeous. It's been exactly thirty-nine days. That's more than stress, don't you think?"

I crinkled my nose. "You are the grossest. I can't believe you've been keeping track of my flipping menstrual cycle, you stalker. What are you doing, keeping a countdown of when you can have sex again?"

"Please, pretty girl. Like your period ever stopped me."

I didn't even blush. The fact that Eric wasn't the slightest bit squeamish—how could he be, given the things we had been through?—was nothing new. And it turned me on. A lot.

Or was that the hormones talking?

I found Eric staring knowingly...at my breasts.

"Hey, boyo," I snapped. "My eyes are up here, you know."

He looked up. "I can leer at my pregnant wife's tits if I want to. Part of the privilege."

I blushed. "You keep saying pregnant, but..."

"Jane, come off it. They are stupid sensitive. You came in literally five seconds downstairs, and you wouldn't even let me touch them last night. Plus, they are about twice as big as normal. Just like last time. You were complaining two days ago about the last-minute adjustments you had to make to this dress, remember?"

I bit my lip. Again, he wasn't wrong. But something in me couldn't quite join him in this playful reverie.

"I'll take a test when we get home tonight," I said. "No use counting chickens."

"Hey."

Eric stopped dancing completely. We stood still in the middle of whirling bodies, the jumbled color of glamor and gleam that was the gala. I couldn't see anything, though, except his steady gray eyes, the warmth he reserved there just for me.

"What if...what if something happens?"

Every fear I had flashed through my mind. That's the thing about trauma. For all Eric's ideas about catharsis and purging, you don't ever get rid of those events completely. You just learn to carry them better.

But sometimes they just won't let you.

Eric pulled me close and drew my head to his shoulder, like I wasn't lacquered and full of hairspray. He wrapped a palm around the back of my neck, soothing me with his touch the way only he could.

"Nothing," he said, "is going to happen. I would die before I'd let anything *ever* happen to you again. Either of you."

I sucked in a deep breath, trying not to cry. Wow, yeah. I really was pregnant.

The truth struck me like a bolt of lightning. But not just with fear. With joy.

I thought of all those still-empty rooms in our home on Seventy-Sixth Street, the ones that I had kept purposefully empty. As if they were waiting for the small people to arrive who would truly inspire them. The rooms ached for a presence the same way I had ached for the child who never came.

Until...now.

I turned my face to Eric's, allowing his shining gray eyes to envelop me with their warmth. *Safe*, they promised. *I'll always keep you safe.*

And I knew he would.

Suddenly, the world seemed full of promise, not threats. Our home called, begging to be filled.

I wrapped my arms around his neck, admiring this man, my partner, my rock, my home. I had never understood how someone else could make you a better version of yourself until I met him. But he did. He really did.

"Well," I said, "I guess that means I need to start calling you 'Daddy.' We can practice tonight."

It was a stupid joke, but a sly grin played over Eric's lips, nonetheless. He tipped his head, then hovered his lips over mine.

"Oh, pretty girl," he murmured. "You better."

Thank you for reading!

If you haven't already you can check out the rest of Jane and Eric's story here: www.nicolefrenchro mance.com/quicksilver

MARRY ME

A QUICKSILVER BONUS CHAPTER FROM
ERIC'S POV

Eric

I almost didn't think it was her.

Aside from the fact that her hair looked like something you'd buy at a cotton candy stand, she appeared so...normal.

Sure, she was wearing all black, with leather pants that made her legs appear indecently long. And yeah, she was still adding an extra inch or two with a pair of chunky black boots. But gone were the chunky studded bracelets, the earrings leading a delicious trail up each earlobe, the heavy black makeup that ringed her cat-shaped eyes. Her fingernails were clean instead of black, and she'd switched her customary concert T-shirt with a sleek silk blouse. Even her chunky glasses had been replaced with thinner, more sophisticated gold frames.

We'd seen each other here and there over the last five years, but just barely, both of us busy with our careers after graduating from Harvard Law together. A lot had changed since then. We'd gone from being law students to being lawyers, and successful ones at that. Skylar and I had even started our own shop just a year ago; Jane had become one of the top Assistant State's Attorneys in Illinois. Whenever she came to see her, Sklyar and her kids (Jane's godchildren), I steered clear of the house. Jane avoided the office I shared with Skylar like the plague. Our paths barely intersected. Until now.

It wasn't really that long ago, but right now, five years seemed like a millennium. Then again, I couldn't remember what I'd worn five minutes ago when she looked like that.

It was still Jane. And I was still an idiot. Because right then I also knew there was no way I would ever pass her by on the street. There was no one, absolutely no one in the entire world like Jane Lee Lefferts, and it had absolutely nothing to do with hair color or clothes or anything other superficial bullshit.

Jane was Jane.

And that was exactly why I was here, wasn't it?

I watched her openly through the window of the hair salon as she paid the cashier, not giving two shits that I was basically spying. Her lips—painted a bright, cherry red—quirked as the guy took her credit card. Her brow arched, and she tapped a long finger to her cherry-red lips. I jerked as a sudden rush of memories flooded my mind.

Jane on her knees, staring up at me.

Red lips, half-open, begging for something between them.

The rap of knuckles on wood. The tap of leather on flesh. The twist of silk on wrists.

You going to be quiet now, pretty girl?

Jesus, had it really been five *years* since I'd called her that?

When she hugged the guy inside, I had to force myself not to growl. Remind myself that he was her hairdresser. And more than that, I had absolutely no right to care.

Fucking hell. What was I doing here?

I was still trying to answer that question when the door opened, and Jane ran smack into me.

"What the fu—oh!" She fumbled with her glasses a moment, then pushed her rainbow-colored locks away from her face and looked up in shock. "Eric?"

Her sharp gaze seared up and down my body. I pulled at the lapels of my suit—a custom gray Tom Ford that I'd only bought a month ago. It didn't matter.

That was the thing about Jane. Her glasses always felt like magnifying lenses, like she could see right through me, past the carefully managed facade with a glance.

How many other women had begged me to open up to them? Pleaded, shouted, cried. I'd always said no? Too many to count. I always knew the second a relationship with a girl went from sex to something else, because she'd start hopping around like a bunny, trying to please. Suddenly, she'd have no opinions of her own. Apologize all the time. Stay quiet or nod anytime I'd act like an asshole, which at some point, I'd probably do just to see what would happen.

But Jane always had a way of poking through my shell with a well-timed glare or sharp retort. And you know what? I actually liked it.

Until, of course, she broke my fucking heart.

Her eyes met mine again, as sharp and curious as ever. And, if I wasn't mistaken, a little pissed off.

One more thing that hadn't changed.

"What the hell are *you* doing here?"

I smiled as her gaze dropped again with transparent appreciation of my suit. Or maybe just me in it. At least the tendency to disorient went both ways. "Nice to see you too, Jane."

She didn't reply, just crossed her arms and stared. Still Jane, yeah. Still formidable. I could see exactly why she'd earned a reputation as some of the best up-and-coming talent in Chicago.

"I'm here to see you," I admitted. "Skylar told me you were having your hair done today."

"Skylar told you..." Jane muttered distantly. "God, Anne of Green Gables is such a damn blabbermouth. She can't ever keep her mouth shut. So, what, you just hopped on a plane to witness my makeover?"

Skylar *was* a know-it-all redhead. Jane's irreverent references usually cracked me up—unless they were directed at me. But then I usually enjoyed making her pay for it even more.

I enjoyed the way her irritation wavered when I smiled. "Well, I was in town, and I asked her what you might be up to. Do you always tell her when you're having your hair done? Seems a little codependent to me."

"Says the guy who stalked me to the salon." She glanced back and forth between us. "God, look at us. We look like fucking Spy vs. Spy, do you know that?"

I glanced down at my custom suit, a light gray Tom Ford paired with a white Oxford shirt I would have liked to have ironed before coming here. Next to Jane's all black, we were a marriage of opposites.

I cleared my throat. Christ, that was almost too literal.

"I'm wearing perfectly appropriate clothes for mid-May," I said. "No one said you have to walk around looking like the grim reaper on acid."

"Whatever you say, Zack Morris," Jane retorted, almost bored as she pushed her glasses up her nose. She was feigning bored, but I could tell she was enjoying the repartee as much as I was.

I pressed a hand to my chest like I was about to pass out. "*Saved by the Bell*? Really? You've lost your touch, Jane. I am a way better dressed than Zack Morris."

"Fine, Preppy. You look like Zack Morris after he dropped out of school and started selling used cars."

We both laughed then, caught up in the stream of insults and nostalgia. It was potent. Almost as potent as the scent of jasmine floating off her. It was the same perfume she used to wear in law school too, the scent that used to linger in my sheets for days, so I'd put off washing them just to remember how she felt in them. Under me. On her knees.

Christ.

I yanked at my collar. "So, what do you think? Do you have some time for coffee?"

Jane blinked, caught up in some sort of daydream of her own. "What? Oh, um...wait, why are you even here? You couldn't have just called me like a normal person?"

I shoved my hands in my pockets. Hard. No, I wasn't going to do this here. "It's not really the kind of thing I can talk about over the phone."

She tipped her glasses down her nose, examining the tells she once knew so well. It reminded me of just how beautiful her eyes were when they weren't obscured by lenses. A gorgeous hazel that opened very, very wide just when she was about to...

I shook my head, trying to get rid of yet another particularly vivid memory. Jane flat on her back. Legs up around my shoulders. Crimson mouth open wide right when I slid deep into her—

No. This was going to work better if we could keep it strictly business.

"Is that so, Petri dish?"

I straightened at the use of the old derisive nickname she used precisely to get under my skin. Well, that was a good way to stick a pin in my libido. The moniker was basically her way of saying I'd slept around so much that I was a walking STI incubator.

I'd heard worse, usually after slipping out of a girl's apartment without saying anything, but the name called back to the reason Jane and I broke up in the first place. Me, flying to Chicago, begging her to make it work. Her, flying back to Boston to tell me she was willing to try. The pair of women's underwear she found in my bed, leftover from a brief escapade during one of our "off" periods. Jane yelling at me in no uncertain terms that I wasn't worth her time and never would be. And later, Jane again, her arms crossed while she stared vacantly into a dark night, telling Skylar, not me, that she wasn't the type who could make a relationship work anymore than I was. Jane, for the first time since I'd ever known her, was unable to look at me in the eye.

Once she knew exactly what she'd get for calling me that. Fifteen minutes back to my apartment. Ten seconds from the front door to my bedroom, two to toss her on the bed, wrap her wrists with a tie, and give her exactly what she was asking for with the leather riding crop we'd bought together *just* for the purpose of making her beg for forgiveness.

She loved it.

I loved it.

Pressing each other's buttons. Demanding retribution. Fucking the rebels out of each other.

Right now, though, I was prepared for her rebellion. Instead, I just waited her out.

A minute or two later, Jane huffed irritably, clearly too interested in my sudden presence to walk off herself. She tossed her hair over her shoulder, sending another whiff of jasmine across the sidewalk.

"Fine," she said. "There's a cafe around the corner. We can talk there."

SHE LED me to some nondescript cafe with pleasant outdoor seating, where Jane's hair matched the climbing flowers. From the back patio, you wouldn't know you were sitting in the middle of downtown Chicago. Not that I cared at all.

I sipped my cappuccino while Jane fiddled with her black coffee, clearly unsure of what to say. She kept stealing glances at me from across the table, that deep gaze peppering over my hair, my suit, my tie, all the little things that were different and yet hadn't really changed at all. I watched her openly, only turning away once she had to reapply her fire engine-red lipstick. *That* was still the same. Jane wouldn't be Jane without those absurdly red, absurdly suckable lips.

Shit.

"All right," Jane said once she'd taken a long sip of her black sludge. "Spill."

I opened my mouth to ask the question I'd flown all the way to Chicago to ask but found I couldn't. Not quite. "Couldn't we go someplace more private? This is kind of personal. What about your place?"

It was odd how much I wanted to see it, actually. Since I'd known Jane, I'd never seen her make a place of her own. In law school, it was the campus housing she shared with Skylar. After that, it was her room in her cousin's apartment here in Chicago. Jane was unique, a creature of style despite the lawyerly career. There was no way a place that belonged to her wouldn't be full of that addictive personality.

She just snorted. "My place currently consists of the couch in my mother's condo. If you would like to meet Yu-na Lee Lefferts, be my guest. But beware, she is the equivalent of the Bermuda Triangle for boyfriends. Once you go in, you may never escape."

She was trying to intimidate me. I wasn't about to tell her it wouldn't work for shit. I remembered only too well how much I had wanted to meet her family, know her entire life once upon a time.

Then again, I'd never let her in that way either.

"We could go to my hotel room..." I suggested, unable to keep the excitement quite out of my voice.

It was clear she and I were thinking the exact same thing. That if we were locked in a hotel room, complete with a plush king bed and all the trapping, there was no way either of us would make it through the afternoon without jumping each other.

Jane crossed and recrossed her legs, leaning over her drink in a way that caused the collar of her shirt to fall forward and reveal the edge of her collarbone. She was tall, but delicate, with skin I could practically see through. I remembered exactly what that hollow between her shoulder and neck tasted like, remembered exactly how the bone curved exquisitely.

Jane cleared her throat, face reddened. "Hey, you came to me, Don Draper," she said.

Inwardly, I smirked. I knew she was off-kilter when her insults lost their touch. The *Mad Men* reference fit the suit, but nothing else.

"What's the big deal?" she pressed. "You worried you're going to get caught? Got a wife at home who wouldn't appreciate you sitting with the town whore?"

The insults to me I could take. To herself, I really fucking couldn't.

"Don't talk about yourself like that, Jane," I snapped. She'd had the tendency to slide in those kinds of remarks when we were dating, and I hadn't liked them then. The only time I really got protective with her was when she beat up herself.

Jane's cherry-red mouth dropped at my harsh tone, and I had to resist reaching out a hand to close it. Desire painted itself across her face like another bit of makeup.

I shivered. She shivered. It was probably seventy degrees out here right now, but we both had goosebumps raised up and down our arms.

Get it together, you moron, I chastised myself.

There was no time for flirting. Or punishments. There was no time for the past. I had a future to contend with, and Jane was the only one who could make it work.

Even now, I was sure of that.

So I shrugged. Now or never.

"Fine," I said. "It's like this. I'm in a bind, and I need some help."

Jane waved a lithe hand. "Intrigued. Do go on."

I sighed. I'd practiced this speech.

"You...remember a bit about my family."

She frowned. "Not really. You barely talked about them. Upper East Side. I assumed kind of rich. And you hate them. Haven't spoken to them for years. Still estranged?"

I grimaced. "Something like that. Well, until last week. I was called home—"

"Called?" She balked. "Like a husky?"

"Like an heir."

That shut her up. For a second, anyway.

"What do you mean...an heir?"

I sighed. This was always going to be the hardest part. "My family is well off. More than most. They own a large company, De Vries Shipping Industries, which makes us wealthy. There's a lot on the line, and after my father died when I was a kid, I became, the, ah, default heir to the family fortune." I gripped my knees hard. I hated the sound of all of this. "You know, I tried to put it all behind me. But last week, my grandmother—Celeste de Vries— asked me to come home for a visit. First one in over ten years."

"And you just trotted on?"

"She said it was an emergency. She's old and sick. So I went." I shrugged. There really wasn't any way to explain my grandmother sitting in the middle of her Park Avenue Penthouse, bookended by her butler and an oxygen tank, not because she wanted to be there, but because she was too frail to go anywhere else. Tiny as she was, Celeste de Vries had only ever been a titan, a shadow of competence and manipulation my entire life.

She was still that. But sick too. And for the first time in a long time, I couldn't say no to her.

"She's old-fashioned," I said. "And dying. And her final wish is to see me—her prodigal heir—married with a family before she goes. Enough that she is threatening to sell off all her shares of the company, including those promised to my aunt and cousins and other extended family members, if I don't get married within six months and stay that way for five years. And try to produce an heir within that time."

By the time I was finished, I'd lost any appetite for the subpar cappuccino in front of me. For a so-called Italian bakery, they didn't know a damn thing about espresso.

I turned my cup in its saucer, then glanced up and found Jane's mouth half-open again, hazel eyes goggled behind her gold rims.

"Produce an *heir*?" she said a little more loudly than was strictly necessary. "Who are you, Prince William of the shipping industry? You have to protect your family's divine right to trade routes?"

A few of the other diners looked up. My hand clenched into a fist.

"Shh! The whole fucking city doesn't need to hear this, Jane."

"Let me get this straight," she continued as if I hadn't said anything, assuming the same position she used to when we were studying tort law. "You're not just Eric de Vries, generically wealthy Harvard graduate. You're Eric *de Vries*, as in *De Vries Shipping*, heir to one of the largest companies on the planet. Have I got that right?"

I shrugged again. She was cross-examining me, and I wasn't interested. "It's just a name."

Jane scowled, now the one to lose her cool. Inwardly, I threw up a fist of victory.

"You don't need to act like I only found out you drink whole milk instead of two percent, Mr. First-in-Line," she said. "It's *not* just a name. And we're not talking a few measly million, are we? We're talking, shit, we're talking Jackson Anderson-levels of cash, aren't we? As much as Brandon, even?"

I shrugged. Again. Brandon, Skylar's husband, was one of the richest men in Boston, worth somewhere between four and eight billion dollars, last I checked.

And he had nothing on me.

"*More?*" Jane pressed, clearly reading me like a damn book. "How—how much?"

I sighed. "Jane, you can look up this information easily on *Forbes* or *WSJ*." Honestly, I was always surprised she hadn't. Jane was smart. She did her research on everything. Except me, apparently. Never me.

She was going to make me say it.

"Yeah, but I want to hear it from the super-rich horse's mouth," she confirmed. "How much does it cost to buy eternal playboy Eric de Vries with a sweet church wedding?"

Sweet. Church. Wedding.

Christ. She really wasn't understanding the point of this conversation, was she? The Jane I knew was quicker than this. She had to know where I was going.

Didn't she?

Maybe I didn't have to ask. Maybe I'd come here for nothing.

Even so, I told her right through my teeth. "Seventeen billion dollars."

Coffee sprayed across the table, forcing me back in my chair. I checked over my suit, but I'd escaped Jane's shock. When I looked up again, she was frozen in place, though her deft mind was clearly moving, processing the magnitude of my family's wealth.

But that was just it. It was my family's, not mine. I was doing this for them, not me. In five years, I'd move on, just like I had before. Go back to the little firm I'd started in Boston. Maybe use my mother's name again instead of de Vries. And Jane and I could go right back to hating each other, like nature intended.

My stomach turned. I chose to sit back and ignore the feeling while I waited for Jane to collect her thoughts.

"Good God, you're really not just a random rich kid," Jane said at last. "You're a fucking dynasty. But who requires a marriage contract to grant an inheritance? The Tudors? Is your grandmother completely batshit or only beginning her decline into dementia?"

And there we were. Back to the cross-examination with a touch of history. Vaguely, I wondered if she used this technique with witnesses on the stand. Smothered them with pop-culture references until they were too flabbergasted to lie.

"She's an old, rich, dying sociopath," I said. "So, it pretty much amounts to the same thing. But it's not about the money. The firm's doing fine with Skylar and Kieran, it really is. I don't need or want to chair the board of directors of DVS."

"Then why do it? You already told your family where to stick it once before, though for what, I don't know. Why pander to this medieval bullshit? You don't even like these people."

I grimaced inwardly. I could go there. Tell her about Penny. About what happened at Dartmouth. About all the reasons why, ten years ago, I'd walked away from my family for good.

But then she might say no.

"I don't even *know* most of them," I said simply. "They are terrible people, all of them. But I don't think that means they should lose everything they have. No one deserves that."

It was the truth. Maybe not all of it. But it was still the truth.

"Okay..." Jane wasn't buying it, but she seemed to remember too when I wasn't going to break. "I mean, it's your choice to sacrifice five years of your life, I guess. But...how come you never told me before that you were the crown prince of New York City? Jesus Christ, Eric. You once invited me home to meet these people. Were you ever going to tell me who they really were?"

I took a deep breath. Yeah, I remembered that weekend. It was when I finally told her I loved her. That I'd been in love with her for three years. That I'd never met a single person like her and never would. I had plans to tell her everything. Throw her to the lions, sure. But only so we could escape the den together and maybe, just maybe, start a real life together.

Instead, she had freaked out.

"I would have gotten around to it," I replied. "But who they are didn't matter then. It matters now."

"Honestly, Petri. I feel like I never even knew you."

I tensed. There was that damn joke again. It really did make me want to take her over my knee.

Still, there was a wistful edge to her voice I couldn't shake off. One that told me she was remembering old times too. Not just sex, but something else. Moments in bed. Gray eyes meeting her hazels. Both of us finally finding a way to stay put with a person for once in our damn lives.

Yeah. I missed that too.

And really, wasn't that why I was here?

"You knew me better than anyone, Jane," I said honestly.

She looked up from where she had clearly been lost in her thoughts, just like me. "Did I?"

"By a long shot."

Jane took a sip of her coffee, then eyed me for a good long time. I didn't move a muscle.

Then I took a final drink of espresso and then a very deep breath. This was the time. It was now or never.

"Which is why," I continued, "I'm hoping you'll be the one to do it."

Jane's brows furrowed. "The one to do what?"

I took my time. Set down my coffee cup. Leaned forward across the table. And made sure I was looking directly at her without a shadow of doubt on my face.

"The one who'll marry me."

The words were bullets, the way Jane shot backward in her chair, like she wanted dive under the table and protect herself from a firefight. Shock played over her expressive face, followed by curiosity, then desire.

And then, as my heart sank, fear.

Because she remembered, just as I did, the way we had burned like rockets, and then crashed just as hard. A different kind of fire-fight. Where we were both the missiles.

"It was five years ago," I pressed on, more out of panic than anything else. "We were stupid twentysomethings. The timing was off. Now, we've grown up, become more accomplished, and there's nothing keeping you from coming back to Boston and marrying me."

Her red mouth opened and closed a few times. Part of me wanted to ask her to wipe off the damn lipstick.

"Wait, wait, wait...you're asking *me* to be your...bride?"

"I—er—"

For some reason the word "bride" had me gasping for breath.

It was what I was asking. But was I really asking for that?

An image of Jane appeared in my mind's eye. Pink hair and all, dressed up in a big white dress, a veil, flowers, the whole nine yards, walking down the aisle of some massive cathedral.

That alone was shocking.

And even in my imagination, all I wanted was her.

She didn't wait for me to answer, and when I returned to my senses, she was bent over the table, cackling like the Wicked Witch of the West.

I scowled. She just laughed harder.

"Me?" she choked out. "Marry you? Playboy, consummate-bachelor, super-bro lawyer, and soon-to-be shipping magnate *you*? You don't even believe in marriage!"

"We've been over this," I grumbled. "I do now. I have to."

"Still, even if you wanted to have a sham marriage and fuck around like other men of your 'station,' those men don't marry women like me. They marry the 'ee'-girls."

I frowned. "'Ee'-girls?"

Jane just snorted. "Yeah. Future Stepford wives. The ones whose names all end with the sound 'ee.' Lindsay. Katie. Sherry. Laurie. They have black Amex cards and love their pearl neck-laces—and I don't mean the dirty kind. Well, not unless you give them some Tiffany's first. Then you'll get a nice, prim BJ before they let you come all over their surgically perfected tits."

I almost choked on my coffee. I don't know why her response surprised me—Jane's insults were always surgically precise. She had no idea how close she was to the truth. It would be easy. Return to the fold as Celeste de Vries's prodigal grandson and heir to the family fortune. I'd have my pick of debutantes, no doubt about it. I could practically throw darts.

It would be easy, yeah. But fun? Not a chance.

"And you...you want to take me, confrontational, unfiltered, half-Korean, candy-haired *me*, home to *marry*?"

Her laughter was echoing all over the patio. I waved grimly at a few of the other coffee drinkers. A studious man in glasses glared at me over his computer screen. Yeah, well, fuck off, man. You try proposing to this one and see how it goes.

Now she was crying, and had to take off her glasses to wipe away the tears and keep them from spoiling her eyeliner.

"Oh, God," she creaked. "Oh, God, that's good. Can you imagine it? They'll think I'm a mail-order bride. I'd be the end of your poor grandmother. Your uptight family would *freak*!"

I grinned. I couldn't help it. Finally, we were on the same page. I reached out and grabbed a strand of her hair—a very, *very* pink strand, woven with blue and green to boot. It looked like a cheerleader's pom-pom, streamers at a birthday party, or something equally loud. Worlds upon worlds away from the antique-laden, beige and cream drawing rooms of the Upper East Side.

"That's kind of the point..." I said, and then before I could help myself, "pretty girl."

Jane's mouth clapped shut. "What?"

My smile curved into a sly grin. Yeah, I knew exactly the effect of that phrase. She called me "Petri Dish," insulted my responsibility and devotion to her. And I would just come back with the last thing she considered herself. Was it infantilizing? Maybe. But deep down, Jane never considered herself pretty. Or particularly girlish. She never saw what I did.

And somehow, whenever I reminded her, I couldn't help reminding her of *exactly* how she belonged to me too. In every way possible.

Her hazel eyes blinked through her glasses, and she bit her lip, sucking in a short breath. My pants tightened. For a second, I considered wrapping my fist with her silky hair, yanking her across the table, and teaching her the lesson she'd apparently forgotten in the intervening five years. I considered conquering that mouth all over again, sucking on that bottom lip, teasing the rest with my tongue until she was breathless and begging for more.

Suddenly, my collar was tight too. Jane's eyes were wide with promise and possibility.

I released her. I needed one thing from her right now, and it wasn't sex. Right?

Right.

We both sank back into our chairs as if sexual tension hadn't essentially handcuffed us together for a few seconds. Still, I kept her hand in mine, unable to stop playing with it completely. Unable to imagine a diamond ring on that finger.

"It'll be mutually beneficial," I told her. "Jane, you're the only one who could make it bearable. I can save my family's fortune and stick it to my grandmother at the same time. What's not to like about that?"

She continued watching the way my thumb pressed into her fingers.

"Right," she said. "Well. As funny as the Christmas cards will be, I'm not sure I want to be a tool for you to engage in some delayed teenage revenge. What's—what's in it for me?"

I took a deep breath. Now was the moment. She wouldn't be asking if she didn't really want to know.

"Twenty million dollars."

The number shocked even me. I was planning to offer five. A million a year would change anyone's life. Instead, I was offering four times that. And, I realized, I'd probably offer more if she wanted.

Jane was frozen. "Come again?"

With some reluctance, I returned her hand and sat back, prepared to go over negotiations like we were at my office. It was better this way. Lay the numbers out. Blind her with them. Make her an offer she couldn't refuse.

"Twenty million dollars," I repeated. "You move back to the East Coast. We get married. You live with me for five years. That's it."

Jane's face twisted. "How romantic."

"None of this is romantic," I agreed, trying not to feel regret. "That's also the point. I don't need someone who is going to get attached, Jane, who thinks I'm her knight in shining armor. I need someone who knows the score. Who knows exactly what kind of person I am."

"You mean the fact that you're a heartless bastard?"

"I wouldn't call it that," I said, more to myself than to her. "But...sure. Someone who knows what I'm capable of and what I'm not."

I didn't move, not wanting to show her how much the accusation hurt. Her words were sharp, no sign of jokes about them. Yeah, five years really hadn't been enough time. We could play cat and mouse all we wanted but when it really came down to it, it was going to take more than twenty million dollars to unbreak Jane's heart. And maybe mine too.

Still, that didn't mean I wasn't up for the challenge. And as I watched her fiddling with her cup, discomfort and bitterness flitting over her porcelain skin, I found I wanted to take it on. I wanted to do whatever I could to make sure Jane Lee Lefferts *never* called me a heartless bastard again.

Still, if it could get her in the door...

"And at the end of five years, you walk away with twenty million to do whatever the fuck you want," I told her, going on a hunch. "Practice law or don't. Design clothes. Open up that shop you used to dream about."

Her head shot back up, tossing her waves over her shoulders.

She was surprised I remembered. I wanted to tell her I remembered everything—every fucking thing—about her. I remembered how badly I'd wanted to make her happy, and how pissed I'd been when I fucked it all up. I wanted to tell her the truth—that this was all a ruse. That my grandmother had handed me an excuse to get Jane back into my life.

Because right then, I knew the truth myself, even if I wasn't ready to admit it: I'd do whatever it took to make Jane's dreams come true. Even if that meant sacrificing every one of my own.

"Come on, Jane..." I prodded gently. "Say what you want, but you and I always did have a good time."

Still she didn't speak, lost in her own thoughts. That beautiful mind of hers always did race, to the point where I could never quite guess what she was thinking. I loved that about it.

Loved. Fuck.

"Jane?" I asked again, starting to get nervous. She still hadn't made a noise, and for someone as vocal as Jane, that wasn't a great sign.

Or wasn't it?

She looked up, an answer at her lips, though nothing emerged.

"Well?" I pressed, unable to hide my nerves. I felt like I was on trial for my life, not for a fake marriage with the former love of my life. "What do you think?"

And it was then I knew that it didn't really matter what she said or how she answered. I'd never stop asking her this same question. Maybe it would take a few months, or maybe it would take ten years. But I'd win Jane back somehow.

Which was why she only surprised herself by saying "I'll think about it" in the end.

I left the cafe feeling like she was already mine, like I was already a married man.

After all, it was only a matter of time.

THANK YOU FOR READING! "MARRY ME" **is the alternate POV version of the first chapter of** *The Hate Vow*, **a fake marriage, enemies-to-lovers, second chance billionaire romance.**

IF YOU'D LIKE **to read Eric and Jane's complete story, check it out here: https://shor.by/thehatevow**

THE NOT-SO-SILENT NIGHT
A QUICKSILVER SECOND EPILOGUE

Hurry, Mama. I can't get out.

I awoke with a gasp, shaking in the night. The bedroom I shared with the slumbering form of Eric, my husband, seemed colder than it really was—odd since at nearly nine months pregnant, I was almost always overheated.

Beside me, Eric shifted in his sleep, as if the moment I awoke, something deep inside him stirred as well. It was always like that with us. After nearly ten years of fighting and fucking, fighting again, and finally admitting that we weren't just in love, but irretrievably destined for one another, some preternatural, unbreakable bond existed between us. Even in our sleep.

"Soul mates" sound cheesy, but there isn't really another word to describe the sensation when another person owns a central piece of your heart and gives you his in return. Even when we hated each other, it was like that. We couldn't stay away from each other. Like attracted like, despite how opposite we appeared. Like something deep inside each other was pulled to the other by an unbreakable chain.

Even now, it was terrifying.

Especially when I was once again about to create that bond with another human being. And I already knew what it felt like to lose it.

I would have smiled, but my heart was still racing. It was that dream again, if you could even call it that. A voice, unnameable, once that I'd know anywhere, but even now, I couldn't quite recall, seeking me out in the dark, looking for comfort, safety, and love.

Mama.

That was the first time I'd ever heard *that* particular word before. But lying here, staring up at our box beam ceiling and counting the glass prisms hanging from the Italian tole chandelier, I knew that voice. I would have known it anywhere.

It was *her*. Him. They. It. I didn't know what to call them, considering this time around, neither Eric nor I had wanted to know anything more about our pending child other than it was healthy. It was as if, by some silent accord, neither of us wanted to jinx the birth. So we knew nothing. Not the predicted size. And definitely not the sex.

I set my hand atop the high crown of my belly, which could politely be called planetesque, so much so Eric had taken to affectionately calling our kid-to-be Pluto. As if to say hello, there was a distinct thump under my palm.

"You all right in there, little bean?" I asked it.

Another kick, small, against my palm. It should have reassured me, but I didn't.

I kept hearing that voice. Wanting out.

With a sigh, I swiped my glasses off the nightstand, then rolled to my side and pushed myself up, doing the best I could not to disturb Eric. He already didn't get enough sleep. On top of the insane hours he worked as the CEO of De Vries Shipping, I knew he struggled with his own PTSD, triggered too by the upcoming birth. We'd come so close to losing everything only a short time ago. Both of us were still getting used to the fact that we could actually be safe. And as hot as it was to give him the comfort of my body on the occasions where he woke in the night, these days being turned onto my knees while he took his pleasure wasn't exactly an option.

Soon, though. My insides ached for need of it. Very soon.

By some miracle, my weight didn't crack the fault lines under our bed, and I managed to make it down the hall to the kitchen while Eric slumbered. Lord, I really was a blimp on pegs. I didn't move forward anymore, just side to side, gradually from one corner of the apartment to the other.

After getting a glass of water, I managed to get myself downstairs to the studio, where the remnants from my final project at FIT still lay strewn over the work table next to my sewing machine and other design materials. I had started my master's at the Fashion Institute in September only to take leave for the birth with plans to return in the summer.

Already people were saying I'd never go back. I knew I would. I loved fashion, and for the first time in my life, I was pursuing a real passion, not just something I was good at. Law had been for my parents, and working in public service had been for my dad. But becoming a designer—that was for me. It was just one of the many ways that Eric knew how to support me. It had been his idea even before it had occurred to me that I could make clothes for a living, not just for myself.

Still, even this room couldn't banish that voice. I needed to hear someone else's. Someone who wasn't me. Someone who would also be up at three in the morning. Who would understand what I was going through.

Nina picked up her phone on the first ring. "Jane, it's Christmas Eve. You should be asleep."

"So should you," I told her. "I'm not the only one with a bun in the oven. And besides, I'm not the one who has to play Santa Claus in the morning."

I could practically hear Nina's grin over the phone. Technically she was my cousin-in-law, but given the way they'd been raised together, she was more like Eric's sister. And these days, kind of like mine too.

Just three months ago, right before I'd been put on the doctor's no-fly list, Eric and I had watched her marry our good friend, Matthew Zola, in a simple ceremony on the Italian coast, discovering only as I was helping her fit her wedding dress that she was also pregnant, albeit a few months behind me. It was heartening, really, to think that like her and Eric, our kids might grow up together. Serve as anchors in this strange world of money and intrigue that had already cost us both so much.

Gained a bit too, though, Jane Brain.

I smiled to myself. The voice of my adoptive father had been popping up more often throughout the pregnancy, as if he knew I needed the extra comfort.

"True," Nina agreed. "But Olivia won't be up until at least nine. And in a matter of days, you'll stop sleeping more than a few hours at a time altogether."

"I know," I said. "But I can't help it."

She sighed. "I know. Neither can I."

And there it was. The acknowledgment that the mind doesn't always follow the body. That even though our families were technically safe from the people who had threatened them—me from an insane biological father who was literally dead, her from her horror show of an ex-husband who was now serving a life sentence —emotionally, we were still a mess.

Because even now, right at the finish line, I was still so, so scared I would lose it. And it would be so much worse than the last time.

"Is it the same dream?" Nina asked.

"Yes."

She didn't make me describe it again. It was always the same thing and had been for months. I was back in that decrepit old house in Korea, drugged and tied to a cot after the baby had literally been taken from my womb. But this time, the baby was still alive, calling for me through the dark.

Yes, I am aware that newborn children can't actually use the words "Help me, Mama." But that doesn't make it any less chilling when they do it in your dreams.

"Have you told Eric?"

"No. He has his own terrors to contend with. And you know him, he'll get all Tom Cruise about it. Rush around trying to beat up the bad guys even though they're all gone. Because *he* took care of them."

I shuddered. Even thinking of that night still terrified me. You don't know fear until your husband has to point a gun directly at you to save your life. Until he has to shoot the captor holding you in close range so that you can both be rid of him forever.

I shook that memory away too. John Carson was dead. My biological father was *dead*, and no amount of dreams, waking or asleep would change that.

"I understand," Nina said. "Matthew was thrilled to get back his gun license last week. I honestly think he feels naked without it."

I could sympathize. Sort of. Like Matthew Zola, I had also worked once as a prosecutor. While I hadn't gone after the organized crime rings that Zola had, I knew other DAs who did and got the personal threats that came with it. They were the ones who often carried their own protection in the event they got jumped coming and going from the office.

"Any news on the Boston DA?" I wondered, looking to change the subject.

"Well, right now the focus is holidays and our first Christmas with Olivia in the morning. She loves Matthew, of course, but it's not even been six months since we moved to Boston. They are still getting used to each other. He's working on getting reciprocity for the bar exam right now, and Brandon offered to connect him with people he knows with the district attorney. But you know how proud Matthew gets. He wants to earn his place on his own."

I snorted. "When will he learn the world is built on nepotism?"

Nina didn't reply. Maybe I'd gone too far. After all, one of the things she liked best about Matthew was that he didn't come from a world of trust fund babies and the Upper East Side. He was a self-made man, through and through, and nothing was going to change that.

"I'm glad he's figuring things out," I said. "And I'm glad you're getting settled."

I drifted a hand over my drafting table, where the last set of sketches was already gathering dust. It would be a while before I could devote myself to a passion beyond what was in my belly. I wasn't sure how I felt about that either.

Maybe the voice calling was little Pluto here. Maybe it was me.

"Duchess? Come back to bed, baby."

Down the line, Zola's gruff voice sounded. Which probably meant that if he wasn't up already, Eric would also come looking for me soon.

"I should go," Nina said. "But Jane, will you be all right?"

"I'll be fine," I told her. "And if we don't speak tomorrow, Merry Christmas, Nina."

"Merry Christmas, Jane. Good Night."

I lumbered back up the two flights of stairs, back to the bedroom where Eric was still dead to the world, even when my cetacean body sunk the bed about four feet as I rolled in. I couldn't relax, though. There, the voice seemed louder.

Help me, Mama.

I shivered even harder in the night. And then I felt it. A grip around my belly, like a vise was placed over those muscles just above my hips and then tightened. Hard.

"Oh!" I cried into the dark, unable to keep quiet.

That was *definitely* not a dream.

"What? Huh?"

Eric awoke immediately, jumped out of bed, and crouched on the floor like a hunter about to pounce. Then he apparently realized where he was and stood. The grip around my belly lessened, giving me a moment to appreciate the shadowed form of my husband, all lean muscle in nothing but a pair of tight boxer briefs. If it were for, oh, impending birth, I would have taken the time to show just how appreciative I really was.

His gray eyes, dark and wild in the night, focused as he woke fully. He shoved a hand through his sleep-twisted hair.

"Christ—did you shout?"

Still tense, I nodded. "Sorry, I didn't mean to wake you up. It was just a contraction, that's all."

His eyes popped open. "What?"

Immediately, he twisted around, looking for clothes.

"They're in the closet, not under your nightstand, you goon," I told him.

"Shit—right—" He jogged into the walk-in at the other end of the room, then jogged out sockless seconds later wearing only unbuttoned jeans and an open button-down and carrying the go-bag we'd put together months ago. "Ready?"

I chortled and lay back on my pillow. "Petri, what in God's name are you doing?"

Eric frowned. "What do you mean, what am I doing? You're in labor. We need to go to the hospital."

"Calm down, Chicken Little," I told him. "The sky's not falling yet. It's one contraction. One. You remember what the doctor said last time. We have to time them."

Eric immediately looked down at himself, as if he would find the time somewhere near his navel.

"What are you looking at?" I asked. "You're not a stopwatch, Petri Dish."

When he looked up again, his bewildered expression had turned to something distinctly darker. And a whole lot more competent.

The go-bag was dropped at the end of the bed as he strode over, then sat next to me and checked his watch. Slowly, he reached out for a lock of my red-streaked hair and tugged on it lightly before tucking it around my ear.

Pending labor or not, it was a direct line to my lady parts.

"That's not fair," he said in a low, foreboding voice. "You can't call me that when I can't do anything about it."

I just offered a smug smile, imagining very well just *what* he would do when I called him that particular nickname. He hadn't stopped until after we got back from Italy and a bad case of premature labor nearly put me on bed rest. The doctor had been very clear—no sex. No orgasms of any kind. At least for me. Which Eric had apparently decided meant him too.

That didn't mean I didn't like to torment him with the possibility, though. After all, misery loves company.

"Well, I had to get you out of that stupor somehow—oh!"

I could barely finish the sentence before another contraction grabbed me.

This time Eric glanced at his watch first. "That was six minutes, gorgeous. We should go."

"Nonsense," I argued, though not very strongly since the contraction was still going. "It's every five. And for two hours!"

"I'm not waiting for two hours just to watch you have the baby in our bed. We need to go to the hospital now. I mean it!"

"Eric, don't be—ah!"

I couldn't finish that sentence before a different sensation interrupted my train of thought. My eyes popped open. It was warm. Wet. And kind of gross.

My husband, alarmist or not, raced to my side. "What? What just happened?"

I looked down at my lap with the approximate expression of a child that just had an accident in the middle of a spelling bee. "Probably a new set of sheets. I think my water just broke."

His eyes popped open. "We're going now. No arguments, pretty girl."

I opened my mouth to do just that but found I didn't want to. That fear had risen in my heart again—the same one embedded in my dream.

Help me, Mama.

Oh God, honey. I'm trying.

"UMBILICAL CORD."

"Heart rate."

"Distress."

Approximately eighteen days later, I could hardly make out

the words said around me, much less to me. My glasses had been cracked beyond use when I'd thrown them across the room in a fit of pain. Bridget, Eric's assistant, was supposedly running over a spare pair, but in the meantime, the room was blurry, my body was throbbing, and I barely knew my own name, much less what else was going on around me.

He was right, goddammit. The bastard was right. By the time our driver got us to Lenox Hill, I was already having contractions less than three minutes apart. My back felt like someone was taking a jackhammer to it, and my insides felt like they were squeezing me to death. The baby was coming. They also said it was coming, much faster than a typical first birth.

But then it just...didn't.

Now the sun was starting to rise over Park Avenue. But I barely noticed.

"Hey, gorgeous."

Eric's voice was preternaturally calm as he sat on the rolling stool beside my bed, took my sweaty hand, and started to massage my palm.

I moaned. "What did they say?"

I knew that tone. I'd heard it before, in the worst place possible. In Korea, when I was lying on the floor, bleeding out after my child.

Fear seized my chest.

Mama, help me.

"They said the baby's stuck," he told me in low, solemn tones. "The umbilical cord is wrapped around their neck. They can't— they can't breathe, gorgeous."

At that moment, neither can I.

"No," I whimpered. "No, not again..."

His hand squeezed mine. "Not yet, beautiful."

"Mrs. de Vries?"

The nurse's voice was chipper. Too chipper for this somber news. My baby was dying. It was dying inside me as we spoke, and I couldn't do anything about it. I didn't even know if it was a boy or a girl. I didn't know anything about it.

"We're going to take you to the OR now."

A few assistants moved to either side of my bed, clicking things and undoing cords.

"You're getting a caesarian," Eric told me as he stood, though he didn't let go of my hand. "We're going in now, beautiful. I'll be right there with you the entire time."

Another contraction shook through me. Oh God, it wanted out.

"Okay," I whispered.

What happened next was a blur. I think I signed something at some point. With shaky hands, Eric did too.

They wheeled me away from the windows and the sunrise to a room on another floor that had no windows at all, but lots of steel surfaces and people dressed in blues and greens. Table everywhere with sharp things. A giant blue sheet splitting me from my belly. Eric gone.

Help me, mama.

"No," I croaked.

"Shhhh. I'm back."

Eric was next to me again, this time wearing scrubs, hair covered with a blue cap and mouth with a mask.

"Here," he said, and set my glasses on my nose. "Bridget arrived. Don't throw them across the room this time, all right?"

The room came back into focus, him most of all. I could barely make out his face—only the high edges of his cheekbones, the top of his knife-straight nose, and his eyes, those steely gray eyes glinting with love, fear, and the promise of protection.

"You're going to be fine," he murmured with a tight squeeze of my hand as he pressed his forehead to mine. "I won't lose you. I won't lose either of you."

Are we about to be lost?

It was all I could wonder about.

Help me, Mama.

"Scalpel."

The voices on the other side of the curtain were talking. The epidural was working—I couldn't feel a thing. I focused on Eric, staring up at him.

"I don't want to lose them," I told him, my voice smaller than I ever remembered.

"You won't."

"But it can't breathe. What if..." Tears pricked my eyes painfully with the unthinkable. But I had to say the words. I had to say them if only to banish them. "What if they don't make it?"

Eric took a deep breath, then lifted my hand to his lips, pressing a long, solemn kiss to my knuckles through his mask. "They will."

"How do you know?"

"I just know."

"No, you don't."

His lips moved into a smile through the mask, as if he had anticipated my recalcitrance, even through my daze.

"Yes, I do," he countered gently. "Because it wouldn't be our kid if they didn't want to fight, pretty girl. Just like us."

I opened my mouth, ready to argue again, but found I couldn't. Instead I blinked through the tears that were warmer, somehow. "You still want to fight with me?"

Eric slid his arm around my shoulder, pressing his face to mine so I could hear him clearly. "Forever."

Security. Safety. Warmth. It all flooded into me. And something else I couldn't put my name on arrived too.

"All right, Mama, this is it."

Eric and I stared at each other, oblivious to the sounds—the heavy ventilation, the footsteps, the slight clinks on the other side of the sheets—or anything else in the room but each other. The truth of what I had struck through my heart like the echo of a gong. This man was immovable in his love for me and anyone else he considered family. He would do anything to protect us. Anything to save us. Even if that meant believing in things when we could not.

And thank God for that.

A cry pierced through the clamor—a voice I had never heard before and yet somehow knew immediately.

My baby.

Mama, I'm here.

KOREANS DON'T HAVE middle names. I didn't either—not really, instead having two last names. My mother's Lee, and father's, Lefferts. Jane Lee Lefferts. I did, however, have a second name, a Korean name that was used only when I was with my mother's family, the ones who didn't speak English at all. I barely understood, them, but I knew my name. Ae-Cha meant "loving daughter," a not-so-subtle reminder of the role I was supposed to have in life.

Upper-crust Americans like my husband, Eric Sebastian Franklin Stallsmith de Vries, are prone to many. Eric's names came from family heritage, albeit no one his father or his mother had actually known. Five-time grandfathers or someone who had owned a ship once.

Mine were simple—names my parents liked, plus the two surnames they provided.

We landed somewhere in the middle, giving him the names of our beloved fathers, whom we had lost too early in life. Jacob Carol de Vries was born at 6:34 A.M. on Christmas morning.

His Korean name was Duri.

Translated, it meant Two.

"EATING LIKE A CHAMP, I SEE."

I looked up to find Eric entering the suite carrying a large paper bag from Citarella. Only after spending the next several hours after the birth with Jacob and me to make sure we were all right, Eric went home to take a shower after I assured him he smelled. He didn't. But I recognized fatigue when I saw it. Eric needed time to decompress just like I did. He needed to go away so he could come back again.

I glanced down at Jacob, this tiny, solid ball of baby who was currently making a meal of my breast—literally. "He's almost as good at it as you are, Petri."

Predictably, Eric's eyes darkened in that utterly tempting way I really shouldn't have been toying with right now. "That name is off-limits for at least six more weeks, pretty girl."

"Pretty, ha. That's a joke." I was a mess. Stitched up the stomach, still exhausted from the birth, my hair a bird's nest on top of my head, glasses askew. But happy. So damn happy.

Eric crossed the room and sat in the armchair beside us. "You've never been more beautiful."

I turned toward him, ready to banter some more, but found I couldn't in the face of the utter adoration and awe written across his strong features.

"Eric," I murmured, unable to help the tears rising again.

This time, however, his eyes watered with mine. Slowly, he took my chin between his finger, then leaned over Jacob's content form and placed his lips on mine, landing a soft, slow kiss that still managed to take my breath anyway.

"Absolutely beautiful," he whispered. "Fuck, Jane. I love you so damn much. The both of you. You know that?"

Finally, a tear fell down my cheek. Then another, and another.

"I know," I said back, rubbing nose to his. "I know."

"I was so scared."

"Me too."

Gently, Eric stroked a knuckle over Jacob's fair head. He was blond already, just like his dad. "But here you are, little man."

I smiled down at the baby, and then at his adoring father. "Here we are."

We both watched Jacob's little mouth working furiously, eyes fluttering closed until finally, he released my nipple with a pop and curled into a tiny, sleeping ball against my chest. Eric continued to stroke his downy head, arching over the both of us with love and compassion.

"Merry Christmas, pretty girl."

I kissed him again. "And a very happy new year."

THANK **you for reading the second epilogue for Jane and Eric's story!**

IF YOU HAVEN'T ALREADY, **consider reading Matthew and Nina's story, starting with The Scarlet Night:**

www.nicolefrenchromance.com/thescarletnight

NEED SOMETHING NEW? **Check out First Comes Love, a secret baby romance: www.nicolefrenchro mance.com/firstcomeslove**

EXTRA SCENES & SNIPPETS

Jane gets picked up

"Jane!"

Eric stood across the parking lot in a summer-fresh suit—all in white—white pants, a white linen shirt, his boyish blond hair brushed back from his brow, his gray eyes covered by a pair of expensive-looking aviators. He looked like an extra in a 90s R&B video, but in the best possible way.

He pushed off the car—another very expensive thing that was too posh for even an intelligible logo on the nose—and waved his hand at me.

"Doing all right there?"

I tipped my oversized sunglasses down my nose and glared at him. "Petri, I feel like a candle that was left overnight to burn. I feel like the Wicked Witch of the West, melting into a puddle of hate. I feel like someone just popped me into a kiln and forgot about me. Summer sucks. End of story."

Eric just smiled, but it wasn't the kind of smile he gave girls at the bars, the kind that almost made him look like a shark. The kind I'd seen time and time again. This one was genuine. I'd once thought it was maybe even reserved for me. At least, once upon a time. Before that idiot dream was blown to smithereens.

"Come on," he said. "You deserve it for taking that sardine can here in the first place. Grandmother has a copter on standby, you know."

I rolled my eyes. "Did you just say 'copter' like that's standard nomenclature?"

He paused and looked at me over the top of the car, which I now saw was a Bentley. "Yeah, why?"

"Just checking. I wanted to know for sure if you had already reached that level of rich-people myopia where things like helicopters have the everyday appeal of an old Dodge Caravan."

"Would you like me to say helicopter awkwardly every time I say it?"

I balked. "Are you going to be saying it a lot?"

He shrugged. "Well, it's going to be ours soon. I might."

I snorted. "Why don't you just say 'chopper' and be done with it. Really lean into the douche factor here."

Eric chuckled. "Whatever you say, Jane. Come on, get into the Benz. "

We turned to a bright white sedan at the end of the parking lot that straddled two full spots.

"What an asshole," I said shaking my head. "These fucin

As if in response, the car suddenly chirped, back lights flashing as its doors unlocked. I jumped, and Eric jangled some keys.

"We're the assholes now," he said. "Get in."

But I wasn't done staring. "This isn't your car."

Eric popped the trunk and lifted my bag inside its immaculate, completely empty space. "My Corolla was conveniently tripled parked at the house. Grandmother thinks it's unseemly for me to seen driving it."

He looked admiringly at the car. Eric had never been one for flashy things, although I did remember he had a penchant for a few luxuries. Skylar had warned me, hadn't she? The obnoxiously priced coffee? Tip of the iceberg. Now that I thought about it, it was true. His apartment in the North End was large and roomy in an expensive part of town. Most of his clothes were plain but understatedly elegant in that way only designer clothes could look. He liked Varvatos for going out, had a weakness for Tom Ford, and had most of Hugo Boss's lines for days in court. He also had a preference for 1000-minimum-count Egyptian cotton sheets. Eric's wealth had never been a secret, but I never suspected it was in the realm of billions.

He swallowed and opened the back door of the car. I realized in the end that there was a driver in the front.

"Backseat," he said. "Security."

My eyes practically fell out of my head. "Who are we, the Kennedys? Is this for real?"

"Grandmother's orders. Too much of a risk."

"You or someone else?"

He smirked. "You know, I think it might be me. Something makes me think I'm considered a flight risk over here."

"Are you?"

For a second, I didn't want him to answer. He could still take it back. We didn't need to do this. He was probably the most eligible bachelor on the East Coast, if not the entire United States.

But Eric just grinned that boyish grin that broke his face.

"Jane, whatever you do, don't doubt that you're the one I want to do this with."

"And why is that?"

"Because you make things interesting."

We rode in silence for another hour and a half. It was a long drive, and more than once, I felt like I was in an F. Scott Fitzgerald novel, Nick to Eric's Gatsby. Or, I wondered, was I the Gatsby here? The poor man who came from nothing, here to put on a show and pretend to fit in with the rich.

"Old Sport," I murmured as we passed mansion after mansion.

"What's that?"

No heart?

Less than five seconds later, he stormed back in. My door slammed against the doorstop, and a second later, a small black object was hurled across the room, right into my lap.

"No heart?" Eric demanded. "No fucking *heart*? Read that, you ridiculous woman. *Then* tell me I have no heart."

Jane's dreams

Dad gave everything he had to make sure I became the lawyer he always wanted to be...but if I had had my way, I would have been a...

My thoughts didn't even finish. I haven't let myself go there for a really, really long time. Once upon a time, I'd wanted to do something else with my life than file motions and pore over depositions. Once I'd wanted to make things. Design things. Create.

Nope. This was *not* the time to be rehashing that garbage bag of a dream.

In another world, the deal required a baby too...

"Kid?" I balked. "What if I don't want to have a kid?"

Eric looked as uneasy at the prospect of parenthood as I did. It was something we had in common—no marriage, no kids. As much as I liked my friends' spawn—after all, my goddaughter, Jenny Sterling, was the cutest damn button on the East Coast, and Luis was a pudgy-cheeked snack cake—I'd absolutely never, ever wanted any of my own.

"Does that...does that mean we have to sleep together?" I wondered before I could stop it.

That look was back. *Pretty girl.* He didn't say the old name again, but I could hear the words anyway. "Only if you want to," he said. "And if you don't, there are other ways to conceive. Surrogacy, for example." He sighed. "Grandmother will probably insist on it if you don't conceive quickly, actually."

Jane's name

"Jane's not a very unique name," I said lamely.

"It is on you." He crawled over me so I was pressed firmly into the pillow. "It's classic. But one of a kind at the same time. Just like you."

I snorted. "A classic?

"A classic is defined as something that never goes out of style," Eric replied. "That's you. In this house, anyway. Not with me."

"Oh my god, you are a corn cob," I joked, but fell flat as I observed the sincerity in his face. I couldn't look away. Not when his deep gray eyes were staring at me like that, holding me to him, willing me to understand his words.

I bit my lip.

"Jane."

"Mmm."

His gaze dropped. "You need to stop doing that."

"Hm? What's that?" I bit my lip again.

What if

"Jane," he asked. "What would you do if someone said you weren't allowed to marry me?"

I leaned back. "Ah...haven't people been saying that from the start?"

He reared back. "Why, what have you heard?"

I furrowed my brow. "Ah...nothing...other than the basic gossip, 'what's she doing with him?', cans of red paint on my dress variety. What's this about?"

Knots

"I have an idea," he said as he tied my hand to one side of the bed.

"Hmmm? What's that?"

I watched him slip the silk around the bedpost, then knot it securely around my wrist. He was so graceful with knots—from climbing, he said. He got a lot of practice.

He slid a leg over my waist so he sat over me, bend over so his bricked stomach hovered just above

I tipped my head and up and licked him. To my satisfaction, he jumped.

"Did you just *lick* me?"

I batted my eyes. "Maybe."

Eric shook his head, clearly fighting a smile. "That's strike two, Lefferts."

I raised my hips, jerking his lanky body. "What's strike three?"

He fell forward, caging me into the bed. "Don't say another word."

I opened my mouth. "Another word."

"That's *it*."

Within five seconds, my pants and underwear were stripped off, leaving me on the bed with nothing but my bra. Eric walked around the bed, examining me. All traces of humor had evaporated, and what was left was a very superior-looking Chairman-in-training. He left his shirt open on both sides, the tease. He knew that somehow, it drove me crazier to watch him strut around half clothed than all naked.

Eric's dominant side

My jaw was seized, and just by that, I was yanked up to meet his violent kiss, bruising and fierce.

"And keep your fucking hands to yourself," he growled, then flipped me onto my stomach so he could pin my hands to the small of my back.

"Well, we have to have a baby anyway, don't we?"

He shook his head. "I'm not fucking kidding here, Jane. You think it's been easy for me? Watching you suck on your fuking lips all the time? Knowing you're out in New York, fucking every man in the city when I know I could be doing it ten thousand times fucking better?"

My jaw dropped. "You *ass*—"

"Shut up, *pretty girl*."

Immediately, my voice was gone.

"Say it," he said. "You know the word."

V-cards

"You?"

I looked up at the ceiling. "I was twenty."

At that, he looked genuinely surprised. "*Twenty?*"

I turned and frowned. "What's wrong with twenty?"

"Nothing. *Nothing*. I just thought..."

"You thought because I was as big a whore as you, I must have started just as young?" I folded my arms and stared back up at the ceiling. "Fourteen. Please. You probably didn't even have facial hair. How much did you weigh, a buck ten?"

Eric cast a sideways glance at me. "I had an early growth spurt. I was at least one-thirty by that age." He rolled over so he was on his stomach and started tracing circles on my arm.

Jane's upset

"I just need to borrow him for a moment," I said through gritted teeth as I grabbed Eric's hand and yanked him through the crowd.

Eric made his quick apologies just before I towed him after me, ignoring the many other people who reached out as we passed, trying to get Eric's attention.

"Jane. Jane! Hey, wait a second!"

But it wasn't I had dragged him down the hall and into one of the several libraries that I finally whirled around. "No, *you* stop it. I feel like such an idiot."

His face turned to fire. "Are you serious right now?"

"Am I 'serious right now?'" I mimicked him. "Yes, I'm serious! Look at me! I look like a powder puff."

"I think you look a lot nicer than that," he muttered, but I just rattled on.

Safe word

"You don't want to talk yet? Fine. We won't fucking talk. Or at least you won't."

He reached around his neck and pulled off his tie—the beautiful, light gray Hermes I had bought him just last week, thinking it would match his eyes. Fucking hell. I was right.

"Turn around." When I didn't, I received a sharp slap on my ass—hard enough that I jumped.

"I don't care if you worked on that dress for a month, pretty girl. When I tell you to do something, you fucking do it."

I turned around, eyes wide, arms bound behind my back. I knew what was coming. I just didn't know when.

"You just dragged me out of a room full of people," Eric said.

Slowly, I nodded.

"You embarrassed me in front of my family."

I blinked away the tears. I didn't mean to do that. "I just—"

"Hush." He turned the tie over and back between his hands, folding it again and again into knot. "What's the word, Jane?"

I stared. He was asking me this *now*? With all these people milling around outside.

Maybe I should have said no. I should have told him to turn around, and we'd continue this conversation upstairs or tomorrow or maybe even never. Maybe it wasn't too late to back out of this whole thing like we were supposed to.

Instead, I muttered our safe word.

A go-word

His hands only tightened further. "You know what to say if that's what you need, Jane," he said. "Or you should." The hand at my chin slid down and wrapped around my neck. "What's the word?"

"Shut up."

He yanked me back against him, and this time his *interest* was quite clear. Right against the small of my back.

"Wrong," he growled.

"There should be a 'go-word' too," I said.

Eric's brow rose. "A 'go-word'?"

I nodded. *Yeah, I like this idea.* "Consent's a big deal, and I take it seriously. And I want to know."

Another instance of red paint

"No!" Jenny cried, but it was too late. The other kids tipped the red paint down, and like a Rorschach painting, it left great splotches of red paint all over my pristine white dress.

Jenny stared at it in horror. "Oh, Aunt Jane."

I just stared at the fabric in horror. All that money. All that time. I hadn't ever cared about fitting in with this family, necessarily. Eric had made it clear that wasn't the point. But did I want to be bullied? Ostracized? Fuck, no.

I cleared my throat.

You're the only one strong enough to deal with them, he'd said. I didn't think it was the kids he meant, but I also didn't think it was the kids who came up with this idea.

I took a deep breath. Then another. And another. This wasn't the first time in my life I'd been ostracized because I was different. Maybe I had hoped that shit would peter out before I was, oh, thirty, but it seemed that wasn't my lot in life.

And I wasn't about to give these bitches the satisfaction of seeing me break now.

"It's okay, Jen," I said. "Look, it's already starting to dry."

And it was. The acrylic paint was drying quickly, almost like it was supposed to be this way. If I wasn't so fucking angry or intent on fitting in, I might have altered the dress in a similar way on my own.

Jenny's lip stopped quivering quite so much. "Are—are you sure?"

I nodded. "It's fine, Jen. Your auntie is used to being the life of the party, right? I'll be fine."

I slipped on my sandals and twirled around, blinking away the tears of frustration while my honorary niece slowly began to smile.

"Go tell Garrett there was an accident up here," I said, and then, thinking it would be best if Garrett didn't have a heart attack upon seeing very blood-looking red flailed all over the bathroom, I added: "a *non*-health-related accident."

Jenny nodded and skipped out of the room to find some help. I gazed at myself in the mirror. The paint was nearly dry. The dress was still mostly white. And my hair...well, my hair was going to have to change too. But I had already planned that anyway.

"I don't *have* another dress," I said. "This was the only one I brought. At least, the only one that's white."

Eric shook his head. "Jane, *everyone* spills on their clothes. This is why I gave you a credit card. You don't need to be stingy with it. There is more than enough."

I glared at him. If I could have, I would have sprayed *his* condescending ass with red fucking paint too.

Jane goes too far

"If this is your version of partnership, it's no wonder Penny killed herself!"

The words hung in the air like fruit, heavy on the vine until one by one, they splattered.

Eric didn't blink. His eyes were wounded.

"Is that...is that really what you think?" he asked after a few heavy moments.

I didn't know what to say. I didn't want to hurt him. I was angry, yes, but that was never my intent. But at the same time...I found I meant it. I could understand now what this family was really like. What this world was like. For someone with less of a backbone, I could absolutely see this kind of bullying driving them to so much worse than breaking a few plates.

Apparently, my silence conveyed my thoughts.

"I see," Eric said quietly. He stood up.

His face fell. And for the first time, so did his mask. Underneath the mask, underneath the cocky exterior was a river of hurt pouring out of those solid gray eyes.

Just the way you are

"I don't want you neat. I don't want you pretty. I don't want you rich." Step. "Polite." Step. "Or cute."

He took my hands lightly in his, and ran his thumbs over my knuckles, then toyed with my fingers, drifting over the chipped black polish. But his eyes, those light brown eyes that were deceptively simple. Brown isn't a simple color at all. It takes a multitude of other colors to make that one.

"I want you just the way you are," he pronounced quietly.

I sniffed. "Okay, Billy Joel. So you're saying I'm not pretty?"

But just like always, Eric didn't waver. His mouth quirked slightly on one side, but his eyes maintained their hold on mine, unwavering. Ever patient.

And like always, it was I who looked away first.

"Jane?"

But his voice, his low, melodic voice that would seriously be able to calm a rainstorm, pulled me out of my self-deprecating spiral. I looked up, and in his eyes was nothing but the words he spoke. And before I could help it, my own eyes started to cloud with tears of my own.

"Eric," I whispered.

He raised a big hand to cup my cheek, brushing his thumb over my cheekbone. The motion pushed my glasses up slightly, and he tugged them back in place. It was just another reminder that he liked them where they were—he liked me as I was.

"I need to hear you say it," he said quietly.

Jane realizes the truth

"You and I were never supposed to work," I bit out. "Don't you see that?"

"Why? What should I see that?" he pushed, crowding me even further.

"BECAUSE I DON'T WORK WITH ANYONE!"

The words left me gasping. Suddenly this shack seemed like a fucking tin can.

But Eric didn't move, his arms caging me against the counter. "I don't believe that."

I narrowed my eyes. "I don't need you to believe what I already know is true. You think it's *my* choice that I'm more lonely at almost thirty than I've been my entire life? People love people like me until they don't. They love a loud mouth. They love a loud opinion. They love the 'sass' and the 'spunk' until I say something they don't like. It happens everyone, and it's going to happen to you too."

He said nothing, of course. Instead, Eric's hard gaze burned through me. I tried to look away, but couldn't.

"What?" I croaked. "What is it?"

Still he didn't answer, his pure, crystalline features cut like stone in the moonlight.

"Tell me!" My voice rose higher, bordering on a shriek. "You heard them. You heard all of them. This isn't going to work. This stupid plan we tried was *never going to work*. So why are you still here? WHAT DO YOU WANT?!"

Not a muscle flinched. Not a wisp of hair. Not a shift of foot. Then, slowly, Eric squeezed his eyes shut, only to open them a moment later, somehow even more zeroed in on me. I felt like I was made of glass. Like with one touch, he could knock me over, and I would crash into a million pieces.

"You."

The word was a bullet. Inside, my chest caved in.

"No," I whimpered, falling forward. "No, you can't."

My fists hit his chest with a thump, and Eric clasped them tight, unwilling to let me pull away.

"Don't," he gritted between clenched teeth, "tell me what I can't do. Especially not with you, pretty girl."

Making peace with Penny's family

Nothing had changed in ten years. The faded sprigged wallpaper. The cracked vinyl booths. The stained Formica counter, behind which still stood Lazaros Kostas, joking and taking orders on a small pad poised over a growing belly. Behind him, overseeing the cooks and checking the orders clipped to the ticket carousel, was his wife, Antonia. Suddenly, Eric felt like he was seventeen again, skipping polo practice to sit in Penny's section and order too many chocolate milkshakes just to see his girlfriend smile. But other than where her photo hung behind the register amidst the collection of signed headshots of celebrities and local politicians, Penny wasn't here.

Penny wasn't here. But Jane was.

And to his surprise, she took his hand. "Are you all right?" she asked.

Empathy. Definitely a good sign.

Eric nodded. "Yeah. It's just a little surreal."

Jane squeezed his hand in solidarity, then released it as the hostess walked toward them.

"Two?" she asked in that brusque tone characteristic of the New York restaurant industry.

Eric nodded. "At the counter, please."

The hostess gestured that they should sit where they wanted. Jane followed Eric to the counter, where Mr. Kostas had his back turned as he jabbered with his wife in Greek.

"Lazaros," she snipped, then in English: "You have customers."

Lazaros barked something back at her, then turned around. "Hello, what can I—oh!"

It had been almost eleven years since Penny's funeral. Eleven years since Eric had stood behind the rows of Greek relatives wailing their disbelief at his girlfriend's untimely death and whispered behind his back. Eleven years since Eric had informed the Kostas that their only daughter had killed herself in his bathtub and that it was probably his family's fault.

Except it wasn't. Not completely. And the Kostas deserved to know everything.

"Mr. Kostas. It's, ah, been a long time."

Lazaros pressed a thick hand to his chest, then raised it and beckoned behind him. "Toni," he called breathlessly, too low to be heard in the kitchen above the clatter of pans and hissing oil. "Antonia!" he shouted over his shoulder, loud enough that nearly everyone in the diner jumped.

A loud clatter of pans crashed somewhere in the back.

Lazaros turned back to Eric with an uneasy smile. "Take a

booth in the corner. We will be right there."

A FEW MINUTES LATER, the Kostas brought over fresh coffee and a platter of dolmades. *Penny's favorites*, Eric thought with a twinge. Mrs. Kostas set mugs on the table matter-of-factly way. Lazaros took his seat across from Eric and Jane, then waited for his wife to join him. When at last they were all seated, had each nibbled at one of the stuffed grape leaves and poured the coffee no one would drink, the Kostases faced Eric expectantly.

Eric took a deep breath. "Mr. and Mrs. Kostas. It's been a long time."

"Since the funeral," Lazaros agreed. "And thank you for paying for that, by the way. We never had a chance to say it. You left so quickly."

Eric's tongue felt thick in his throat. He remembered the clouds that had never rained, but threatened it just the same. He had left as soon as it was over. Left New York. Left his family. Everything.

"You didn't even come to the *makaria*," Lazaros was saying. "We held it right here in the restaurant. Toni made very nice salmon. Everyone came." He pushed his wire-framed aviator glasses up his thick nose. "The whole family. But not you."

It was all Eric could do not to hang his head. "I..."

"Zaro, give the boy a break," Antonia put in with a smack on the man's wrist.

"He's not a boy anymore," Lazaros grumbled. "And it's been ten years. It's about time he answered." He turned back to Eric. "What would Penny think?"

Eric opened and closed his mouth a few times before he finally managed to answer. "She'd..." He rubbed his face. "Well, Mr.

Kostas, she'd be ashamed of me. She'd wonder where the hell I'd been and why I hadn't checked on her parents sooner."

Lazaros examined Eric for what felt like several minutes, his time-worn face unmoving until, all of a sudden, he burst out laughing and smacked the tabletop. Beside Eric, Jane jumped, but Antonia smiled warmly. Eric relaxed.

"Good for you," Lazaros said. "Better late than never, right? Isn't that what they say, Toni?"

His wife nodded with satisfaction. Eric smiled. This was the warm family he remembered.

"So," he pressed. "How are you?"

"Oh, it's been fine, fine," Lazaros said, still chuckling. "It was hard for a few years there, of course. We miss her so much, but we will see her one day again, God willing."

Beside him, Antonia crossed herself right to left, Orthodox-style. Just like Penny used to.

"Toni's niece came to help with the restaurant a few years ago," Lazaros continued. "That's Steffy over there, from Philadelphia." He gestured towards the hostess, who was wiping down another booth. "She's single, in case you're—"

Jane suddenly cleared her throat, disturbing the entire table. Eric muffled a laugh in his napkin.

"I've been a bit rude, Mr. Kostas," he said. "This is Jane, my wife. Jane, this is Lazaros and Antonia Kostas. Penny's parents."

For a moment, there was a different shine in Jane's eyes when he said the word "wife." "It's lovely to meet you," she said kindly, shaking each of the Kostases' hands.

"We saw you in the papers," Lazaros replied. "But we weren't sure you were still married, I'm sure you understand." He held up his hands, as if to say, "can you blame me?"

Jane chuckled. "I understand. I'm not sure what I was thinking, but I still agreed to marry him."

"You were thinking..." Eric drifted off, trying to find the words to defend himself, but taking too much joy in Jane's sudden playfulness. Would it remain after they left this place? God, he'd be the butt of any joke she wanted if she would just keep looking at him like that.

"Eric."

Everyone shifted at the sound of Antonia Kostas's direct tone. Eric blinked. Lazaros might have forgiven him for his absence, but Penny's mother was a different beast.

"Why are you here?"

Unlike her husband, Antonia Kostas had a thick Greek accent that wasn't smoothed over by serving the front of the restaurant for forty years. Her dark eyes focused on Eric. It was obvious that she still carried considerable grief over her daughter's death and the role she believed he had in it.

"I came to say..." Eric rubbed a hand over his face again. "Look, Mr. and Mrs. Kostas, I came because I never did apologize. But I also have new information about Penny's death that I believe you have the right to know."

The Kostases glanced at each other, then turned back to Eric and waited.

Eric took a deep breath. Under the table, Jane squeezed his knee lightly.

"She...well, there's a man. A man who hates me and my family. Who seems bent on destroying any good thing that happens to me, for reasons I don't fully comprehend yet."

He took another deep breath, then continued, retelling all of the story as best he could. His father's friendship with Carson. Their business dealings, gone south at some point. His relationship with Jane's mother. And, eventually, his recruitment of Eric to the Janus society.

"I must beg of you," he said quietly, "not to mention the society to anyone. For your own safety."

"Did...did Penelope know about any of this?" Lazaros asked, understandably flabbergasted.

Eric swallowed. "I don't think so. But she was a smart girl, Mr. Kostas, and we were together when I was recruited. It's entirely possible that she figured it out, and I just never knew."

God, he could see her now. The vision of her, the stained bathroom tiles, the cold chill of the room, even on the late spring day. The metallic scent of her blood. The glaze over her open eyes.

He had to tell them.

"Mr. Kostas, Penny didn't kill herself. She was murdered. By a member of the Janus society, probably sent by John Carson. It was only a few days after I was fully initiated and maybe a month after my family cut me off for deciding to marry her. I thought at the time it was my family's ostracization that caused her to do it—the note, which now I see was clearly forged, indicated as much. But Jane and I both heard her killer confess. It was part of a larger scheme to bring me to heel. And for this man, John Carson, to punish me in my father's stead."

For a long time, both of the Kostases sat silently, digesting the revelations. They murmured to each other in Greek. Under the table, Jane reached for Eric's hand.

"That was very brave," she whispered.

Eric darted a look her way. "Thanks, pretty girl."

Jane's cheeks flushed.

"I don't understand," Lazaros pulled their attention back. "What does this man have against you? Why would he...do that... to my daughter?"

"Because the only thing John Carson cares about is power and control," Eric said. "Mr. Kostas, perhaps you remember. When I decided to marry Penny, my family cut me off. I accepted that because I loved your daughter, and I knew we could make a good life without my family's fortune. But I believe now that those terms were unacceptable to John Carson, who needed those resources for his own plans. The fact that it only continued torturing me in my father's place was a bonus."

Lazaros just shook his head, now tearing at one of the napkins on the booth. Antonia's face didn't move at all.

"I don't understand," Lazaros said, over and over again. "I don't understand."

"Mr. Kostas."

Jane's voice surprised everyone, low and unassuming. She placed a hand on Lazaros's wrist, which everyone stared at before she withdrew it.

"You might have known this about Eric, Mr. Kostas," Jane said quietly. "But he's one of the most independent people in the world. When he makes a decision, it's *his* decision."

Next to her husband, Antonia nodded. Respect entered the older woman's dark eyes. "Yes," she murmured. "I remember."

"Unfortunately," Jane continued. "He also was born into a world where, because of his family's expectations, many of those decisions were taken away from him. When he tried to shirk their guidance, people weren't happy about it. Especially my father."

"Your father?" Lazaros seemed even more confused.

"John Carson is Jane's biological father," Eric said quietly. "We didn't know—she never knew—until we were engaged. Until he announced it himself and forbade our marriage, purely out of spite. A decision that we also did not accept. And for which we were also punished."

The Kostases just stared, clearly shocked. Beside him, Jane shuddered.

"Look," Eric continued, more hurried now. "I still can't claim Penny's death wasn't my fault. The truth is that had Penny never known me, she wouldn't have been on John Carson's radar. She would probably still be alive."

Eric's chest felt heavier than ever, but he forced himself to meet Lazaros and Antonia's grief-stricken gazes head-on.

"Yes," Lazaros agreed after a minute. "She would be."

"But she didn't kill herself," Eric said. "That's what I wanted you to know."

"Well, of course she didn't kill herself," Antonia said abruptly. "Penelope was my daughter. I know she would never do something like that."

"Ah, yes," Eric said. "That's right, Mrs. Kostas."

Antonia turned to her husband. "I knew it. Didn't I tell you, Zaro? Penelope would *never* have done that. I *told* you!"

Lazaros was shaking his head in disbelief. "You are sure?"

Eric nodded. "I'm sure."

"And this man? This..." Antonia turned to Jane. "Your father? He is a killer and he is just running free?" She turned back to Eric. "You would marry a murderer's daughter?"

The lump in Eric's throat disappeared, burned away by sudden anger. "Now wait a second, Mrs. Kostas, Jane is not—"

"I get it." Jane's voice cut across the noise with the precision of a knife. "But Mrs. Kostas, I understand your grief. I truly do. I understand it because I've experienced it for myself, by the hand of the same man."

Mrs. Kostas said nothing. Jane chewed on her lip, staring at the edge of the beaten Formica.

"Jane," Eric said, "you don't have to..."

But Jane shook her head with sudden vehemence, and instead of shrinking into herself yet again, she leaned across the table and took Mrs. Kostas's hand.

"Five weeks ago, I was pregnant. My mother and I were both kidnapped, and by the time Eric found us, I wasn't pregnant anymore. John Carson made sure of it." She sucked in a deep breath. Her body vibrated with contained rage. "I misspoke before,

Mrs. Kostas. John Carson is responsible for my existence because of one night with my mother, thirty years ago. But he is no father to me." She released Antonia's hand and tucked her own back into her lap like a maimed animal. "Just a monster, plain and simple."

The Kostas both stared at Jane as a single tear trailed down her cheek. The hand still in Eric's clenched so hard, he knew he'd see marks from her nails later.

But he wasn't letting go now.

"Oh, my," Antonia breathed. "Oh, my, I'm so..."

"You don't need to feel bad for me," Jane said. "I can't imagine it compares to losing a fully grown daughter."

"A loss is a loss. Just because my husband and I lost our daughter doesn't mean we can't feel your pain as well. We are so sorry." Antonia turned her brown eyes on Eric. "For the both of you."

Jane looked up. That flash. That spark. That fight. He hated that it had taken something like this to bring it out again, it was still there. And he had never been so relieved to see anything in his life.

"John Carson will meet justice for what he's done," Jane said. "Eric and I—we have resources too. No one is going to let that man go for what he has done to so many people. We can promise you that."

Jane dyes her hair

"What are you doing to your hair?"

"Oh, my God, what are you doing here? Do you stalk me to hair salons or something like that? Do you have a secret fetish for hydrogen peroxide and bad gossip?"

"Jane, what are you doing?" Eric sank into the chair next to me and stared.

"What does it look like I'm doing? I'm getting a haircut and dyeing my hair. We're having our picture taken for the society page of the New York fucking Times in three days. Do you want me to do that looking like a giant ball of cotton candy?"

Eric crossed the space of the shop in less than three seconds, and multiple heads turned in his wake. He sank into the empty chair next to me and just stared. His eyes, normally a soft gray the color of a drizzling cloud cover, had turned darker. Steely.

Finally, I couldn't take it any longer. "What?" I demanded. "*What?*"

He opened his mouth, but it took him a few more breaths to speak. "I like your hair just fine the way it is," he said finally. "Don't do anything to it."

It was the last thing I expected him to say. All he did was tease me for it. He teased me for everything. The black polish. The

Or did he?

A small voice in the back of my head—one that sounded like an irritating mix between my mother and Skylar—asked the question again and again. And just then, I couldn't come up with any good example to defend myself.

Did he have a problem with the way I looked, dressed, spoke, acted? Or were those just doubts I put on myself all along?

I picked up a strand of my hair, the wet pink that lay in dark, rose-colored strands over my shoulder, and examined it. "Eric, I can't have my picture taken looking like a character in Rainbow Brite."

"Why not?"

"Be...because, all right?" All of Skylar's warnings about this crowd, the need for armor, the way she had warned that my exterior would serve as a sort of armor against their cunning flew

QUICKSILVER   303

through my mind. And out again. How could I tell Eric, someone who had chosen me for this ridiculous ploy precisely because of my cheek, that I needed to dye my hair a strong, solid, formidable black because...I was scared?

"Jane?" Eric pulled me out of the spiral of equally black thoughts.

"What?" I asked, but the acidity had melted out of my voice. How weak I sounded. How...small.

"I like you just...the way...you are," he said slowly.

I sighed again. Part of me wanted to say "fine" and be done with it. After all, my roots weren't grown out too badly yet, and really, I *liked* the pink hair, or I would for at least another few months. I'd gotten it precisely because I wanted to look like an eighties kids' cartoon. It was the first time in five, almost six years that I'd been free to do it. For most of my twenties, I'd been locked behind a desk, chained by the pressures and decorum of court, Chicago politics. I didn't have to do that anymore.

But...

There was Skylar's voice again. *This is protection,* she'd said as she piled silk tops and designer, only once recognizing that she was doing exactly what her mother—a sneak if I ever met one—had done for her when she had entered a similar world with Brandon. *This keeps them from making a fool out of you. It will keep your respect.*

Pretty girl

"Why did you call me "pretty girl?""

Eric rolled over. "Why wouldn't I?"

I shrugged. "I don't know. Maybe because I'm not really that pretty?"

He frowned. "Jane, what the fuck is that nonsense?"

"I'm serious. And I don't mean it in a fishing-for-compliments, woe-is-me kind of way. Look at me, though. I'm not Cindy Crawford.

"Well, I hope not. Cindy Crawford is about fifty years old. I'm very, very glad you're not Cindy Crawford."

"I mean...I'm not like...Okay, I'm not like Skylar, for instance. I don't open my pink mouth and have men running for me."

Eric screwed up his nose. "Crosby? Seriously?"

"Come on. You're a guy. You can't tell me that the first time you saw her, you didn't think she was beautiful."

"Skylar's not...my type."

"Leggy redheads are not your type? You probably need to get on pornhub, dude."

He shrugged. "Skylar's so damn condescending, she's basically the older sister I never had.

"I thought you had an older sister."

"Younger, actually. And she's condescending, but unlike her, Skylar cares."

"The truth? Skylar's pretty, Jane. But I met you both that day at orientation. And you were the one I couldn't stop looking at."

I blushed, for the first time since the fourth grade.

Jane gets caught with a vibrator

The was a sudden knock at the door.

"What—*wha!*"

"Jane?"

I tried to turn it off. I really did. I practically jammed my thumb inside the damn thing, but it just. Kept. Buzzing.

"You fucker, *stop!*" I hissed at it. "Come *on!*"

"Jane, are you all right in there?"

There was another knock at the door.

"I'm–I'm fine!" I croaked, but only after the door opened. Suddenly, I was tossing the bedding around like a tornado, flipping sheets and —anything to distract from that fucking buzzing noise and the fact that I was currently sweaty and bothered, having been brought literally *right* to the brink of an orgasm before this fucker decided to do a wellness check.

"Jane?"

I flopped the covers back down. "*What?*"

Eric stepped back, looking over the room mildly. "You were kind of moaning in here. I just wanted to check if everything was all right? What's that noise?"

"What noise?"

"That noise. That buzzing noise." He looked around the room, his nose in the air like a damn bloodhound. I opened my mouth to tell him it was a *noise*, not a smell, so if he really wanted to play Pluto over here, he needed to stick his ear out and listen. But, of course, that was only if I wanted the attention.

Keep talking, I thought to myself as I continued to jab at the button on my vibrator.

―――――――――

"JANE," he said, stopping my babbling. "You're saving my life. You're saving my family's life. It's just an orgasm, all right? And since you already know that I'm going to do it a hell of a lot better than any piece of mechanized silicon, stop the fight and let me do it, all right?"

His silvery-gray eyes were firm, but not unkind. This wasn't Eric the dom, though he wasn't completely absent—it was Eric, my friend. Eric, my once lover. Eric, someone who didn't

"Okay," I assented, feeling the stress flow out of my shoulders the second I said it. I had forgotten how good it felt to give in sometimes. To give in to *him*. "Let's see if you still got it."

He leaned down. "It smells good. Are you going to make me wear a dental dam again?"

I giggled. I *had* once made him wear one while he went down on me, more out of spite than anything else. It hadn't lasted long. Aside from the fact that neither of us could stop laughing long enough to do anything resembling oral sex, the stupid thing wouldn't stay in place anyway.

"Eric," I said. "Just get down there. I could have come at least three times by now, broken motor or not—ooh!" I squealed.

"Jane," he said. "I'm going to ask you this nicely since I'm apparently not allowed to tell you. Please shut up."

FIRST COMES LOVE

AN EXCERPT

Oh, God. Oh, *God*. I stared at my drink. The bubbles ran to the top of the glass with the same urgency I had to run out of this party.

But my feet didn't move.

When had my feet stopped moving?

When had my body stopped listening to me?

Maybe when I started hallucinating the father of my child suddenly appearing at a random party? Yes, that was it. I was cracking up from lack of sex and fun. Kate was right. I was too hard up to think straight, and celibacy had finally taken its toll.

"Francesca."

Oh. My. God.

Gradually, I looked up. And up. And up. I was five three plus heels, and just like before, he was a wall of lean muscle swathed in a black suit that perfectly fit a pair of impossibly broad shoulders, a tapered waist, and long legs that stretched for miles. His square jaw was dappled with stubble, shadowing full lips and high cheekbones topped with a shock of inky black hair that shone under the lights of the party.

He cleared his throat and tugged at a tie that matched his eyes. Oh, those *eyes*. Dark blue pools of charisma that I had wanted to dive into the moment I met him in a crowd thicker than this one, though much less formal. That was when I knew it was really him. They glimmered with promise and mischief, with the confidence of a man who knows he's attractive and knows the woman he wants thinks so too.

They glimmered like the last five years had never happened. Like he'd never sent the letter that broke my heart. And I'd never had his baby without telling him.

I swallowed. Opened my mouth.

Absolutely nothing came out.

"Frankie," Matthew was saying as he looked between Xavier and me with growing recognition. "Do you know him?"

Shit. Oh *shit*. Sofia might have been a secret from Xavier, but she wasn't from the rest of my family. Back then he was Xavi to me, but at home he was "the devil incarnate," "good for nothing shitstain," or "dickhead," depending on who you were talking to. You try keeping so much as your diary a secret when you share a room with at least two other women at any given time.

All I needed now was for my brother, already strung tight as a violin, to realize this was *the* Xavier who had knocked up his baby sister out of wedlock and given him two extra mouths to feed on his public servant's salary.

Xavier might have been a giant, but Matthew was a former Marine *and* he grew up in the Bronx. He knew how to fight dirty. In the mood he was in tonight, I doubted he would hesitate.

And so it was for that reason, more than any other, that my body somehow found its power of speech and movement again.

"Get lost!" I hissed as my hand flew out and shoved Matthew back a few steps.

His brow furrowed in surprise, but I gave him my best "don't cock block me" look. His expression morphed from confused to knowing.

"Going," he said, but not before he gave Xavier his patented big brother glare. "But my two cents? He's too tall for you anyway."

Before I could snap that my height or anyone else's was absolutely none of his business, Matthew disappeared into the crowd, sure-footed as a cat.

"Francesca? Is it really you?"

Trying not to shake, I turned. Around us, the party was launching into full swing. Champagne glasses were clinking, people were laughing a little too loudly. It should have been fun, like one of the balls Austen wrote about so much. But I couldn't hear anything other than Xavier's deep voice, Queen's English heavily overlaid by South London. Yes, I knew the difference. That's what twenty-five years of being an Anglophile gets you. *Way* too many Saturday nights binging BritBox. I don't even want to get into my obsession with Regency adaptations.

"Hello, Xavier." My voice was low, barely a whisper. Oh my God, Frankie, *talk.* He's a man, not a phantom.

And yet, was there a difference when it came to him?

He looked good. Edible, even. Somehow better than I had imagined over the last five years.

I shifted from one foot to the other. Suddenly, my dress was a bit too tight, and my skin tingled with anticipation. I felt drunk, despite only one glass of champagne.

"What—what are you doing here?" I managed to get out.

Stupid question. Xavier quirked a black brow and glanced around as if the answer was obvious. I suppose it was. It was a party. Why else would he be here if not to enjoy himself like everyone else?

Most of the guests were too absorbed with the free-flowing champagne, music, and well, themselves to take interest. A few, though, had definitely noticed him. More than one woman was eyeing Xavier over their flutes of Cristal.

"Business." Xavier pulled me back with a smile. It looked like he was trying to be nice, but something about his expression looked forced, like it didn't come naturally. It was distinctly...predatory.

What did that make me? His prey?

"I'm finally opening that restaurant in New York," he continued. "De Vries is one of my investors, and he invited me tonight."

"De Vries?" I frowned.

Xavier waved a casual hand toward the crowd. "Eric? The host? He and I were at university together when I did a semester abroad at Dartmouth. What did you do, sneak in with the caterers?"

I flushed. Did I stick out that much? I wasn't dripping in diamonds or couture, but I thought I looked respectable. Audrey, Matthew had said. But maybe he meant like in *My Fair Lady*. Before the makeover, when she was still the homely flower girl with the Cockney accent and rags for wear.

"I—no," I stumbled. "He—Eric—they're friends with my—"

I stopped, took a deep breath, then tried again. I could do this. Hold a conversation. I was a teacher, for goodness' sake. I basically herded cats for a living.

"I came with my brother, Matthew," I clarified. "The guy who was with me before. He's friends with the de Vrieses."

Translation: *I'm supposed to be here.*

Was it my imagination, or did Xavier's massive shoulders relax a little? That smile peeked out again, this time looking a bit more natural. Still an imitation of a shark, though.

I suppose that made me the minnow.

I swallowed the rest of my third glass of champagne immediately.

"Your brother? Do I get to meet him?"

He swung around, looking for Matthew. But thank God, he had disappeared into the sea of glitter and money.

I shrugged, then lunged for a glass of champagne on the tray of a passing caterer. "Hold on there, buddy," I said as he started to walk away. "One more for the road."

The waiter took my empty glass with a wry look and moved on.

I turned to find Xavier watching me intently. One side of his mouth twitched, like he was about to smile. But he didn't. I took another long draught of champagne. His gaze traveled with the glass to my lips and stayed there for several seconds until, again, he cleared his throat and pulled at his necktie.

"Too tight?" I asked.

He frowned. "What?"

I nodded. "Your tie. You keep adjusting it."

His hand dropped. "Eh. Well. Hate these things, if you want to know the truth. Like a bloody noose." He exhaled slowly through his nose. "Christ, what have you been up to? It's been, what, five years?"

I took another deep swig of champagne. Feeling lightheaded was better than feeling starstruck. And for some reason, every time the muscles of his neck tested his collar like that, I didn't quite feel steady on my feet. "Some-something like that."

"Did you finish school?" he pressed. "You were studying literature, correct?"

"Um, yes. That's right." I stifled a smile. "Good memory."

"You were writing your thesis on Austen. Something about Mr. Darcy and his evolution in the modern age, wasn't it?"

My mouth fell open. "You remember that?"

He took a step forward, closing the space between us enough that I caught a whiff of his scent: a touch of cologne atop something clean and slightly spicy. A chef's scent. Same as before.

"I have an excellent memory." His voice rumbled low.

"Like...for what?" I knew I shouldn't have asked. Or even cared. But his eyes were pulling me in—or up—and I couldn't look away.

"You have a London Fog every morning," he informed me. "Love peanuts, but hate peanut butter. Your favorite poem is 'Frost at Midnight.' In fact, you love all the Romantic poets except Wordsworth. Thought he was stodgy."

I gawked. "How in God's name do you remember all of that after five years?"

Again, that sharkish almost-smile appeared. "Oh, I remember everything about you, Ces."

Ces. Pronounced "Chess," a shortened version of my full name that no one had ever used but him.

My entire body shivered.

I was Frankie to everyone else in my life. Friends or coworkers, mostly. Frances sometimes (usually to a priest or my grandmother). Fran, maybe even Franny to Mattie or my sisters.

But with Xavier, there had been no in between. It was Francesca, my Christian name, when he wanted my attention. His eyes would glow, and his mouth would twist the word like it was wrapped around a ripe strawberry, luxuriating in each syllable with that wicked tongue.

And then there was this. When it was just us two, and he looked at me like he loved me, like I was the only one in the world.

A nickname that belonged to him and only him, as intimate as anything else we had done together.

Ces.

As his gaze traveled up and down my body, it was quite clear just what *else* he was remembering.

I should have been appalled. But then again, I was remembering it too.

Xavier cleared his throat once more. Yanked the middle of his tie this time instead of the knot. "So. Are you a professor now? Should I call you Dr. Zola?"

I swallowed. Of course, it was *that* remark that made my cheeks flush again. With shame, not excitement. "Um, no. I, ah, actually left school to deal with some, um, family stuff. I teach third grade in Brooklyn."

"What's that, primary?"

I nodded. "Yeah."

My eyes darted around the room, looking at the splashy modern art hung on the walls. Toward the sound of breaking glass somewhere near the dining table. Anywhere but him.

When I finally found the courage to look back, his eyes bore down at me as intently as before. "Well, it's still teaching, isn't it? Do you read them any of your poetry? I seem to remember some rather racy bits in that journal of yours. Anything about me?"

Again, my mouth fell open. "You haven't changed either, have you? Just as arrogant as ever."

He was too. And I *hated* that it turned me on so much.

His sapphire eyes glinted, though suddenly, he turned away. "Well. I've earned it."

Before I could ask how, another caterer appeared.

"More champagne?" she asked, tittering up at Xavier.

"Sure."

I couldn't help feeling slightly jealous when an actual smile appeared for the stranger carrying drinks instead of me. It wasn't a real smile, at least. Xavier hadn't smiled much when I had known him before, and it seemed like he did it even less now. The shark made yet another appearance, without an iota of warmth or kindness.

If it had been directed at me, I would have been terrified. And maybe the waitress was too. But she was also clearly entranced as she handed Xavier the drinks, unable to look away.

"When you take those back to the kitchen, can you just bring us a bottle? Thanks, babe."

The waitress giggled and stuck out her considerable chest before turning away.

And just like that, his spell over me, at least, was broken.

Babe? Really? Sure, he had always used that term the way Americans say "man" and "dude." And once upon a time, I had liked it when he called me that too, among many other things. It was the familiar. Open.

Right now though? It made me sick listening to him flirt so openly with another woman, even if with the warmth of a brick wall.

Frankie, stop. You have no claim over this man. You don't want this man. You do not.

By the time I was done with my internal pep talk, I turned to find Xavier staring intently at my mouth. His smile had vanished, replaced now by a small indentation between his brows.

"What in God's name are you looking at?" I snapped a little too harshly.

Again, one side of his mouth twitched. "You still chew on your lower lip when you're thinking." He leaned down as he traded my empty champagne glass with a fourth serving—or was it my fifth? His scent, that intoxicatingly spicy blend, wrapped around me like a mist. "And it still makes your lips look like strawberries."

Another full-body shiver coursed through me. "I—you —what?"

His cheek brushed mine, and his voice dropped to a rumble only I could hear. "What do you say when that bottle returns, we find someplace a bit quieter? Somewhere we can catch up. Get...reacquainted."

He stood up straight, expression as stoic as ever. At first, I wondered if I'd imagined it. There was no emotion in his face. No sign he had actually proposed what I thought he had.

But he had. His blue eyes dilated with clear, hypnotic desire as he waited out my response. And I knew the same expression was echoed in mine but couldn't quite hate myself for it. Whatever pull he once had on me, it was still here. I was once again a moth drawn to a bright blue flame.

Slowly, as if to touch a wild animal, Xavier reached out a finger and hovered it over my jaw, above my chin, down my neck. I could feel goose bumps rising, despite the fact that he didn't touch me. Not yet. It was a tease, a preview of what he might do. A reminder of what he had once done.

But as soon as his finger made soft contact, just in the hollow above my clavicle, I remembered.

This wasn't a dream.

This was real.

Xavier was here and clearly as icy and dangerous as ever.

Touching me.

Wanting me.

And through this growing haze of champagne, there was absolutely no way I would be able to keep the secret I'd been holding for years if he did more than that.

I couldn't just think of myself here, I had someone else far more important to protect. I had to think of Sofia.

"No," I said clearly, jerking out of reach. "Oh, *no*. I—"

I cut myself off, looking around. Lord, where was my overprotective brother when I needed him? But all I saw were nameless faces, people awash in alcohol and laughter, riches and wealth and confidence that had absolutely nothing to do with me.

I turned back to find Xavier still watching me with a different kind of expression. Not one of patient waiting. But instead, like a victor. Like he had walked out of one of my beloved Austen novels. But he wasn't the hero. He was the villain who had just captured his prize.

"Shall we?" he asked as the waitress returned, giggling with the requested bottle.

I blinked between him and the girl, who looked like she would be more than happy to share the drink with him in my place. And he wasn't exactly correcting her either.

"No, I don't think so," I said.

And then I turned on my heel and left.

www.ingramcontent.com/pod-product-compliance
Lightning Source LLC
Chambersburg PA
CBHW051956240626
47153CB00005B/1779